ALSO BY ELIZABETH GRAVER

Have You Seen Me?

UNRAVELLING

Elizabeth Graver

HYPERION

NEW YORK

Library of Congress Cataloging-in-Publication Data

Graver, Elizabeth, 1964–
    Unravelling / Elizabeth Graver.—1st ed.
      p.   cm.
    ISBN 0-7868-6281-5
    1. Women textile workers—Massachusetts—Lowell—History—19th century—Fiction. 2. Mothers and daughters—New Hampshire—History—19th century—Fiction. 3. Women—New England—History—19th century—Fiction. I. Title.
PS3557.R2864H86   1997
813'.54—dc20   96-18002
                                                                              CIP

FIRST EDITION

Designed by Gloria Adelson/LuLu Graphics

10 9 8 7 6 5 4 3 2

For Ruth

This for the two stones inside me,
The two shadows gone from me—
That they may begin to understand.

At night, because it is summer and the air is hot and close, the mosquitoes float like snowflakes over the bog. I step onto the peat, which gives like a mattress, and the insects circle me in clouds. When I was a child playing here, my flesh was plump and sweet and they flocked to me and drank my blood; now I am no longer a girl, but still they swarm me. On my bog there is heat lightning, and lightning bugs too, blinking across the pond which grows bigger one year, smaller the next. In the beginning I thought that pond would mark my life, its circle growing smaller every year, hemmed in by the peat until it was only a puddle, a drop, a memory in the sludge. Then I noticed how the mass of floating land inched forward one year only to inch back the next.

My mother liked to say that life is a long straight road if you live it right, but mine has turned and tumbled. In 1829, when I was born, she picked my name from an article in *The Ladies' Pearl*. Aimee. At Factory Improvement Circle, I learned how in French it meant Loved. My mother did not know.

"It was a lady's name," she told me. "You were born with fingernails like a lady's. You waved your fingers in the air and howled like you owned the world."

First I was loved, like my name. Then I was unloved. Now I have Amos and Plumey who visit me, the village cripple and the village orphan, as they are known in town. I have my rabbits who give me fur to spin into yarn. I have my house, built to last, chickens who leave me eggs, clear vision and a strong back, a mother I never see. Amos brings me trinkets and sings me songs about pretty girls, though I have lived thirty-eight years on this earth.

In beauty I am no longer a great believer, nor proud the way I used to be. It is a fact that I was prettier than most at the factory, pretty as an angel, I was told. When the strangers came through, the factory owners from England looking at how it was done, I was one of the girls who was led to the front looms and asked to demonstrate. When the men from Washington came through, I was one of the girls to carry the banner: "Welcome to the City of Spindles." We wore white muslin dresses with blue sashes that day. We carried parasols edged in green. We marched singing to the factory: "How Doth the Busy Bee." Afterwards they made us give the dresses back.

I wove that, I wanted to say, or if not that one, then one like it. I knotted the knots when the thread broke, and ran from one crashing loom to another, and threaded the two thousand weft threads until my fingers swelled like rising dough.

Mine, I wanted to say.

I only looked like an angel.

Perhaps if I had been named something else, things would have turned out differently. I might have been named Charity, or Faith, perhaps, or Grace. But Grace can go crooked and Charity is often no more than a guilty conscience, and of Faith I have my portion—or would I still be waiting every day?

This morning, like most mornings, I make my way over the peat and wash my face in the dark green water of the pond at the center of the bog. Once a fortnight in the mild seasons I bathe there, too, and if I raise my leg to see the kiss of a black leech or feel a water snake circle my ankle, I do not shriek the way I would have as a child, do not flounder and splash and make the birds cock their heads toward my voice. A leech is a leech; a water snake, a water snake. I am in the habit. My body in the water is as bare as when I was born, and if they come while I am bathing—if the tribes of boys or some hunters spot me there—I try to take no notice, but keep cleaning myself with my sponge of brownish moss.

The hunters, when they see me bathing, crash like awkward bears into the woods. The boys, when they come, usually hide behind trees and peek at me, but today they grow brave and start to chant:

There once was a woman
and what do you think?
Bok bok bok!
She lived upon nothing

but victuals and drink.
Bok bok bok!
And though victuals and drink
were the whole of her diet,
this dirty woman
would never keep quiet!

Then they stick out their necks, fold their arms into their armpits and flap like chickens. "Never mind them," I can hear Amos saying, though he is not there. "Just a stupid song they'll sing about anybody. They didn't even make it up."

But later, when they are gone and the song is still circling my head, I must wonder: What do most people live on? What do I?

"Victuals," I might have told the boys, "and drink and love."

The chickens and rabbits are scrambling with hunger, so I feed them. The twig brooms I started yesterday are crooked, so I trim them. In this way, the hours pass. It is almost noon when Amos comes to me with blueberries and sits down for a cleaning. They did a poor job of it, the doctors who cut and sewed him up. Over the years the skin on the end of his thigh has healed in deep folds like the inside of a navel. Amos will not clean himself, says it makes the bile in his stomach rise. He sits on a log stool by my door and unpins his coverall leg, and I lower myself down, kneel, and lean over the place where he lost his calf to gangrene, the surface veined and marbled with a month of stubborn dirt.

"You'll lose the rest of it," I tell him, "the way you treat it."

"Clean," says Amos, "or I'll throw the berries to the birds."

He tries to whistle a birdsong, but it comes out thin and plain.

"The blueberries come in strong this year?" I ask him. I dip my rag in the water he has carried in a bucket from the bog pond and begin to wipe.

He shakes his head. "I found you all there is in the state of New Hampshire. Spent a week going after them."

"I found some myself," I say, "with Plumey—the low, wild ones. We meant to pick enough for a pie, but we kneeled right down and ate them there."

"If you have found honey," Amos tells me in his holy voice, "eat only enough for you, lest you be sated with it and vomit."

He was studying to be a preacher before he lost his leg, and with it the love of a woman and all faith in the workings of the Lord.

"Stay still," I tell him, for he is squirming, the skin still tender, he says, after all these years, the ghost of his leg still begging to be scratched.

The bog water is cloudy in the bucket but clear on my rag—strong, preserving water; bodies in the bog do not decay. Cows have been found along the bottom whole years after they went missing, still with flesh on their bones and their brandings left intact. People, too, though not in my lifetime. A witch, they say, with recipes for potions scratched needle-thin up and down her body. A hunter with his quiver of arrows still strapped to his back. No maggots and worms do their speedy work here. Water like this does not forget.

I pour the water over the skin, into the scarred folds so that they fill like rivers at melting time, then run into a water-fall down where his calf should be. Between my fingers I mash some jewelweed and rub my fingertips stained green with juices along the ridges of his stump to keep the rash away.

Month after month I have tended Amos's leg, year after year. In the beginning, he would hardly look at me, his mouth pressed in a bitter line, but then one day he must have felt how my hands were touching him where he would not even touch himself, for his hands moved from where they were clenched at his sides to rest lightly on my head.

I did not smile or look up, except deep inside myself. I cleaned.

He did not ask me to do it, the first time—so many years ago by now. He had fallen in the woods, not far from my house, and I found him with his wooden leg cradled in his arms, his wound new then, the bandage come undone, attracting flies. I brought a bucket of water to where he was, cleaned him off, wrapped him up. He was silent, went off just like that, but the next month he returned with a jug of cider strapped to his back, sat by my house and rolled up his trouser leg. That was the start of us; soon the town was talking. Soon Amos was staying through the night.

"Say another part of the Book," I tell him now, not because I want to learn how to walk on the righteous path, but because I have been hearing those words for longer than I can remember and love the turnings of his voice.

He grins, shifts on the log that is his seat, and says, "Your lips distill nectar, my bride. Honey and milk are under your tongue. The scent of your garments is the scent of Lebanon."

"Another part," I say.

"Why not this?"

"No nectar in the cupboard, and I'm not a bride."

And Amos answers, "All right, the scent of your garments is the scent of your rabbits?"

I cannot help smiling.

"And you have snakes under your tongue?"

I open my mouth and lift my tongue. Amos peers, but when he gets close I clamp my mouth shut.

"Nothing," I say. "No honeybees or snakes."

"They're just hiding," says Amos. "Let me see."

He cups my chin and tries to kiss me.

"Stop," I laugh. "I have to wash you. You'd think we were children."

"Come here, pretty girl."

"I'm no girl."

"But pretty."

I believe Amos when he says he likes how the skin around my eyes shows the prints of where I've been. We get better and better, like fine wine, he said to me last week, and I pictured how vinegar turns to cider, cider to wine—rich, full, and only slightly bitter. Time, I thought, as I lay in Amos's arms, is supposed to smooth the edges of all things, so why am I so jagged sometimes, still, so filled with shards?

Now I lean forward and run my finger down his face, over the curve of his steep nose, along the cleft above his lip. He is older than I am by four years. His face is scarred from the pox, lined from the weather; his hands are rough from work. But his eyes are the deep, keen gray of slate after a rainstorm—slate flecked with the yellow hanging-ons of moss.

"Can't stay," he says, nibbling my palm. "Too much work to do."

"It can't wait?"

He shakes his head.

"What is it?"

"A new henhouse door at the Bacons'. A fox keeps getting through."

"The Bacons?"

"They came a few months ago, related to the Prescotts somehow, living over on Osterhold's land."

"How many of them?"

"A Mister and Missus and four or five little porkers. And the mother, they brought her along. I saw her coming from the church."

"An old lady?"

He shrugs. "Not so old, old enough. Like some other mothers." He pauses to let his silence gather, but I will not linger there.

"Time to go," I say briskly, though we both know he is not going anywhere. I must still wind his leg with bandage, pick up the wooden part, strap it on with the leather thongs and let the blue cloth fall. I must cover him up until he becomes something the people will look at when he goes to town. I will wash him clean as the inner petals of a bud.

"Get along," I say, but I take my own sweet time.

On the beams of my house are things I have not thrown away: a shell comb, a brooch pin wound with hair, a blue sash, letters from my mother. Over the door hangs my rifle, my powderhorn, and bullet pouch. At night, sometimes, I bring the rabbits in to sleep with me; there are foxes in the woods, and owls. In the twelve feet by twelve feet of my house, my rabbits eat from my hand. I give them oats and barley, apples, corn and carrots. Outside, milkweed and lupine could kill them, mudholes could suck them down. "Shush," I say, stroking back their ears. Near the door I have hung a salt lick on a piece of wire. When I set the blind one before it, she lifts her nose and sniffs, then licks, and I watch as she tastes comfort in its roughest shape, the salt of tears and skin.

Plumey, who has no parents, sleeps in town, in the Doctor's house. Amos sleeps, most nights, in his cottage at the foot of Red Skunk Hill. My father is under the ground, not preserved in the bog. My brother Jeremiah died of consumption when I was still at the mills; my sister Harriet died of a thickness of the blood after I had come back and moved into this house. They lie beside my father in the churchyard. My brothers Thomas and John live out West—a place I cannot picture and will never see. And my mother? Just through the fields, over the hill, living out her days with my brother Luke in the house where I grew up. A few heartbeats, a short walk, an impossible distance away.

Still, it must be said that in my way, I am rarely alone. My thoughts have been dense with voices, thick with bodies, and I have heard coughs and hiccups, breaths and cries and other things. Sometimes the crowd inside my head makes the days move faster. Other times the days move slowly, and I worry that I am nothing but a stubborn woman spiraling in on herself—the way they must think of me in town.

Mostly the days move like days, and sometimes I gather things to eat or tend the animals, and sometimes I sit with Plumey on the bank, and sometimes I lie back on my bed with my knees bent up, as if I were birthing. Or I lie on my side with my head bowed and my knees tucked to my chest, as if I were waiting to be born.

Once there were two little girls,
Margaret and Kate.
And every day they went to school
And never went too late.
One day the girls did stop awhile,
A dolly game to play,
And as the dusk fell on the land,
The daughters lost their way.

We would lie on our wide straw tick mattresses in the attic—John, Thomas, Harriet, Jeremiah, and myself—and our mother would stand on the ladder leading up so that only her face showed, and sometimes one of her hands, rising up to stress a point.

The night was black, the grass was high,
The rain began to fall.
The mother looked for them awhile,
Through darkness she did call.
She found them both and took them home,
And after that dark night,

They never stopped to play that way,
But always acted right.

"Good night, chickens," she'd say then, and I'd watch as her chin disappeared down the ladder, then her nose, her forehead and the straight part dividing her hair. By that time, the younger ones would already have fallen asleep, and I would be running the words together in my mind, trying to make them stop meaning: thenightwasblackthegrasswashightherainbegan . . . I had heard it too many times.

We slept in two beds—John and Thomas under one of the eaves, and Harriet, Jeremiah and I under the other, with Jeremiah between us for when he had his nightmares. Sometimes our mother tried to put Jeremiah with the other boys, but he always crawled back to us. Luke was not born yet, and Anna had Blossomed on Earth to Bloom in Heaven. Forever we had slept like that, and their bodies were like my body, the heel of a foot in the crook of my leg like my own fist there. Later, when we got a little older, Harriet and I moved to one shared bed; then, when Harriet turned twelve, we each moved to our own. But in the beginning I slept with my brother and sister like a litter of pups, in a damp, tangled pile.

Only Jeremiah would wake me sometimes, coughing into his cupped hands as if he could save the cough and use it later on. Harriet would hear him and tunnel her head under her pillow. John would turn over and groan. Only I would find myself tugged from sleep—by chance, I think, the first time, but later I grew to depend on being my brother's nurse and to love, especially, those moments afterwards when he had stopped coughing and the two of us were awake in a sleeping world. If the coughing got bad enough, I would lie him down on his stomach on the pine floor and pummel his back with the flats of my hands until he cleared the insides of his throat into a handkerchief he had wadded by his mouth.

"Shush," I would tell him. "Shhh."

Sometimes in summer we crept downstairs, then, and out into the dark, where we sat in our nightclothes on the stone wall. We didn't talk much, usually, sitting there. We listened to the bullfrogs' calls—pent-up and thick with sorrow, coming to us all the way from the pond. Sometimes he would tell me things I had said out loud in my sleep—words I could not make sense of, the names of people I was sure I did not know. Jeremiah and I would invent whole dreams to fit around these people. My family probably thought I was taking care of my little brother; I thought so then myself. I think only Jeremiah himself really understood how comforted I was by the pale blond down on his head, how much of my time was spent searching for him, even when I thought I wanted to be alone.

We all knew he would be the first to go. It was not so much that he was built frailer than the rest of us as that living made him tired. When I rolled down the hill with my arms twisted around my body and my legs locked tight and lay at the bottom watching the tilting grass and sky, Jeremiah walked slowly down, placing his feet on the hillside with the greatest care, like an important old man. We were almost twins; he was only a year younger than I was, but I was half a head taller and could run twice as fast. Often he annoyed me with his carefulness, and I grew sharp.

"Like this," I would order him by the brook. "One foot here, one foot there, then there. Go—"

And he would dare his foot out to the first mossy rock and then withdraw it.

"Just do it!" I'd tell him. "If you slow down, you lose your balance. Watch—"

I'd leap over the stones to the other side, then back. *Quick girl, graceful girl,* I could hear the grasses say. He'd try again, send his foot out slowly, then hurl his thin body forward in an act of will. He always ended up with one leg soaked to the knee, shivering, glaring up at me.

"Go on home and change, or you'll get sick," I'd order him, though I did not really want him to leave. He was the only person who could read under my words. He never stopped following me, and when I grew a little older and actually forbade him from coming, he became quite deft. That was fine, for then I could feel alone and not alone, could walk with only the trees and sky in front of me and sense my brother hovering nearby. Sometimes it would take me twenty minutes to be sure that he was behind me as I wandered through the barn, along the road, down by the bog, up the hill to where the black-berries were—all over the eighty acres that was our land. Other times I'd think I was alone, then see him at supper with his hands and lips stained deep purple and know that he had followed in my wake.

Harriet played dolls—dolls made of cornhusk, or rag, or one she had gotten for Christmas, with a china head and round, black eyes like holes. I pretended to be bored by dolls, but actually they scared me—the emptiness of their stares, their fixed smiles, how they were almost people but not quite. Often she and her friend Lily would tie a string to our brother Thomas and lead him around with them. Sometimes he was the father, sometimes the baby, sometimes the family mule. Once in a while, when our parents were in town, Lily would smear mud on Thomas's face and pretend he was her slave.

"Say Master Lily!" she'd yell, and whip him with a flimsy reed, and Thomas would laugh and try to eat the mud, too young to understand. Our parents never knew how she tied and dirtied him. Harriet always saw to it that Thomas was scrubbed and fed when they got back.

I was the girl in our family who might go bad, the one who needed to hear the warning bedtime stories, right from the beginning, but my mother also seemed to love me best. Then, I thought myself the most deserving of her love—I was, after all, the prettiest of her children and the quickest at school. She had given the rest of them ordinary names; for me she had picked Aimee. My name, I reasoned, began with the same letter as her own, Ann, but then became fancier—Ann with a curtsy, dressed in lace. My mother made Harriet keep her hair cut above her shoulder blades so it would grow in thicker and find some curl. My hair, which was thick and wavy, she let grow and grow, and when she brushed it out and braided it up, I could feel how precious I was in the motion of her fingers lifting and weaving through the strands.

Also she loved to sigh and say my name: Where has Aimee wandered off to? What did Aimee do with the box of pins? Aimee, stop that sucking on your finger. Harriet, run up to the henhouse and tell Aimee those eggs will hatch by the time she gets around to bringing them back. I could hear her saying my name even when I was not there, could feel it running through her thoughts, picking at them like a comb. As I read in the barn or hunched in the corner watching my father slaughter the chickens, I could feel how I lived in this place and my name was everywhere. So were the names of the others: Thomas, Harriet, Jeremiah, John, even Anna, buried in town by the church, but my name had the best sound: *Em-MAY*, like nothing you'd ever heard.

My father took each chicken and stuffed it upside down into a metal cone hanging on the wall. Then, with the chickens' legs scrambling and scratching, their wings beating NoNoNo, he pushed their heads through the bottom of the cone and took their necks off with his ax.

I watched to prove to myself that I could, and because the blood poured like water from the cones, and because even though he had done it hundreds, thousands of times, my father's hands seemed to tremble as the blood came down (or was I seeing things?), and he looked away and muttered something, probably a prayer, and then I saw him as someone I might be able to know.

One time I watched him kill a sow, end her life with a bullet aimed right between the eyes. The sow he had shot kneeled down, not leaning to one side or the other. Then her hind legs gave way and she rolled onto her side, her legs pedaling for a minute as if she were still trying to walk.

I watched my father go into the pen and cut the neck veins to help keep the meat free of clotted blood. As the blood spilled to the ground, the other pigs hurried over to drink it— the blood of their mother, their sister—eagerly, as if it might save their lives. Then my father and brother hoisted the sow from the pen and over to the chute leading down to the scalding tank. The air filled with a bitter smell. When she came out, they swept her bristles from her with a metal brush, leaving her as hairless and pale pink as a baby.

"Tell your mother seventy-five pounds, each half," I remember my father calling out to where I stood by a pile of wood, as he bent to fix a stretcher between the pig's splayed legs. "That should put some meat on your bones."

My father would not look at me. Even when he spoke to me, he looked over my head, as if I made him nervous or he was not sure I was real. Back in the kitchen, I pictured myself with the gun, how steady I would hold it—if I were ever allowed—how true my aim would be. It was not that I wanted to kill that pig, exactly, although I would not miss its presence.

I wanted to make my father look inside me—not through me, or around me, or even at me, but inside to where a sure, small double of myself was standing with her feet planted firmly, her eyes in a squint, her finger on the trigger of a gun.

Watch, I would say, and he would look up with startled eyes and see that I had someone inside.

Mostly he was there but not there, hoisting, cutting and reaping during the day, tired out at mealtimes, his thick hands hanging at his sides. Like Jeremiah, really—tired from living—though Jeremiah was small and white, and my father large and red. He did not love me best, did not know how to talk to me, because I was a girl. He loved John, who was strong and quiet, and Thomas, who was still a baby and could be held and called soft names. I know he held me, too, when I was very small, because I can still remember the color and smell of his lap—how wide it was, how blue, smelling of grass, sweat and horse. I would sit high up in the cradle of his arm as he ate and watch his big hand lift the spoon, move it toward his mouth, tip the contents onto his large pink tongue. Sliding down into his lap, I would watch his jaw rise and fall as he chewed. Even then I knew I did not have to be afraid of him, for he held me as if at any moment I might sink my teeth into him—as if I were a tamed wild animal who might one day remember the woods.

My mother teased out my splinters, scrubbed my crevices, burned ticks from my skin and peered down at my droppings to make sure they were the color they should be. She knew that I had not come from the woods, but from inside her. I had much more reason to live in fear of her, for she did not live in fear of me.

──✦◆✦──

There were always people in the house, animals in the barn. Even in the fields, where I lay down and sucked the juices from the spores of the purple clover flowers or chewed on wheat kernels to make gum, insects would crawl over my eyelids, red ants bite at my legs. Somebody—in the barn, in the house, perched like a sentry on the stone wall—was always calling out my name, "Em-May! Em-May!" For most of my childhood I did not mind such company—did not mind Jeremiah, though sometimes I pretended to. But the summer I turned fourteen, a great exhaustion, a sleepy, waterlogged idleness invaded me, and the world became an itching, prying thing. Even when I was not in the fields, my skin tingled as if covered with invisible insects, and I began swatting at the air. One day when I felt Jeremiah lurking several yards behind me, I stopped pretending not to notice him.

"Leave me alone!" I said, swiveling around to where he stood behind a shed before he had time to hide. "Stop spying on me."

"I'm not spying."

"Then what?"

His sharp shoulders rose and fell.

"Well, stop."

"I can go where I want. This isn't private property."

"Oh no? Who owns it, the President?"

"We own it. Our father."

"Oh, really?" I shook my head slowly back and forth. "I had no idea you were so smart. You should study to be a preacher or a doctor, instead of playing at being a spy."

Then his breath started coming fast, his chin trembled.

"Oh, for goodness sake," I said.

But his body had taken over in the way it sometimes did, everything usually tight and careful shaking into motion like a machine turned on—his teeth chattering, his chest heaving, liquid rushing from his eyes and nose.

Your fault, his body said, though his voice was silent. Because you're cruel to me. Because you're fast like a boy, easy on your feet, and I'm thin and little like a girl and not meant to stay on this earth.

I stood and watched until the heavings grew smaller and he began to swipe at his nose with the edge of his sleeve. Then he started to cough again, his throat all clogged, and I lay him down in the grass and thumped his back.

"I'm sorry," I muttered when finally he had stopped heaving and lay with his head facedown in the grass. I was not sorry, really, for he always coughed and heaved when he couldn't get his way, and I was tired of being made to feel so wicked. But I understood, even then, the tremendous power of thought, and I knew that if I didn't say I was sorry and something awful happened to my brother, I would have willed it into happening by my thoughts.

Also I knew I still needed the shadow of my brother—always there several steps behind me, as if my life were full of interest, somehow charmed. My hair and eyes were dark—I should have been the shadow—his hair as white-blond as milkweed puffs, as fine and full of light. He pulled himself up, came to where I was kneeling on the grass and began to undo and rebraid my hair. Harriet had taught him how to braid when he was still almost a baby, and though he could not cross a brook, could not jump from the hayloft down to the empty stall below, his fingers could navigate my hair like a boat on a river with three currents. The braid when he finished was glossy and tight. He bound it with a piece of long grass, and when I got up and walked toward the North Hill, my brother did not follow me, but sat gazing down at his hands.

"Come on, then," I said, turning to him, but still he did not rise. "What is it?"

Jeremiah looked up at me, but his gaze was distant, and I saw how he, too, had places still and private where no one else could go. I did not like to see my brother so sad and oddly old.

"Race you hopping to that pine tree?" I asked.

"No."

"Oh please?"

He stood and raised up one leg like a funny little bird. He smiled at me, a tilted, crooked grin. And then we were off, and I did not so much let him get ahead as simply not try too hard. My brother when he won was flushed and panting.

"Now you need to kiss it," I told him after I caught up.

He sank down onto the pine needles. "What?"

"The tree, for letting you win."

He squinted at me. "Did you?"

"Not me, silly. Her." I pointed at the pine tree.

"Thank you, Miss Tree," he said, rolling over to plant a kiss on its trunk.

"Oh!" I said, making my voice as barky and treelike as I could. "My first kiss! Can I have another? How old are you, little boy? Is it true you're almost thirteen?"

Jeremiah scowled. "Your braid came undone."

"It doesn't matter."

"I'll do it again."

"No," I said. "No no no!"

And then I was off and running, my hair whipping loose across my eyes.

Places I tried to be alone: the road from school to home, where, if I stayed late to help the slow ones with their lessons, sometimes I would be the only one going in our direction, and I would walk slowly with my new body, my hands like sandbags pulling down my arms, my eyes trying hard to stay open, longing so to close.

The fields at dusk, where I would stand in the grass as the cows nosed over to the salt licks and worked grooves into them with their pale, fleshy tongues. Something quieted in me, then, as I watched the cows' necks bend and saw the calm, essential pleasure they found in something as simple as salt. I loved how long it took for the block to change shape; how the cows seemed drawn there, as if by a magic source. Once I stood between their flanks and ran my own tongue along the salt, but it was covered with slime and stung my mouth, so after that I simply watched.

The bog, off on the edge of our land. There I would poke at a brown cattail until it exploded in a fluff of white, or peer inside the shed that stood on the bog's edge. Someone had built it as a hunter's shelter long ago; now it was tilted and full of used-up things—charred bits of log, a broken fishing pole, an empty whiskey bottle. When I was younger I had tried to make a home there: a stump for a table, empty flour sacks for curtains, a broken wooden spoon to stir the soup. Harriet would come with me sometimes, and Jeremiah. He was the baby, Harriet the father or daughter. I was the mother— sometimes stern, sometimes kind and singing—or, when things got too quiet, the wolf who came howling at the door.

Later they stopped coming with me, and the scraps from our games got mixed up with all the other objects that had blown in or been left over the years. I stopped playing house, but even when I was thirteen or fourteen, I always hoped I would find something extraordinary there: a pan full of gold ore, or an Indian baby gazing up at me through inky eyes. Instead, I found a place where I was the only person breathing.

It was either a lovely feeling or a sad one—I couldn't quite decide. I stood in the dark, pretended I was blind, and ran my fingers over my eyelids and into the softness of my mouth.

In bed at night, though I was not alone, the others lying nearby, I could *feel* alone after they had fallen asleep—my eyes the only open ones in a room of steady breathing and closed lids. I was tired when I should have been awake, awake when I should have been tired. My hands could not stop straying toward my body, though I knew it was a sin, inching toward where I had begun to change—the places that Harriet hid from me on her own self, and where now I was rising and swelling and growing hairs.

What did I know of my changes? So little—just that they made me feel lived-in, as if something were prodding me from inside, and that my father grew deeper red when he looked at me, and my mother, when she heated the water for my bath, now hung up a curtain and turned her head away. Sometimes, when I was sitting in the privy, I looked down at myself, but there was hardly any light in there, and I could not see what was happening—just the folds of my skirts, pushed up, and my bare knees like scrubbed potatoes in the dark. I watched my sister, but Harriet moved carefully and changed clothes under the tent of her dress, and anyway she had always seemed more like a woman than a girl.

I had seen couplings on our farm: the black bull heaving his heft upon the back of the brown cow, then pulling back to reveal his tool—sharp and pointed, an angry dark red-pink. The ducks on the pond, how sometimes the male would chase and bother the skittering female, jump on her back, bite down on her head, push her underwater until I was sure she would drown. How, other times, the female would glance over her shoulder as if beckoning him. Nature, I had noticed, did not stop to watch these scenes. The other cows chewed their cuds and swished their tails; the other ducks stared straight ahead and held their heads up high.

I had seen the glistening hidden pinkness of dogs and cats, so startling when it showed itself, so raw and hairless. I had watched snails lock horns in the dirt of the herb garden, so that you could not tell if they were caught in war or love. The next day, when I returned to plant some seeds, I pushed aside the soil to find hundreds of shiny silver eggs. I had seen cows and ewes grow slick with sweat, roll their eyes into their heads and push their young into the world. I had watched a cow who had just freshened walk around for a day with bits of the afterbirth, a mess of richly colored innards, swinging from between her legs. Later I had watched her eat the afterbirth. In my mind all this meant violence, but also change. It meant unseen workings, places I could not see. I walked the farm in search of more, but the ants seemed always to be carrying scraps of food or dragging dead relations, and the dogs, though often sniffing at their secret parts and mine, had their meetings when I was not there.

On mornings when the sun was out, I had sat in the privy with the light slivering through the cracks and peered down at myself to see how there were five hairs in the place I should not look, then ten hairs, then a mass of patchy wool like the coat of a sickly black lamb. I knew the Lord would shun me for this looking, but I could not help it. In the attic I sprawled on my stomach on the hard floor and pressed my growing self into the wood.

Of men and women together I knew little, heard no murmurs from my parents down below, no sounds of strain or pleasure, though I would not have known exactly what to listen for. And yet among the women I knew, there was always another baby on the way. I knew how it got there, vaguely, from talking to girls at school. And I knew, through the steam of boiling water, the weight of wet rags and the cries of my mother or aunt in the next room, how it came out.

I was alone most often in my thoughts, which the others could not read, and in the second hayloft, where I climbed when I had finished with a long list of chores—up the ladder in the barn, then past the new hay to the next ladder, which took me even farther up. This was where the old hay was—dry and flammable, hardly even smelling anymore, hollow pale gold husks. We were not allowed up there. The floorboards were loose, and the hay could slide and cave in with no warning, drowning you. But no one ever seemed to know that I was there—the loft so far up, so far back that not even my father ever went up except to fill it, or every once in a while to send hay down the trap door into the stalls.

Afternoons, when I had done my chores, I climbed up and lay on the hay, feeling the heaviness of my limbs, letting the bits of straw poke and prod me. Each time I shifted, the whole surface moved beneath my weight. I could hear them calling me from up there, but I did not have to answer; it was as if I did not exist. Sometimes I brought magazines sent to us by my mother's sisters in Biddeford and Albany—*The Saturday Evening Gazette* and *The Ladies' Casket*—the pages worn from use. There were pictures of ladies inside, of new bonnets, pointed shoes, potions, salves and balms, corsets to reduce the waist. There were poems and songs, true stories about Paris and India, drawings of the latest in machines. In one of the magazines I saw a picture of Lowell, Massachusetts, the City of Spindles—brick building after brick building, the flowers in their window boxes, the girls coming home after work by the canal, arm in arm.

Often I would start to read the magazines and grow drowsy. It was warm up there, even in autumn. Mostly I slept, or watched the swallows navigate the rafters of the barn with a series of rapid turns.

Sometimes I daydreamed about places I might go and people I might meet.

"Aimee," I would tell them. "Not Amy or Emmy, Em-MAY." And they would ask where I got such an unusual name.

Sometimes, the sun slanting through the dust to light the place, I lifted up my skirts and looked. A pinkness, I found there, a hidden thing. It made me sick to look at it, but in the dizzy, ringing way of a fever. I buried it back in my skirts.

I do not know when Jeremiah began to spy on me. I would have never thought it possible; the ladder was tall and steep and he so scared of heights. I have no idea how long it had been going on when finally I caught him; I always felt eyes upon me, but for a long while I thought they were the ones my mother swore she had in the back of her head, or the all-seeing eyes of the Lord.

Yet he was there, my brother Jeremiah, hunched on the ladder, his eyes peering over the edge of the loft. He was silent and still, perched there hour after hour. Watching. He, who was as clumsy as a newborn calf, as fragile as a web, one of the meek who shall inherit. But what of his devil's store of patience, his sharp and curious eyes, the rapid turnings of his brain? He found his balance on that ladder. He did not stumble or fall. Not even a board creaked for the longest time.

I did not know he was there. First I slept, and then I woke, and then I lay rocking upon the heel of my hand, and (I did not see it happen; it happened, and then I saw it, as if it were a picture in a book) his head must have appeared over the edge, his shoulders, and all the rest of him, for he was there with his back hunched, his eyes fierce.

He did not want to move, or talk, or do anything but stare at me as if he had never seen me before, had never felt my hand thumping his back, or heard my sharp tongue, or run with me in the woods.

"Go back down!" I whispered, but then I realized he would tell what he had seen, and I would be dragged from the barn and placed with my burning fingers in the church.

"Stay," I whispered, and he inched toward me on his knees and held his hands up in the air in front of himself, trembling, as if he were considering touching something dreadful—a rotten piece of meat or a severed snake with its insides hanging out like string.

I showed him everything. I don't know why. I slid off my underthings and let my knees fall apart, and he sat on his hands and looked. Then I covered myself, and he lurched toward me as if he were falling. By then I was crying—loose, ugly tears, my mouth slack and wet—and he wiped my nose with his sleeve and said, "Don't cry, Aimee."

How things begin is the strangest thing. My brother and then not my brother, Jeremiah and then someone I did not know at all.

For one minute, two minutes, for what must have been no more than five minutes, he ran his hand up past my skirts and touched the aching place, and I pulled down his trousers as if I were about to bathe him and touched between his legs—like an earlobe it was, that sort of softness. So small, for he was just a boy and young for his age; it curled inside my hand. My mouth tried to touch his mouth—the mouth of my brother, of a boy we all knew would never live to be a man—but he pressed his lips together and turned his head. He buried his face in my hair, the hair he had braided so many times, and my hands on his back felt the sharpness of his shoulder blades, which were not the ones I knew, but those of someone else, a stranger—a boy still, but almost not.

He touched me as if I were the last thing left on earth—carefully and with the greatest attention, and not the least trace of timidity, so that I wondered if somehow he had touched this way before. He touched me as he might touch something unexpected he had found in the woods: the bleached, perfect skull of a deer; an Indian Pipe plant, translucent, veined and curved. He was quiet and calm, but my breath came fast and my head hurt as if someone were tightening a band around my brain. He did not speak. His breath when I smelled it was the breath I knew, of my brother—faintly sour and smelling of cornmeal and milk.

Then I breathed through my mouth so I would not recognize his smell.

For seconds or minutes—I am not sure—we touched, until his hand was webbed with the stretched, glittering threads of something issued from inside me.

Then we stopped. My hand returned to me, my brother's hand to him. The hayloft returned to me—its thick smells and colors—looking sharper and brighter than before, and at the same time more distant, a place I was already remembering from far away. I was not sure what had just happened, or why, or how, but I knew that from that moment on, I would begin to live a lie.

I pulled down my skirts, spit into the hay to get the taste of sin from my mouth, and prayed rapidly for forgiveness. I had brought sewing up there with me, a piece of quilt, and I took the needle from where it lay stuck in the bear paw pattern and drew blood from my finger, blood from his finger—on the hand that had not climbed beneath my skirts. Then I mixed our blood and swore him to secrecy.

"God in heaven will make you wither and turn gray if you tell what we just did," I said, and he did not tremble and look down as I expected, but nodded solemnly, like an adult, and licked the spot where our blood had mixed.

"What will you do now?" I asked, and he said supper, because it was that time.

Then he climbed down, and I climbed down after him, and at supper he ate one spoonful after another, and I felt a fever blotching my cheeks and said I was ill and could not eat.

Upstairs, my mother came to me with a cup of Number Six, a dark liquid made from herbs according to the directions of Doctor Thompson, an herbalist whose recipes she followed. I did not like these mixings up of flowers, barks and leaves, but I drank the mixture when she handed it to me, its taste moldy and full, like ripe fruit covered in soil. As I swallowed it down, I thought how it tasted too much like the touching I had just done.

"Too much sun," she said, and I said yes from where I was sitting as far back in the eaves as I could fit, my back pressed up against the wall. "Is that it?" she said, so I knew she knew it was not, and I said yes again.

That night I pulled my mattress to the far back corner of the loft, away from them, lonelier than I had ever been before, though it was nothing to what I would know later on.

It was the first of my lies.

Or no, not the first. The first was much earlier—I was eight—when Marshall Tabor accused me of taking a one-cent multiplication table from his desk and tearing it in half. When I denied the deed, Master Shattuck, who was short, jolly-looking and wicked, lashed at the palms of my open hands with his leather strap until I gave in, whipped into a lie, and said I'd done it, though I had not. It was one small lie, but one is just the beginning of a sum. My schoolmates asked me, "Why did you not say sooner that you tore it up, and save yourself a whipping?" My father said, "Do you know what becomes of liars?" And all I could do was shake my head and hold my striped hands behind my back and lose my voice until I knew that I had done it, if not in this world, then in the world inside my mind. Later I held my hands up in the air and told Harriet how I had torn the paper in half *like this* because Marshall Tabor was a fat, stupid boy with rotten teeth.

My brother stopped following me, though I could tell he was still tracking my every motion in his mind. My body swelled, itched and heaved all that year. When my blood came, a few months after Jeremiah found me in the barn, I did not tell my mother, but swaddled myself in tow-cloth rags the way I knew my sister did and leaned quietly over the fist of pain opening and closing inside me. I could not wash the rags without my mother knowing, so I balled them up under my dress and buried them in the woods.

"You've had your bleedings," she said to me after the second month, one day when we were sitting in the kitchen making pies. I said yes, but it didn't matter, I knew what to do.

"You're earlier than Harriet, the same age as me," she said, as if I were supposed to answer, but I stared off into the distance and focused my ears on the steady hacking noises made by my brothers chopping wood.

Raspberry leaves, rosemary and nettles for the cramps and swelling, my mother told me. The rags had to be washed in the creek, not in the basin in the house, or ill fortune would come, and even more important, they had to be washed when no one was around, especially no man, and then they must be left to dry on a line she had rigged up for that purpose in the lean-to by the tool section of the barn.

"If you scrub it between two flat rocks in the sun, it will all come out," she said.

"What about winter?" I asked.

I pictured the creek covered with snow, my blood staining red upon white the way the dogs stained brown and yellow with their leavings. My blood bearing into the snow, drilling red-rimmed holes.

"In winter we boil them," my mother said quietly. "But when your father isn't home."

She peeled an apple with one swift circling of her knife, and I watched the skin curl in a ribbon by her hand.

"It's all so simple, once you get in the habit. Nobody has to know when you're in your time."

I did not ask her how she knew. It was nothing that surprised me; she had made me and had eyes in the back of her head.

She rolled out the dough, then went to the hutch and came back with the Bible, whose pages she had marked in advance with fresh oak leaves, the spiked ends sticking out from different sections of the Book. I read:

"From the lips of a loose woman drip honey, and her mouth is smoother than oil, but in the end she is more bitter than wormwood, and sharp as a two-edged sword." And marked by another leaf, and by my mother's outstretched finger directing me to the verse: "Who can find a virtuous woman? for her price is far above rubies. The heart of her husband doth safely trust in her, so that he shall have no need of spoil. She will do him good and not evil all the days of her life. She seeks wool and flax, and worketh willingly with her hands. She is like the merchants' ships; she bringeth her food from afar."

Then my mother came to me and held me, which was rare for her, and I felt how my new bosom pressed up against the bosom that had fed me, and how her hands, splayed on my

back, were tensed with the burden of her love for me. Though I
tried to hug my mother, my body would not help me. I stood
stiffly for a moment, then moved away. My dress, when I took
it off that night, was marked by the blurry flour shadows of
her palms.

3

Plumey walks and the earth shakes; I can hear her coming long before she stops, thick and stolid, by my door. I say hello, but she doesn't answer; I am used to her ways and do not mind. As a child I would have scoffed at her and called her names. I would have found her silence jarring; with the other children, I'd have tried to taunt and prod her into words. Her thick stare would have made me want to shake her, to jolt some movement into the stubborn blankness of her eyes. She comes from the Maine coast, Amos told me, from a house caught fire, a family eaten up by flames. When the townspeople searched for traces among the ashes, they thought they found the bones of all the children, but three weeks later a creature crawled into town, its hair matted, its skin the color and dusty hardness of dry clay. The pastor's wife planted it in a tub of steaming water and removed layer after layer to find the girl unbroken in her pale white child's body, but with no voice. What happened? asked the town. Where have you been? How did you get out?

But she could not seem to find the words.

They sent her south, here to New Hampshire where she had relatives, the childless Doctor and his wife. Her uncle and aunt treated her well, dressed her up, but she was too old to be a baby for the Doctor's wife, and too young to be a companion. They talked to her, but her own words, when finally they came, were thin and halting and usually made no sense. They put ribbons in her hair, but she had probably never been a pretty child, and now, though she had lived through fire, she looked pale and bloated like a creature too long underwater. Only her name, Plumey, held the promise of something still unfurling in her—that, and a certain rare flicker in her eyes.

She comes to see me on her way to nowhere. I never know if she is coming to see my bog—a puddly reminder of the Maine sea—or myself, but she always comes first to my door, dressed in the brightest calicos, a starched ribbon mocking her lank, blond braid. The Doctor and his wife don't know what to do with her or how much is working in her head, and so they leave her be. When she first arrived, Amos says, they took her to the schoolroom, but she got up and wandered out the door during the first lesson. The teacher thought she had gone to the privy without asking, but she never came back. Later they found her sleeping by a brook. At home they gave her small chores, but she sewed the two edges of the pillowcase together with jagged

stitches and gave the cat cough remedies to drink. Now—
she must be ten or eleven—she lives in a world without ex-
pectations, with no school to go to, no chores to do, no one,
aside from my own self and her memories, to visit. And yet
she is a busy girl and must have a purpose, though I do not
pretend to know it.

The air today has a chill, but I look out the door to see
her panting, sweat beading her brow and her upper lip.

"Plumey."

I peer at her cupped hands.

"What have you brought?"

She shows me a spool of thread, deep pink and of a
fine quality. Her hands and pockets are full of treasures. I
do not know if they are given to her or if she steals them,
but I do know she lets go of them easily, with a kind and
generous hand. Now she leans into the doorway, sets the
spool in the middle of her wide palm and holds it out.

"For me?"

She nods. I pat her hand as I take the spool, and her
eyes smile for a brief instant, though her mouth stays
pressed in a tight line. I back into the darkness of my house
and tuck the spool in a basket in case she remembers to ask
for it in one of her rare moments of speech.

"Spool?" I will say. "What spool?"

I am not trying to trick her; it is simply a color I like
well, and it means nothing much to her.

She is outside, still leaning by my door, and so I join
her, and we sit on the two log stools. From her deep pocket
she pulls a pouch of sugar. Yesterday I gave her a straw
broom to trade for it. Now I can make cranberry bread.

"Thank you," I say, and hand her a tiny pine needle
basket for her trouble.

Thank you, her eyes say back, and the basket disappears into her skirts.

Sometimes it is as if I am her sister, though we are decades and decades apart. Then we sit quietly thinking of nothing in particular, so comfortable, as though we were both too old, too tired, to bother with conversation—or too young to know yet how to talk. Other times, Plumey pounds at the air or speaks nonsense to an invisible presence at her side. Then it is as if I am her uncle, the Doctor, and I stare at her and wonder what she hides inside her wide brow—if words are left inside her, refusing to come out, or if her insides have been charred beyond repair.

It is not as if she cannot talk sentences, for talk, or chant, she does—long lists, drawn from the papers, I suppose.

"Healing Lotions," she chants in a thin, high, pretty voice, and I picture the balm on my sore back, and then, in a voice much quicker and brighter than the dullness of her eyes, she singsongs, "Excellent Vanilla Anti-dyspeptic Bitters Family Groceries Last Chance Summer Boots Four Cent Reward Chairs and Tables Rooms to Let Periodical Pills New Music Ladies' Slips Misses Ties—"

"Shush, Plumey," I tell her after a while, for she gives me sick headaches, but she cannot seem to stop.

"—Feather Renovators. Corn Plaster Worm Lozenges Old Rags—"

My mother used to say that you are known by the company you keep, and that the apple never falls far from the tree. I love this Plumey, as if she were my own. I love her because she has nothing to do with her days, and yet she is a busy girl; because she is not fair of face, and yet she fills her pockets with treasures and moves through the world with an open hand. I love her because she has lost her own village and sea, flesh and blood, and yet she knows the path to my bog and will sit and chant to me.

"You're a good girl," I tell her.

"Good," she mouths back to me, though no sound comes out.

I say it again—"good"—hoping she will echo me, but she purses her mouth as if I have forced her to swallow something sour.

Because I feed my rabbits and chickens, offer them shelter, worry over them and hold them in the night, they give me fur and eggs. I save some eggs for myself, put the rest in a wire basket and give the basket to Amos or Plumey when they come. Sometimes I put other things inside it, or in a burlap sack: twig brooms; small, tight baskets woven from pine needles or rushes; mittens and stockings made from rabbit fur; little cloth sacks that I have sewn and stuffed with herbs. My mother taught me to make many things; the rest I have taught myself.

If one of my chickens dies, I scald it, pluck its feathers and put them in a bundle to sell. If the bird was not diseased, I trade the meat with Amos for some venison or pork. Sometimes, if I am very hungry and Amos does not come, I will eat the chicken, but I do not like to do it—these creatures are my constant company, too close to family to me. Once in a while I find hawk or eagle feathers and cut their tips into fine quills. From barley, wild cranberry, bog myrtle and honey, I make a drink, halfway between beer and fruit wine.

Every three months I shear my rabbits, then spin their wool into the softest yarn. When the does multiply, I fatten the young ones and send some of them off with Amos, who sells them for their meat and fur. I keep ten does at a time, no more.

Also a buck, off in his hutch. At first I didn't like to take the young ones from their mothers, but if I didn't remove them as soon as they were weaned, more kept coming, since I couldn't always tell the does from the bucks when they were young. Now I ask Amos to go in and collect them.

When I want a doe to kindle, I scoop her up and carry her to the buck. Sometimes she kicks and scrambles as I try to put her in his hutch. Other times she arches toward him. I do not mate the blind one; she is too frightened a creature, nervous and darting, her eyes a milky gray. Once I put a few kits next to her to see what she would do, but she only made small grunting noises and moved away from the babies tunneling into her side.

Amos and Plumey take away my eggs and rabbits, wine and brooms. I used to go to town myself, but they don't seem to mind, and it is easier this way. When they come back they bring me other things: kerosene for my lantern, canning jars, a pail of milk, or perhaps a slab of cheese. Nut coal to burn, some pine knot and tallow candles. A cracked mirror once—to see your face, said Amos, but I propped it up behind a candle to multiply the light; only now and then do I steal glances at myself. When I was a child I loved mirrors—the way they showed me to myself from the outside. *This girl windblown on a ship*, I'd picture. *This girl flying on a sleigh.* How did I get from there to here, I wonder sometimes, only perhaps I am the same old me, for my eyes, when I look, stare gray and watchful, as they always have.

Before Plumey leaves for town, I stand before her and say what I need three times: *Needleneedleneedle. Sugarsugarsugar.* I must repeat it, because I do not know how her mind is working. Sometimes I feel her laughing at me, watching me as if from very far away: Who is this woman who speaks to me in echoes, as if I were a fool?

But other times she comes back a few days later and hands me something I never asked for. Once she held out a worn, eyeless rag doll she must have taken from some other child, since the Doctor and his wife would never give her a doll like that. I had not asked for a doll, but for a bit of cloth. If it had been the fancy doll of a rich child, I might have taken it or let Plumey keep it for herself; a rich girl would get other toys in its place. But this was the doll of a poor child, made from rough sheeting and dressed in a filthy piece of sacking cloth. For a moment I thought it might have been her own, a survivor of the fire like herself. Then I remembered that Amos had said she had been naked and empty-handed the day she reappeared in her old town.

"Is that yours?" I asked her, and she shook her head.

"Then you need to take it back."

She held it out again. I had needed cloth to mend a hole in my dress. For days I had waited, hearing my instructions— *clothclothcloth*—in my mind.

"No," I said, trying to keep my voice level, ending up sounding sharp. "No, it's not what I needed, and you took it from someone. You need to take it back, Plumey, understand? You take it back right now."

She nodded and smiled, smiled and nodded—no anger on her face—but she did not stay to visit, and as she walked away, just as she was almost out of sight, I saw her twist the doll's neck around until the head was facing crooked above the spineless back. Then she lifted her arm above her head and pitched the doll into the bog.

I made her a doll from cornhusks to give her the next time she came by. I filled its head with lavender, peppermint and lemon balm, to calm the nerves, and gave it hair of corn silk, a braid on each side like Plumey's own. I bound the ends of each braid with a knot of pink thread, but how to draw the face?

If it smiled too much, she might think it was laughing at her. If it frowned, she might feel disapproval in its gaze. I remembered the dolls my sister had played with as a child—the way their eyes bore into me, their smiles more like sneers. I left this doll faceless, like the one Plumey had brought me. When I gave it to her, she tucked it quickly into her apron pocket, and her own face twitched for a moment into an expression I could not read.

It is the deepest mystery what goes on inside her—inside anybody's—head.

Amos brings me things he thinks I need. Sometimes it is nails and boards to patch up a gap in the roof. Sometimes it is cloth for a winter dress. Once it was chocolate. I had not seen chocolate for so long, I didn't recognize it.

"What's this?" I asked him, staring down at the small cube wrapped in brown paper.

"Open it," he said, and I tore loose the paper and saw a block of something sitting there, deep brown and perfectly square. I turned it over in my hand, hefted its weight, felt how it grew softer as I touched it, oily. Then a memory came to me, so carefully put away I had to tug to let it out: Something this size, one Christmas season when I was around seven or eight. Something in paper like this. My father had taken me on his lap, unwrapped the paper, broken a chip from the cube, and told me to taste.

It was so smooth, that chocolate, so rich, so unlike anything I had ever eaten, that I leaned down over my father's palm and snatched the rest of the cube into my mouth like a starving animal. I felt my teeth graze my father's palm, tasted the chocolate bulky in my mouth.

And then he slapped me, sharp across the side of my

cheek so that I bit my tongue and felt the heavy taste of chocolate mix with the silvery taste of blood.

"Spit it out!" he said, and his wide hand closed tight
around my chin. "Go on and spit it out!"

His thumb and finger closed around my jaw, pushing on
the bone until my mouth opened like a puppet's and the mess
of chocolate spilled out into his other hand. Still he pressed on
my face until I thought my teeth would break. I felt a cry rise
up, but something stopped it. Finally, he released me. I sat
rigid on his lap, straight-backed. We both looked down at the
chocolate as it sat in his palm like a lump of fresh, unhealthy
dung.

His voice was loud and breathless with disgust. He said,
"You greedy thing." He said, "Half for you, half for Harriet,
and now you've gone and ate it all!"

Mouth big enough to sail a ship in. Appetite like a pack
of starving wolves. I don't know if my father said these things
just then. These things were said to me when I was a child,
more than once. I always ate a lot, more than my brothers. It
was not so much that I was hungry as that I was afraid (though
it never happened) that we would run out of food the next day
or the next. We were not poor, but my father had been poor as
a young boy, and we lived surrounded by want. I saw how he
ate as if someone were about to snatch away his food, and how
many of the children at school found nothing but a heel of
bread inside their pails.

"Count every blessing on your plate," my mother said
each night at supper, and I would stare down at the potatoes,
the chicken leg, the pile of peas and start, silently, to count,
beginning with the big food, moving on to the difficult peas.

But I also ate so much because I loved the look and taste
of food, the texture—the way the peas were first round, then
bursting, then flat upon my tongue; how the potato skin tore

open to let steam float up into my face. The deep red of cranberry relish, the pink of ham, the yellow-white of new corn with its neat rows of teeth.

My father pushed me off his lap, or perhaps I scrambled down. I know I saw his heavy boots surrounded by a puddle of water where the snow was melting off. I swallowed to get the chocolate taste from my mouth. Still it lingered; still part of me could not help loving it and wanting more. I watched him push back his chair, stand up tall, bend toward me for an instant as if he might strike me again.

I backed toward the door, watching my father as warily as if he were hunting me. *Careful, you don't know him*, I remember thinking, almost in my mother's voice. I had seen him take the heads off chickens. And then my own voice: *Yes, but neither does he know me*. I locked him in my gaze, and I knew I had nothing more to fear when he was the first to look away.

He smeared the mess of chocolate onto the brown wrapper, balled it up and hurled it toward the fire, but it wobbled on the edge of the hearth and then stood still.

I'll get it, I thought. After he is gone.

Instead, as soon as my father left the room, my bones grew soft, and I found myself kneeling on the floor, crying in loose gulps. I pictured myself snatching the wrapper from the edge of the hearth, hiding it upstairs in a cranny between beams, sneaking moments to taste and smell it. But I knew I would not touch the chocolate, not with my face throbbing and my father nearby. I wanted, then, to push the wrapper into the fire and watch it burn, but even this I did not dare to do.

When I dried my tears and went into the kitchen, Harriet looked up and said softly that my jaw was turning purple. They must have heard the whole thing, my mother and Harriet. I lifted my face to my mother, the tears starting up again now that I knew I had a mark to prove my pain. She handed me a warm cloth to hold against my jaw, but she would not comfort me. I do not know if she thought my father was in the right, or if she disagreed but would not cross him. My father's will did not show itself often; perhaps she was as surprised as I was. What did she know of the man she lived with? Was he a gentle man with sudden, rare spinnings into rage, or an angry man who mostly held himself in check?

I have always thought that he gave up on me that day, washed his hands of me, though I could not have been more than seven: *Like an animal, where did she come from?* As I fell asleep that night, I was angrier at my mother, who did not come to rescue me. Who loved chocolate—I was sure she did, though she would never say. My father never gave us sweets again at Christmas, and he never struck me again.

Amos brought me chocolate as a present—as an opening, a bright pinprick into a world that was not the useful world of nails and kerosene. His gift had taken planning and money, more than the worth of my eggs.

Taste me, the chocolate said to me. Smile and taste me, then thank Amos, who has been so kind.

I could not.

I could hold the cube, even bend my mouth into a grimace of a smile, but I could not put that chocolate in my mouth. That many years later, my father's ghosthand on my jaw. But something else, something more. Chocolates from France, *Bon-Bons de Paris*—in a box, wrapped not in brown, but in silver paper that reflected, distorted, my eyes as I held it up.

I have worked hard to reach a quieter ground.

"I—" I said to Amos.

"It's just candy," he said gruffly. "I picked it up in town."

I nodded, tried to eat it, but far as I was from those other times, I felt my throat close up, then the taste of cornmeal and weak tea. I touched my neck, shifting on the stool, and the chocolate fell from my lap and landed in the dirt.

I do not know how long I sat there like that; perhaps I fell into a kind of sleep. When at last I looked up, the sun seemed lower in the sky and a chill had come up, making goose bumps rise along my arms.

And Amos? Gone, but what did I expect, the chocolate still lying there, half-melted now, mixed in with dust and grass. I gathered it up: a handful of ants, dirt, stickiness, brown paper wrapper. Slowly, searching for my balance, I walked out over the peat and threw the whole mess into the bog pond.

Most of it went down.

I pictured the chocolate bumping up against the lips of the hunter, sweetening the old witch woman and the rag doll, coating the udders of the cow. To keep the witches from walking after death, the people pinned their bodies to the bottom of the bog with oak stakes. Later, peatcutters found them in the layers of peat, their limbs still whole, the sticks still poking through. There are stories: How one was found with a sack of human eyeteeth around her neck; how one nursed a wolf pup, its snout still clamped to her breast.

That day I crawled into bed when the sun was still on its way down, wrapped my arms around myself and rocked.

I'm sorry, Amos, I said, but to myself.

If we had not each been so skittish, I might have turned to him and told him; he might have pretended not to hear, then nodded and moved into my arms. But he was not there, did not live by my side. Like water bugs we darted towards each other, then away.

Amos did not come back for some time after that. He let me run out of things and reach a point where I considered going into town myself. Each time I prepared to make the trip, I pictured how people would stare—*The bog lady, remember? So rare that she lets herself be seen.* In fact, those times I did go to town over the years, nothing ever happened. *May I help you?* asked the man in the store, and my bag filled up with things. Sometimes on the street a woman would glance at me, raise an eyebrow, draw her daughter close: *See what happens if you stray?* Or perhaps—probably—I imagined it. How silly, I'd tell myself, walking home, to think these people had you on their minds.

Somewhere hushed inside myself I knew that wasn't it. On the other side of my parents' land, the acres stretching out to the west, to the north of this bog, my brother Luke is living, and my mother. If I go to town, I might see her. She might look right through me—or stare into my eyes.

I ran out of cornmeal. I ran out of candles, flour, grease to cook my eggs. At the last minute, Amos came. Silent and with a bag full of necessities. No presents.

"Sit," I said. "I'll get you some tea."

He threw down the bag.

"I was about to go myself," I told him, but he only pivoted on his crutches and left.

Two days later he was back, and that night he stayed—salty, sweet—in my arms. There is no room for grudges the way we live; he knows it as well as I. I am carving him a chicken out of balsam wood, have been working on it for months. A M O S, I carve on its wing. For eyes I put in tiny chips of acorn shells; this bird has a bright and seeing gaze. For claws and a beak, I carve sharpness; it must be able to worm, root and find grubs. I will put it in the sack with the brooms I have made. Amos will go away, and the next time he comes, he might not thank me. That is fine.

Somewhere—next to where Amos eats or sleeps or takes

off his wooden leg to let his skin breathe air—my chicken will sit near him. Things I have made with my hands are everywhere in this world: my brooms sweep, my baskets hold trinkets, my preserves draw children with their colors and put sweetness in their throats. This is how touch travels, from me to you to you.

4

It is important to know where and how and when you were born.

My mother said I was born in her bed on July seventh, Eighteen hundred and twenty-nine, just before dawn—that time when the air seems loaded with black dust and it is difficult to make out anything at all. I was born in the house I grew up in, in the string bed my father built. I do not know if I was a difficult or easy birth; my mother did not say. She said I howled and waved my arms when I came out.

During my fourteenth year I became an expert with my rags. I went to school, came home, did my chores, dressed and undressed under the tent of my gown. For hours at a time, I helped my mother in the kitchen: blanching ham, grinding spices and green coffee, cutting and pounding loaf sugar, sifting heavy flour, soaking oatmeal overnight, shelling nuts, seeding raisins, making and nurturing the temperamental yeast.

Blue Monday was wash day; Tuesday we ironed, two days buried under clothes. A poor girl down the road wanted to help for a little money, but my mother said no. She never said why, but I was sure it was because she did not want someone else's hands touching the clothes that touched our bodies. Even the way she folded the boys' clothes was different from the way she folded her own, Harriet's and mine; her hands sped up, became more careful when she came to the undergarments of my father or brothers. Her eyes stayed raised as if she hoped to forget what she was touching and not draw attention to her hands. To bother her I would linger slightly, as I ironed, on my brother John's trousers. I would hum, lean over and examine the fabric for wrinkles while I pushed the heavy nose of the iron up a leg.

"Hurry yourself up," my mother would say. "You'll scald it the way you go so slow."

Sheets seemed to be her favorite thing because they had no holes, no places to come undone, and belonged to no one in particular. Folding them between us was like a kind of dance—leaning back to pull the wrinkles from the fabric; stepping, then, toward each other, arms upraised, faces almost touching as the two sides of the sheet embraced. Backing up again as the fabric caught a swell of air and lifted in a puff.

My mother's hair was always curled from the steam of the iron, her cheeks flushed so that she looked young and excited. Sometimes I would feel a sharp, painful dart of love for her—this woman retreating from me with her hands gripping the sheet, then coming at me again, sometimes playful, waltzing, mostly just anxious to get done. I was always sorry to see so much made into so little, to watch my mother turn away from me to other things. We began with a huge, billowing wilderness between us. We ended with a cold, white cube.

Nights, I wedged myself back into a far corner of the loft, sleeping alone on a cornhusk pallet with a thick down quilt. Harriet slept in the other corner by herself, leaving the boys in a heap in the middle of the room. Jeremiah and I skirted wide circles around each other and never met each other's eyes.

Outside the kitchen, I did other tasks—milked the cows and fed the chickens, finished a sampler, in perfect cross stitch: *Welcome Tired Stranger to Our Home.* I went to church on Sundays, and after church I walked with the other girls my age along the river. I was quiet while they chattered; everyone seemed to have forgotten how much I used to talk. Sometimes I went visiting at my friend Eliza's on Sunday afternoons; she lived on the farm down the road and was a year behind me in school because she had started late. While I looked older than my years, Eliza looked much younger—tiny and thin, with huge, fast-blinking eyes and quick hands. She did not seem to notice my changes, and often we cut figures out of catalogs and made paper dolls together. We never played with them, but just kept making more stiff people and letting them drop to the floor.

One day before church, Eliza took me aside and told me she couldn't visit that afternoon. She was ill, she whispered proudly, from her You-Know-Whats. After that I couldn't stop thinking about it, all those women, everywhere, with darkness trickling between their legs. All those bodies letting go that way, without the permission of their owners. Rag after rag after rag. Why blood, I wondered. Why not just water or tears? Though it had been some time since my bleedings had started, I was still bothered each month by the sight of that redness, so *red*, my insides turning out. I would sit in church and look at all the girls and women sitting calmly, hands clasped in their laps, and wonder who was in her time.

I sat calmly. I clasped my hands. In church I was a good girl and did not bring my family shame, but still my mother must have worried at my prettiness, for she made me pull my hair back into a tight bun in public and wear dresses that did not press tight. At home I was there and not there, pleasant one moment, sullen and sharp the next. They simply came upon me, those moods, and when they arrived I could not make my fingers stitch another stitch or pluck another feather. Then I would drop my task and rush outside, only to pace in a quick circle around the barnyard and into the kitchen again, my mother's eyes pulling me back like a magnet. She never asked me questions, but I could hear her anyway: *You used to be so happy at my side, what has become of you? Why don't you ever sit still?*

Boys in our town looked at me; I noticed out of the corner of my eye. They were all friends of my brothers or brothers of my friends—lank, splotchy-skinned boys with Adam's apples jutting from their throats as if something they ate had lodged there like a pebble. I looked at them as little as possible, but I did watch a few men in the town, or not men really, but parts of them: The arms of the blacksmith—how, when he lifted things, his muscles shivered like the flanks of the horses he shoed. The large shoulder blades of my father's friend Samuel Plain poking at his shirt like the beginnings of wings, and the heart of sweat that bled onto his broad back when he heaved lumber. The long neck of the minister, and his jawline, tight and wedge-shaped as an iron. I would have touched those things, but not their owners.

Inside, something was slow-rising in me, putting pressure on my bones, crowding my blood, making me short of breath. Sometimes I thought it was my sin and lying. I never looked at myself anymore if I could help it. I never touched my hidden parts, not even when I was alone. My baths, when I took them, were short and angry, but I preferred not to take them at all and would only strip behind the curtain and kneel in the tub when my mother started remarking on my smell. It was not that I thought I was ugly. I knew I was not. But I could feel how my sin had been written on me—how my mother, if she poked her head around the curtain to hand me a cake of soap, would be able to read it in the way my lap-hair grew sleek underwater and my breasts blushed and hardened in the cold air. What did she know that she was not saying? I hunched over and scrubbed my legs and arms, my shoulders and the middle of my stomach, the safe places, the ones that had not changed.

Jeremiah grew half a head in half a year. The sound of his cracking voice and the sight of his body lurching into manhood disgusted me. His skin, so white and smooth before, burst into redness. His arms grew too quickly; his white wrists hung from his cuffs like things not meant to be seen. Though he still walked around with a handkerchief balled in his fist, he began to look more like my father or brother John, or like the boys in town. His neck thickened; the hair on his head started to darken and curl.

Worse, he would not talk to me, did not need me. At night

he still woke coughing. I lay silent in my corner, part of me wanting to pound his back and sit with him outside, the rest of me wishing he would take his hacking sounds and go away.

No, I told myself then, each thought of his leaving like an omen of death, one I had wished upon him myself. Instead of pounding on my brother's back, I reached over the edge of my mattress and knocked softly on the wood planks of the floor to keep my evil thoughts from coming true. After a while the thoughts came so quickly, so fiercely, that I could not prevent my hand from knocking. Often I lay that way for hours— imagining his doom, my parents', my own—then tap-tapping it away.

I knew this was plain superstition and would be frowned upon by the Lord and my mother, so after each knock I said a little prayer, and soon my ritual grew longer: thought, knock, prayer, and then again. In the hayloft I had not been able to keep my hand from myself and my brother; now I could not keep it from the wood. Sometimes in daylight I looked at my own hand and felt it had been added onto me as an unkind afterthought, something to sin with, to hammer against the world until my knuckles grew scraped and raw.

The part about touching, the part I tried to forget, still came to me in the briefest slivers. Mostly when this happened I grabbed onto something quickly—a song, a prayer, the numbers backwards from one hundred. Sometimes I was not quick enough, and then something would rise in me until a bitter taste curled my tongue.

His hand and my hand, his softness and the liquid I made, foreign as the juice of the pomegranate fruits I had read about in the Bible: "Your two cheeks are an orchard of pomegranates, an orchard of rare fruits." I thought, then, of those other words, "bitter as wormwood," and of my mother—how once she had loved me best, and how she knew now, though she did not say, that I could not look at her with a steady gaze. I thought, too, of my father. He would not let me watch him at work anymore, told me it was not fitting for me to hang around like a barnrat when I could be helping get supper in the house.

Fine, I told him. I was just on my way inside.

For the first time, I found my stomach turning at the smell of the animals—the cow barn so sweet and heavy, ripe feed mixed with the edge of fresh manure; the hen house sharp with the smell of chicken and old egg; the sheep, wet after a rainfall, stinking like mildewed clothes and burn ointment. Even the animals themselves disgusted me, the way they nosed over looking for food each time I walked by, the way they lifted their tails before the whole world and pushed their droppings out their ugly knotted holes. They knew nothing but the pens where they had been born and would die their stupid deaths.

And then the world. I could feel it waiting, just over the rim of the hill, round like a fruit—an orange or, better yet, a pomegranate (which I pictured like an orange only deep, deep red)—ready for me to cup it in my hand. In my mind this world was spacious, yet full of people. It was big enough to hold me, but small enough for me to hold, filled with dresses I had cut from catalogs and countries I had traced from maps. The animals in it were camels, elephants and monkeys, and they had no smells. Ships sailed across this world, clocks chimed from belltowers. Girls wore white and walked with their arms linked together, like daisy chains.

Different things happened to the girls in our town. The poorest girls never went to school, or dropped out at nine or ten and went to help on the farm. The next poorest girls stayed in school until thirteen or fourteen. Then they helped on the farm, or stitched boots piecework at home for a factory in Boston, or plaited bonnets from palm leaves brought all the way from Cuba by traveling men. Sometimes the girls were sent as house servants to the bigger towns. Some of them got married at fourteen or fifteen. Some waited a few years. A few never married and became spinster ladies, maiden aunts spinning at their wheels.

The rich girls—and there were only a few—were sent to Boston, Albany or Portland to live with relatives and attend schools for ladies, where they learned to play piano, speak French and hold their forks. At holidays they would come back with the newest in bonnets, fur muffs, shoes with buttons made from pearls. I knew one girl, Annette, because her father bought her a foal from us. She wrapped her shoes in burlap before she would walk across our field. Her face looked bleached from where she had tried to hide her freckles with powder. Miss Hoity-Toity, we called her behind her back. Miss See-How-I-Stick-My-Pinky-Out-to-Lift-My-Little-Cup.

I was not one of the richest, not one of the poorest or the next poorest girls. Our farm, which had been my mother's father's farm before that, was medium-sized and holding on with a little left to spare. Now my grandparents had sold their grain mill and moved to Biddeford with their youngest daughter, and though they claimed they made the move because the winters were too hard on the farm, we all knew they thought my mother had thrown away her life in marrying down. Most of my aunts and uncles had moved to the city or gone West, taking my cousins with them. "Spread all over the place," my mother would say, flinging out her arms.

Sometimes my father hired other people's children during harvest time so we, so I, really, could stay in school. Harriet was not a good student, and John had already begun apprenticing to learn the blacksmith trade. Jeremiah was always sick.

When I was fourteen, my mother had Luke, and my sister, who was good with children, began to stay home to tend the younger ones.

I was the quickest at my lessons. I was to stay in school and apprentice myself to my teacher until I got a little older and a post opened up for me in one of the nearby schools. My mother had been a summer schoolmistress for two seasons before she met my father. She spoke of those days often, and as if they had been a decade: The time we painted a map on a sheet, the time lice got into every head and the room reeked of kerosene for months, the hymns I taught them, the spelling bees we had, their handwriting, perfect as a queen's.

My mother could not spell; I knew that. Her handwriting was even blockier and more awkward than my own. During her second summer at the school, she met my father in town at her father's mill. He had come from the neighboring town. I don't know what happened. Did they look at each other and fall in love? Did she marry him to escape the schoolroom? I knew he brought her flowers once. Within a month, they were engaged. Married within three. My mother told me the dates when I asked, but she never told me how or why.

You'll just teach until you marry, she said.

I was fourteen and a half when I turned from pupil to apprentice-teacher. *You'll just teach until you marry*, but I knew I could not marry a boy like my brothers, with yellow teeth and splotchy skin and eyes that saw no farther than the next big hill. Everywhere I looked, I saw nothing but such boys. And so, though I did not say so to my mother, I knew I would become an old maid, a maiden aunt in that schoolroom. I would not have memories of spelling bees and maps on sheets. Spelling bees would be my life.

The smell of the classroom—of chalk and wet wraps and the wood stove burning, the acrid smell of ink—began to sour my stomach. The sound of the chalk screeching over the board began to tear at me, until I would have to dig my fingernails into my palms. The sight of the heads of the other students, bored, dull and sleepy, made me want to stand up in the middle of a lesson, howl and lift my skirts above my head.

For years I had liked school—the books, anyway, about places I had never been. Now, as a teacher's apprentice, even the books seemed to taunt me. I could not be a teacher and rap knuckles with a ruler, could not go through the tables of arithmetic and teach how to spell "separate" and "yield," only to come home at night coated with chalk as if my skin were turning to dust. I could not mark off who was there and who was not, who was sick with the fever, whose drunken father had kept him home to tend the animals. I could not, especially, use that chalk, which coated the hands and filled the air with dust and the mouth with a white panic.

I had seen drawings of the factory towns.

Brick upon brick, four stories high, and in front, a paved street. In front of the street, rails where the trolley ran, and in front of the rails, trees—as straight and even, as city-careful as the bricks. On the rooftops, chimneys—not just one or two, but chimney after chimney, and every so often a belltower, where a bright, plump bell hung waiting to be rung. Flower boxes on the windows, vines trailing down—not too far, but delicately, like ladies' fingers. Down below, tiny people—in buggies, on horses, on foot. Men with wheelbarrows and boys with hoops. Women with waists you could circle with your hands. And girls—everywhere—walking in groups of two or three or four, out on the streets or hidden behind walls, invisible, a honeycomb of busy bees. Tending the flowers, tending the looms, improving themselves, making enough money to buy the bonnets in the pictures and the parasols, and tickets to Boston and beyond.

Other things I had seen: pieces of the money the girls earned there—not real money, not like the bills we used, but play money that worked as real if you used it at the company stores. Lily Perkins, Harriet's friend, had a sister, Helen, who let us see a bill when she came home from the mills for a funeral. She held it up, only touching it at the edges as if her fingers might soil it—or as if it might soil her fingers, it was hard to tell. *Look*, she said. *Don't touch*. Fives all over it, fat and rounded, their edges shaded so they looked like heavy objects you could shift from palm to palm. There were coins printed on the bill, each coin with its own five. The coins were arranged in circles like the petals of a flower. Manufacturers Bank. On Demand.

And printed in the middle, a girl who looked nothing like the other girls I went to school with, but something like me—dark eyes, long curls, that certain proud tilt to her head. She was gazing over her shoulder at two little children who stood with long spools cradled in their arms. Her hand rested on a big machine. Next to her a man bent over the machine, and behind her the light poured in, bathing them like angels. They were surrounded—that girl who was me and that man—in every direction by the number five.

"Doffers," said my classmate's sister, who was holding up the bill.

And we all nodded as if we knew exactly what she meant.

First my mother told me I had a bee in my bonnet.

"Get that out of your head," she said. "You're not going anywhere. You're training to be a schoolteacher, which is more than most girls get to do with themselves. You die of lung diseases in those factories. Those girls dip snuff just to get the lint out of their throats. That cotton gets inside your lungs and makes a cocoon from the inside out, and you choke to death inside your own lungs."

Then, the summer I turned fifteen, an agent from the factory came to town, and I stood in the kitchen of my friend Eliza's house while he talked to her parents in the front room and showed them drawings.

"I don't know," Eliza and I heard her father say in his gruff voice. "Awful far off to send a girl so young."

The agent wore a city hat. We had never seen him before, but he seemed to know everything about us:

Look at the Watkins girl—one year and already saved enough to pull her father out of debt. A new barn they're building now, with their daughter's help, to house some forty head of cattle. Look at the two McDuffy sisters, from New Milford. They were wild ones before they went off, everyone knew it. Now Annie was fixing to marry a schoolteacher she had met down there, and little Maddy was rising quickly through the ranks and already managed her own looms at the Boott Corporation.

"Our Eliza's not a wild one," her mother said, and Eliza poked me.

"Of course not," said the agent.

"She helps out a good bit about the home, always has," her mother said.

"And Alice is the one beneath her?" said the agent. "I hear she's a mighty big help herself. They've got to grow up and go off on their own. I know it myself. My eldest has been working down there for two years now. I shed a big tear when she left the home, but to see what it's done for her . . ."

"But you live down there," Eliza's mother said. "She can stay with you. It's having them so far off—"

"Oh, but I'm a traveling man, ma'am," said the agent. "And my wife, bless her, went to her Maker two years ago. To know that Marybeth is in good hands in her boardinghouse when I go traveling gives me the greatest peace of mind. Did I show you these? Take a look here."

Silence, then, and though I craned forward toward the edge of the doorjamb to see what they were looking at, Eliza clutched at my arm and yanked me back. Anyway, I already knew from my magazines—the neat row houses, the canals, the girls walking home after work.

It's a moral education, we heard the agent tell Eliza's parents. It's an education in a trade. The girls take classes when they're not at school, and they form sewing circles and learning circles, and they are always home by ten at night and at church on Sundays, no running around tolerated, not even the littlest bit.

"Eliza doesn't run around," her mother said.

"Which is why I came to you," said the agent. "We know which girls would do the best with us, and the schoolteacher told me how fine a pupil and young lady your Eliza was."

"She's not so grown," said her father. "Still more a girl than a lady." He snorted. "Don't figure she'll ever be much of a lady, we're farming people, always have been. But we'll think on this mill thing and see after a few years."

"Most girls send home a dollar a week at the beginning," said the agent. "By the end many of them have saved several hundred dollars, sometimes more. It makes a nice nest egg for when they marry, especially if you start 'em out young. Not that you all seem pressed for money—this is a mighty fine place you have here. Is that a Connecticut Clock on that shelf? I sure would like a piece like that in my parlor."

I knew what he was looking at—the Thirty-Hour Clock a peddler had convinced Eliza's parents into buying on credit—a cheap clock with a shiny face and wooden movements inside that swelled up when the weather changed, so that now it was always seven past three. The "parlor" was where Eliza's parents and the youngest two children slept. Eliza was one of the next poorest girls; she would not get to be an apprentice teacher. No matter what, this would be her last year in school.

"We get by," said Eliza's father.

"Would it be too much trouble for me to talk to the girl?" asked the agent. Beside me, Eliza drew in her breath.

"She don't need convincing," said her father. "She's already got it in her head, from the girls around here who've gone. It's us that thinks it's not the best idea."

"Just to meet her," said the agent, "having heard so much about her."

"Who do you have talking this town up over at your factory?" Eliza's mother said. "You sure have managed to find out a lot about us, not being from these parts."

"Only good things," said the agent. "They tell me she's fit as a fiddle and steady as they come."

Her parents were silent for a moment, looking at each other, I imagined, trying to decide something with their eyes. Then her mother called for her.

"Liza-Jane! Get on in here. We know you're listening on the edges!"

Eliza dug her fingernails into my arm, then went into the front room. Her voice when she spoke was so soft I could hardly hear it, just a few yes sirs, and thank you sirs, and I sure would like to see what it's likes.

"And where's your friend Aimee gone to?" I heard her mother ask after a few minutes. "She had a friend back there, a girl from the farm up the way."

"Back sewing," said Eliza softly.

I started pinching my cheeks to put some color in them.

"Aimee!" her mother called. "Come in here a minute. We got someone for you to meet."

I walked out into the front room, feeling how I was too tall, all arms and legs, my tongue thick inside my mouth. But it was only a matter of seconds before I saw how the agent's eyes took me in with one glance. I had seen that look from the boys in town, but this was a grown man. He smiled nervously then, and looked down at the ground. All at once my limbs came back to me—cooperative and graceful, the perfect length. My mouth wanted to tug into a smile, but I kept it in a careful pout. Where had I learned it, this game, this dance? From my mother, my sister, my romance stories? I was sure I had been there before.

The agent leaned forward and said what a true pleasure it was to meet me. He smelled like medicine, minty and sharp. What was my name, again? he asked, and when I told him, he repeated it slowly and said that sure was unusual and pretty—Aimee.

Which family, he asked, was lucky enough to have a fine girl like myself?

Double-tongued, I thought. The kind of man who'd sell you a horse with a hidden disease or make people who can't read sign away their houses with an X. I had heard about men like him, the kind who always had their fingers crossed behind their backs. A song-and-dance man, my mother would say. I stood taller, then, and told him my parents' names.

"You and Eliza go to school together?" he asked, and I nodded.

"You're a little older though."

I nodded yes.

He stepped closer, and I could feel how the air stretched and tightened. He was double-tongued, but his eyes were a deep green shade and he was aiming them on me so that I knew that I could not look down, for to look down would be to lose with him. I stared at him steadily. Deep green with a little yellow in the middle. It was unfair, those brilliant colors on such a snake.

Don't blink, I told myself. I could feel how I was hypnotizing him. It was as if the others in the room were not even there.

"Sixteen?"

"Fifteen." It felt almost like a lie, for my birthday had just come a few weeks before, and I was not yet used to my new age.

"You don't say. I'd have pegged you for sixteen, even seventeen. From around here your whole life?"

I nodded. My eyes were watering from not having blinked. I let them shut for an instant. When I opened them he was smiling a tiny, hidden smile.

"You ever work a loom?" he asked me.

"No, sir."

"What do you see yourself doing the next year or two— before you settle down to raising a family, I mean?"

"Oh, she's quick as a whip," said Eliza's mother. "She's training to be a schoolteacher."

"Right here in town?"

I nodded again, met Eliza's eyes for a moment and looked down, holding in an urge to laugh.

"The big new thing with the girls at the factory," he said, "is learning a million different languages. You should hear them, chattering away in French and Latin and Greek. You can't find a group of smarter girls."

He was pretending to talk to all four of us, but I was quite sure that really he was talking to me. I could see it in the way his feet were pointed, in how his eyes stumbled on my eyes when they made their way around the circle of people, as if each move away from me hurt. He kept leaning slightly toward me. Somehow I had unsettled him. Sweat showed on his brow.

Eliza stood next to her mother, tying her handkerchief into knots. I'm sorry, I thought to her. Later I'd be sure to cut the agent into little pieces and tell her how stupid I thought he was. But for now I had to keep playing the game of looking into his eyes, not down on the ground. He was not a boy like my brothers, not stretched and gangly the way they were. He was a man; I could not tell how old exactly, except to put him in that far-off place of someone much older than myself. He was a man in a suit with a carrying case full of pictures. Cuff links studded his cuffs. He would think about me later, I was sure he would. After he left, he would try to piece together my face, the sound of my voice.

I wished, then, that my hair were not pulled back in a bun that showed how my ears stuck out, that my dress was not made of such a brown, dull stuff, that I were cleaner and had not avoided a bath.

It was not that I liked him. I did not. Never trust a man who wants to sell you something, my mother said, and for once I knew she was right. I knew, too, how whatever it was in my face or person that made him lean that way was not a picture of my soul, but a skewed picture, one which might lead me astray. *From the lips of a loose woman drips honey, and her mouth is smoother than oil, but in the end she is more bitter than wormwood.* It was like those drawings we used to look at in school: What Is Wrong With This Scene? The ax handle would be shaped like a pump handle; the shoes would have no laces; the bird would be flying upside down. And yet at first glance, if you just looked quickly, it was a perfect drawing of a sunny day.

Suddenly I found my voice. I read somewhere, I told him,

that they make enough cotton yearly in those factories to wrap twice around the world. Could that be true?

"Quick as a whip," he said. "I guess you truly have been doing some reading. Sure, it's true—close to two million yards in a week. Enough in a year to wrap twice around the world and more."

It had bothered me when I read it—first, how anyone could have figured such a thing out, and then the thought of the world all bandaged up, double-wrapped in white.

"And the girls sometimes travel to Europe on the money they've earned?" I said.

He glanced at Eliza's parents. "Not Europe, usually, no. Not that far, but you gather up a nice little nest egg. What have you been reading, miss?"

I shrugged and met Eliza's eye. She was stone-faced; I could not tell what she was thinking.

"Just magazines," I said.

There was a thick silence. Finally Eliza's mother coughed and said she'd better go check on the baby.

"Well," said the agent, picking up his carrying case and glancing at the clock as if it told the correct time, "it sure has been a pleasure to meet you all. I'll leave you my address, and if I'm not unwelcome, I'll stop by again on my next trip through town."

Eliza's parents only stared at him. As he gathered his pictures from the table, he pretended to forget one, of a girl standing under a bower of grapes. But I saw how his eyes lit on it and then passed it over. He probably did that everywhere, to make people think they'd gotten something for nothing. He probably had stacks of that one picture in his case and thought of it as the Picture to Forget.

"You left this," I said when he was almost out the door. I

took it from the table and held it out. He turned. When he reached for the picture, his hand grazed mine.

"Why, I guess I did. Thank you," he said, but then he handed it back to me. "You know, why don't you girls keep it, as a little souvenir?"

Bowers, heavy with grapes, and on one side, a perfect rounded beehive, and on the other, a church steeple. In the middle, in front of the big brick mill with a cross on its roof, a girl in a pinafore, a shawl draped over one hand, a book in the other. Not a pretty girl, not like on the money. This girl was plump, bland and pale, with a gentle smile on her lips. The drawing was in gray and black, but somehow I think I could tell, even then, that her sash was blue.

"You keep it," I told Eliza when we were alone in the sleeping loft of her house, leaning over the picture, but she shook her head.

"I don't want it," she said.

"But it's yours. He came to your house."

"You found it. I didn't even see that he'd forgotten it. He left it there for you."

Her voice was tight; I was afraid she might start to cry.

"I don't want it, though. It's yours," I said. "He forgot it on purpose. He wanted us to think his shoes were new, but I could tell how they were buffed with tallow candle, around the edges. Did you see? He might as well come from around here with shoes like that, and pretending he knew us all."

She looked down at the picture. As she stared at it, the baby downstairs began to howl, a sharp-pitched, determined scream.

"Colic," she said. "It never shuts up. I'd like to wring that little baby's neck."

"Did you hear the way he kept buttering up your

parents?" I asked her. "I thought your mother was about to burst."

She had turned away from me and was looking out the tiny window below, where the gables met.

"What?" I said to her, but when I put my hand on her shoulder, she jerked away.

"What is it?" I said again.

She spoke so softly that I had to put her words back together after they came out, as if I hadn't heard her.

"I'm going."

"Huh?"

"To that mill."

"What do you mean? You can't. Your parents won't let you. Your father said maybe in two years—"

"They'll let me. They worry I'll never leave this stupid house, with no dowry or anything. Once they think on it a little, they'll let me go, the way the crops have been."

"But what if you get there and they won't have you? You could get sent back."

She turned to look at me. "So I'll see, right? Lots of girls go and see. It can't hurt to see for myself."

She was small and pale and could not look a stranger in the eye, but she knew what she wanted and she knew how to go about making it hers. I had seen it before—in school, where she crept up quietly when slates were being passed out, but always managed to get an unchipped one. In recitation, where she would begin so softly you could not hear her, but end in a voice so strong and steady you had to wonder where she had found it. My mother would say she had Resources, but I thought of it more as a solidness inside her, something strong and alive, like a growing tree. All she had to do was look inside herself and feel its limbs stretching, its sap pushing through her veins.

Sitting there next to her, I felt a sudden envy, made all the stronger by the fact that I had been standing in the front room feeling like the chosen one, the one with the world in her hands. My outsides were pleasing, but I could see, even then, how my insides were full of confusion—nothing knew which way to grow. I had brambles inside me, burrs and thistles, poison ivy. I had a mother who could see right through my skin to the mess inside and who would never let me go away. I wished for a moment that my family were as poor as Eliza's, so my parents would need to let me go. Then I knocked on the floor plank to chase away the thought.

"What?" asked Eliza.

"What?" I asked back.

"Why'd you just knock?" Nothing ever passed her by.

"I made a wish," I lied, "that your parents would let you go and it would turn out fine for you."

Then I made a tiny invisible knock with the bottom of my foot, to make that wish come true. I could feel my lies building up in my throat like wax.

I knew he would come to the house.

I thought he would come the next day, so I bathed and put on a nicer dress, though I knew I was being vain and stupid. I hovered over the kettle to make the tendrils around my face curl and chewed on a stalk of licorice to freshen my teeth.

Then I thought he would come next week, so I stayed home with the baby, who was sick, when the others went to church, and I planned what I would say.

Stupid Aimee, I told myself. Stupid, stupid, stupid, to care about such a fool coming to your house. No, said another, kinder voice inside me. You care because you want to go to the mills. A means to an end. A way of getting there.

Mostly I wanted to see that agent watching me again. In his watching, I might stare back and see reflected the power of my own eyes.

He did not come. A month passed, and then another month. At school I stopped listening, and when it was my turn to run the younger ones through their recitations, I snapped at them if they stumbled and forgot things. Then I felt terrible and gave them more points than they deserved. Eliza went to the mills. A tree fell on her parents' house, and everyone said they let her go because they needed her to send home money for repairs, but I knew she would have gone anyway, somehow, once she had made up her mind.

"Crazy," my mother said, "to let her run off so young to such a place."

At church one Sunday, Eliza's mother showed me a letter from her, which I read aloud because I was not sure Mrs. Briggs could read: *There are lots of girls from all over . . . the work is hard . . . I share a bed with a girl from North Adams, Masachewsets.*

Then, in a more formal hand, a poem:

> *I want to see you more I think*
> *Than I can write with pen and ink*
> *But when I shall I canot tell*
> *But from my heart I wish you well*
> *I wish you well from all my heart*
> *Although we are so far apart*
> *if you die there and I die here*
> *before one God we shall apeare.*

"Bless her," Eliza's mother said. "It's a wonder the way she put together those words."

I did not say I was sure she had copied the poem from somewhere. Eliza's mother did not, like my mother, have eyes in the back of her head.

"You going to join her, Aimee?" she asked. "It'd be nice for her to have a friend down there."

"Don't know," I said and shrugged. I could hear how sullen I was becoming, how something was going rotten in the sound of my own voice.

Once, when I was bored at home, I tried talking to Jeremiah, who was hunched over in the barn.

"What are you doing?" I said, keeping my distance, standing several feet away from where he sat.

He looked at me as if I were a fool and held up a length of leather.

"A bridle? How'd it break?"

He shrugged. His hands were pulling and stretching at the cracked leather, trying to work it back around an iron ring.

"You going to school tomorrow?"

He coughed a fake cough. "Maybe not."

I swooped up one of the barn cats as it wandered by, held it against my chest and ran my chin back and forth along its gray fur. "Well, you're not missing much, staying home so much."

Leave me alone leave me alone, I could feel him thinking. The half-grown, wiry cat was squirming in my arms.

"Stop that, you," I said to it.

My brother looked up. "That's Indigo. She hates to be held."

"Huh?"

He scowled. "The cat."

"It has a name? You named it?"

None of our barn cats had names. There were too many of them, and they disappeared and were replaced in such a steady stream that naming seemed beside the point.

He nodded. "C'm here, Indigo," he said in a soft voice, making clucking noises with his mouth.

I brought the cat near my brother, kneeled and set it down on the empty stool beside him, and for a moment we both petted it, my hands smoothing down the fur on the bottom of the jaw so that the creature tipped its chin back in bliss. Jeremiah stroked the gray back and swaying tail. His hand, I saw, was bigger than mine now. Though his face was redder than it used to be, his hand was still pale against the fur.

For a perfect moment, sitting there, he was just my favorite brother. It was as if the barn where we were sitting did not have a second hayloft, as if I had never climbed up. I realized, then, how much I had missed Jeremiah since the day in the loft, and how tired out I was from living with him as if he were not there.

I thought out a sentence, then said it:

"I'm walking to town to get buttons for a dress Ma's doing over, if you want to tag along."

As I lifted my head to speak to him, our hands brushed accidentally on the cat's back. We stiffened, and the animal leaped up and ran into a stall.

"Indigo!" Jeremiah said, throwing the bridle down to run after the cat. "Come back!"

He stood frozen for a moment at the dark beginning of a stall, where a mare's tail swished harsh among the flies. He peered in and kicked the side of the stall with his boot.

"She'll get kicked back there," he said. "You scared her off."

"She *lives* in this barn," I said. "She won't get kicked. She's never been kicked a day in her life."

"You don't know anything," my brother said. "Why don't you just stop pestering me?" He looked the way he used to when he was about to cry, except I could tell he wouldn't cry now, not in front of me. He hit the planking of the stall with a tight fist. "I can't believe you scared her off like that. She's only a kitten."

And he edged past the mare and disappeared into the darkness of the stall.

I walked to town alone, kicking up dust along the way. Inside the dry goods store, hundreds of buttons lay piled on each other inside tiny wooden compartments: white, black, red, cloth-covered, wooden, metal, bone. Standing over them trying to choose, I pictured them running in a line up and down my back, studding my spine, trapping me forever in one dress. Then I saw them sewn onto my mouth, sealing it shut with a row of brown dots like rotten teeth on the wrong side of my lips, a girl turned inside out.

"What can I find for you, Aimee?" asked Mr. Curtis, the small, stooped man who ran the store.

I must have looked up with a dazed expression, for he smiled a careful, false smile.

"What are you looking for?" He peered at me. I was taller than he was and could see a piece of fuzz resting on the top of his bald head. My throat was closing up; I had to leave the store.

"No, I mean, I looked already," I said quickly. "You don't have what I need—"

"We'll get in more next month."

Next month, I thought (and then was surprised at how strong the thought came out, how sure), next month I'll be gone.

At home I told my mother they had run out of black buttons. The lie slipped from my mouth with such ease that I believed it myself.

"Out?" she said. "It's the most common thing in the world. They always have them."

"Not today."

She looked at me, then, long and hard. She put down her sewing, smoothed her skirt, and looked at me with such steadiness, such a desire to know, that I turned away. My mother was beautiful. She had wide-set clear eyes, a firm mouth, and thick hair a little lighter than my own. Even as I fixed my gaze on the floor, I could feel her looking at me, could feel us standing there: the girl with her face turned down, jaw tight, feet planted, hands fisted at her sides; the mother, staring, wondering: How has she grown so far away from me? What has infected her soul?

"Lord help me, but I just don't know what's gotten into you," she said.

And I found myself screaming, hitting the table with my fist, hearing my words ricochet off the wooden walls.

"I told you! They—don't—have—any—buttons!"

I hit the table harder, but it was as if my fist were made of iron and could not feel. Then I spoke again, quietly, between clenched teeth.

"Nothing's gotten into me. Please just leave me alone."

And she did, and Jeremiah did, and they all did, for hours and hours as I sat in the barn and thought about how I had been blessed with a family that did not beat me and gave me food to eat and loved me, and still pricked against my skin, somehow, like a hairshirt, something I had to strip off.

It's your own fault, said a voice inside me. For wandering where you should not have wandered. Only I knew that wasn't the only reason, and I pictured the ships I longed to sail on, the distances I wanted to travel, the places I might see that they had never seen. Sometimes one of our dogs would cock his ears, sniff into the wind and then *go* in a stretching-forward run—for the brush of air, the change of pace, because he *wanted* to.

With the hayloft above me, I could not stay in the barn any longer, so I went up to the hill, and when it began to get dark, down to the toolshed where tow-cloth rags were hanging in a line. White, my mother had scrubbed them. Whiter than snow, whiter than teeth, white as only something cleaned by my mother and bleached by the sun could be. No stains any-where—from the baby, from the kitchen, from my mother's own two hands. Some of the little cloths might have been her monthly rags, but she had left no traces so I could not tell.

I slept in the toolshed that night, determined not to go into the house until someone called for me. *Please call for me*, I thought, but no one did. The house was connected to the shed, which was connected to the barn in an L shape, but it didn't matter—I might have been miles from my family, in another town or land. Though the barn faced north to protect the house from wind, still somehow the wind came through the tool-shed, rustling the teeth of the dry straw brooms, playing on the metal of the rakes. I spread out some hay and slept inside a burlap sack, and when I woke shivering in the middle of the night, I pulled the rags, now dry, from the line and draped them over the sack, and slept again.

My mother was not always far away and knowing. When I was very small, she used to talk to me—loosely, freely, at dusk in the heat of summer when we sat, just us two, hoping for a breeze in the field. Sitting there with her, it was almost as if I were an animal—hardly a person, hardly a little girl, just something warm and breathing, a creature with two ears. She must have been sure I would not remember what she said or how we sat there with the grass itching our legs and the wind moving across our skin.

I did, I do remember—not everything, but shards like the bits of china we'd find sometimes mixed in with the garden dirt, from plates my mother probably ate off as a girl. She told me things about her courtship with my father: "Brown-eyed Susans, he brought me, said they were like my eyes, did you ever hear of such nonsense?" She sang me songs in a low voice which cracked sometimes at the high parts:

> *Here we come up the green grass,*
>> *Green grass, green grass*
> *Here we come up the green grass,*
>> *Dusty, dusty day.*

> *Fair maid, pretty maid,*
>> *Give your hand to me,*
> *I'll show you a blackbird,*
>> *A blackbird on the tree.*

> *We'll all go a roving,*
>> *Roving side by side.*
> *I'll take my dearest Adelaide,*
>> *I'll take her for my bride.*

Some of the tales she told were regular stories about girls on farms, where people did their chores, got lost and found, and lived in a world I recognized—a world where the only things that sprang from the ground were plants, and an empty pot stayed empty until you filled it yourself with water, soup or stew. These were the sorts of stories she told to all of us while we lay in bed at night as little children. She had to stay with this kind, then, because if magic came into a story, my brother Jeremiah would grow too scared to fall asleep.

But every once in a while when I sat alone with her on those heavy summer evenings, she used to tell me different kinds of stories, ones filled with singing bones, hairy men and stolen fire. I never knew where she got those stories—from her own mother, or from a book somewhere, or from inside her head. She always told them in a careful voice at first, but then she would forget about me. Her voice would quicken and rise, and she would begin to tell them for themselves, or for herself, in the same way she told about my father courting her or her brief days as a teacher at the school. There was one story that stayed in the back of my head even when she had not told it for a long while, because I was sure whoever had invented it had meant it specifically for me.

"Remember, it's only a story, goose, about make-believe people," she would say as if she thought I would be scared, even though I always leaned into her voice, my jaw and toes tight, and if she stopped, I begged her to go on. I knew how it ended—it always ended the same terrible way—but I couldn't help wanting to hear it just the same.

Once, my mother told me, there was a good daughter, a bad daughter and an old woman. One day the old woman took the good daughter deep into the woods. As they walked into the thickets, the thorns parted to let them through, and they passed two arms which were fighting, and further on, two legs, and then two fighting heads without bodies, and the heads said, "Good morning, my child, God will help you." Then they came to a house and the old woman sat down near the fireplace, took off her head, and began to delouse herself, throwing the lice into the fire, where they turned into fireflies and flew off.

She gave the good daughter a dry bone to put in an empty pot, and the girl did it, and the pot was full of good meat. She gave her a single grain of rice to pound with the pestle, and the girl did it, and the mortar grew full of good rice. After they ate their supper, the old woman said, "Pray, child, scratch my back." The girl scratched her back, but her hand got all cut up, because the woman's back was covered with broken glass. Then the old woman blew on the hand, and it was cured.

When the girl got up the next morning, the old woman said to her, "You must go home now, but you are a good girl. Go to the chicken house. All the eggs that say 'Take Me,' take. All the eggs that say 'Do Not Take Me,' leave. When you are on the road, throw the eggs behind your back to break them."

The girl did as she was told. As she walked, she threw the eggs and pretty things came out. First diamonds, a white horse and a dress of blue silk; then a path that led to a castle, and in the castle, a velvet room, and in the room, a prince and a long and happy life.

When the other daughter, the bad one, went into the woods, all the same things happened, but when the eggs said "Take Me," she looked at them—all covered with chicken leavings and bits of matted down—and left them, and when the eggs said "Do Not Take Me," she slid them—all white smoothness—into her apron pocket and went away.

As she walked she broke the perfect eggs onto the road, and from the gold sacks of their yolks and the clear slime of their whites came snakes, toads and frogs, which began to run after her, and whips, which lashed at her skin, and voices, which shrieked in her ears.

"She ran and ran," said my mother, "but the thorns closed around her so she couldn't leave the forest, and that poor girl couldn't outsmart those whips or run those voices from her ears."

I must have been between one and eight when I heard those stories, no older, for she stopped telling them to me when I grew big enough to spend much time away from her side, as if she feared I would repeat the tales to my father, the schoolteacher or my friends. I might have been still nursing from her breast at the beginning, her voice floating over my head as I swallowed down her milk. Perhaps at first she spoke simply to hear the rich sound of her own voice. As I grew up on those stories I fed on them, the way I sometimes snuck spoonfuls of molasses from the jar—a treat that could turn sickly sweet and clog my throat if I had just a drop too much. The next day, the next week, years later, her stories still hovered as pictures in the back of my mind. I could pull them forward, and their colors would brighten, but if I looked at them too long, they took on the bleeding reds and blacks of a bad dream.

Mostly, listening by her side when I was six, seven, eight—just before she decided to stop telling me stories at all—I wanted to know who was who. For I knew, even then, that for my mother, everything held a lesson. The old woman might be my mother, the way she seemed to know everything, but then why was her back jagged with broken glass that cut the girl's hand? And why was she called the old woman, and not Mother, and why, if she was their mother, was she so bent and old? The good daughter might be me, since I was the one who got to hear the stories, and since I longed, more than Harriet, for things like carriages, diamonds and blue silk. But such greed would make me more like the bad daughter, hungry and grasping.

If something says "Take Me," I asked myself, would you want to take it?

And I knew I would grow bored and leave it there.

If something says "Do Not Take Me," would you want to take it?

And I knew how badly I would.

Harriet did not sneak molasses. Harriet did not have a mouth that ached for chocolate, or teeth that could not stop biting on fingernails and chewing on blades of grass or strands of hair. If she had strong hungers and sorrows, they lay buried so deep inside her that I could only guess at them. Sometimes she would wince just the slightest bit, let show the tiniest stiffening of her shoulders if I did better than she did on a lesson in school. Once she got up suddenly in the middle of supper, her blue eyes blurry and confused with tears; I never did figure out why. Mostly she held herself inside herself, her hands capable and swift, her voice kind. Even when she was ten, she seemed like someone closer to my mother's age. An egg that said "Do Not Take Me"? Harriet would leave it in its bed of straw.

And so I decided that the good girl was Harriet, and the bad girl, me. Only still it was not simple to figure out, because I also knew that just because I was the bad girl didn't mean my mother loved Harriet better, though that was how it worked in fairy tales. There was such sadness and kindness in my mother's voice when she talked of the poor bad girl and how the thorns closed round her so she couldn't leave the forest, but had to keep running circles from those whips. I knew my mother herself could not have been a bad girl—it was impossible—but perhaps, every once in a great while, she had thought a bad girl's thoughts. Or maybe she had known a bad girl very well as a child, and that girl had died an awful death. That would account for the trouble in my mother's voice when she told the story, and the way that, as she neared the end, her hand sometimes closed quietly around my wrist, as if to steady herself with the living flutter of my pulse.

The other story I remember best was not about me, not then. I don't know why she told it, quite, except that my mother had a way of seeing far behind and far in front of her.

And I don't know why it stayed with me, except that even then, I sometimes squirmed inside my skin as if it were a wool dress on a blistering hot day, and I knew what it was to want to leave yourself behind.

One day, my mother told me, her fingers darting in and out of a buttonhole she was sewing, one fine day there was a man who rode up at night to a cabin on the edge of the deep woods. He was hungry and he said aloud to himself, "If I can get a hunk of bread and a slice of bacon, I don't care what I pay!" And a little woman came out of the cabin. She asked the man to come in to get some supper, and he liked it so well that they married and he stayed there with her eating her good food.

And so at first they got on nicely together, but then he noticed something funny about the little woman—how a few times, when he awoke deep in the middle of the night, she was not in the cabin. Then in the morning, she was back. One night he made up his mind to spy on her, and he lay down and pretended to sleep. When she thought he was dreaming, she jumped up and pulled down a grid-iron from the side of the wall, put it on some coals, and pulled out the big spinning wheel from its corner by the hearth. Then she sat herself down on the grid-iron, and as soon as it was red-hot, she began to spin the skin off her body with the spinning wheel.

> *"Turn and spin, come off skin—*
> *Turn and spin, come off skin."*

And the skin came off the woman's body, beginning with her head—came off as slick, as easy as the husk peels off an ear of overripe corn. She took her skin and put it under the bed, then she climbed out the window and was gone.

And as soon as she was out of sight, the man jumped out of bed and took the skin and filled it with salt and pepper and threw it back under the bed. Then he watched through the latch-hole till, much later, he saw his wife coming up the path, and he crept quickly back to bed.

She laughed while she bent to rake the skin out from under the bed, and she laughed while she shook herself into it. But when she felt the salt and pepper, she laughed on either side of her mouth, and then she moaned so you could hear her all the way to town.

But she couldn't get out of her skin, that woman. It burned her and burned her until she fell down shaking and died there on the floor.

I would lie in the parched grass as the wind tickled the blades against my legs, and my skin would itch and ache. I would gaze up through the gathering night at my mother, who had looped-stitched four neat buttonholes during the story, and she would look small and distant, like something far down the road. Sometimes she added another ending, how the woman prayed to the Lord just before she died, and how she went to heaven where she wore the white robes of an angel and her skin no longer hurt because she was a Blessed Soul. Other times, if I did not look at my mother, but stayed still and quiet in a tight ball at her side, she stopped with the woman dying on the floor.

Then a picture would stretch across my brain: My mother buried stiff and dead in the churchyard, green copper pennies on her lids. For it seemed to me that the woman in the story might be my mother, and I wondered if she, too, went away in the middle of the night, leaving her skin in a wrinkled pile in a corner of the house. And if she did go—out the window, into the dark—what did she turn into without her skin? All blood, like a cut, or taut and blue-white like a stretched pig's bladder, or as changing and uncatchable as air? Once, after she had told me the story, I put salt and coarse black pepper on my tongue until my cheeks puckered and my nostrils flared, and then I tried to picture it everywhere—inside my fingertips, behind my eyeballs, inside all my holes, burning me to nothing.

If the woman in the story was my mother, then the man was my father and someday he might do that to her skin. I thought of my father leaving a bruise on my face and wondered if he had ever hurt her. It was hard to imagine—mostly my mother told him what to do—but still I looked at him differently after I had been thinking about the story. His own skin was so pink, so thick, as if he were skin all the way through and could never lose his covering. My mother's skin, when she lay her arm belly up on the kitchen table, was thin and blue-branched, like my own. I could press down with my thumb on one of my fat veins and it would turn from blue to nothing. I could let the life rush back—as simple as that—with a mere lifting of my thumb.

I did not repeat the stories to anyone, for I feared that if I did, my mother might have pepper rubbed in all her raw spots simply for telling them, and it would be my fault. Instead, I repeated them, over and over, to myself, and yet still I did not know exactly what to make of them, or who was who. What I learned from my mother's tellings of these stories, one thing I learned, was that I did not know her—not if she could be how she was during the day with us, so careful, so efficient and calm, and still hide stories like that under her tongue.

Later, I wanted her to talk to me again the way she told

those stories. I wanted her to talk to me like that when I was a girl trying to go to the mills, and I wanted her, still more, to talk to me like that when I came back. But my mother chose her life carefully and she lived it carefully. Sometimes, right after Anna died when I was nine, she would cry out, despite herself, in her sleep. At first they would be simply cries—animal sounds, sharp and full of pain, but later in the night the sounds would turn to angry, frightened words and thrashing noises, as if she were trying to brush biting red ants or the fingerprints of the devil from her skin.

"Get away! Get off! Oh Lord oh Lord help me, no!"

From where I lay in the loft I would hear my mother calling out, then hear my father waking her, telling her to shush, it was only a dream, and her soft, embarrassed words of apology. Then there was silence, but I knew my mother was not sleeping. Like a board she was lying, stiff and knotted, trying to tell if we had heard.

Jeremiah could not stand to hear such sounds coming from our mother. When we were little, before the time in the hayloft, he would get me to clamp my palms over his own hands, which were clamped over his ears, to make a double shield. But I could not stop listening, my ears straining open, could not help wanting to find a way into her pain. Mornings, after hearing her, I would wake to see her differently—her motions now those of a woman who was caught inside herself, so that as I watched her lean into the dough, or attack the wood of the table with a bristlebrush, or shake the tablecloth until it made angry snapping sounds in the wind, I saw rage and longing in every motion of her hands.

They did not last long, these moments. My mother grew still and quiet again at night. I forgot, for long stretches, about her calling out. My mother crept back inside herself; I crept back inside myself. Mostly she was as far from me as the moon, and still I would gaze at her and see myself and not myself, my world and a world apart. And she would gaze at me, or glance, really, at moments when she thought I was not paying attention, her looks full of worry, or sometimes envy, it seemed to me, or sometimes pure and simple curiosity.

No one has ever talked to me the way my mother did when she thought I was too young to understand. It is the way I talk to my rabbits now, thinking they do not really hear me. Perhaps they hear me—the blind one, anyway, her ears sharpened by the lack of sight in her milky, pale-blue eyes. It is talking but not talking, saying things I might never say out loud to someone I thought could understand. Often in summer I wear no shoes, and I let my hair hang down my back, but I am, in some ways, as careful—more careful—than my mother in all I have kept to myself.

When I feed my chickens their own crushed eggshells to make their new eggs strong, I think of the eggs who said "Take Me" and "Do not Take Me." When I break an egg on the hard edge of an iron skillet, I think of diamonds and silk dresses, snakes, toads and whips.

When the egg begins to sizzle and the edges grow hard and lacy—caught—I think of voices you cannot leave behind because they are inside you, and everywhere you run, they run.

I knew he would come to the house.

It took him three months—of other girls, other towns, other tables where he could leave a copy of his picture of the factory girl and the beehive before he stepped out the door. A traveling man, a busy man. During those months I forgot that I had not liked him, forgot, too, that he saw pretty girl upon pretty girl in every town he visited. Instead, I convinced myself that he thought of me sometimes when he leaned back in the bouncing coach between towns, shut his eyes, allowed his prepared speeches to float to the dusty corners of his head and be replaced by something else: a dullness, mostly, a sickness at the smell of the stagecoach and the taste of dust coating his tongue. He shut his eyes to the passing view of village green, red barn, saltbox house after saltbox house, pigs nosing their way through mud. I was sure he preferred the darkness of his own eyelids to the sight of another farm town.

Sometimes, I told myself, I had to tell myself, sometimes he felt something else—a break in the pattern, a place where the coach rounded the bend and came to a pond flecked with light or horses cantering along a ridge. A longing. Then he would see my face.

He came on a Saturday in early September. Everyone but my mother, Harriet, me, and the baby, Luke, had left at dawn to go work in the fields. We were cutting vegetables when the knock came, Luke feverish and fretful, the rest of us grateful that his cries had hiccuped into whimpers. I knew it was the agent from the sound of the knock on the door: firm and polite it was, friendly and determined at the same time. A practiced knock that listened to itself, not like the thumping of our neighbors, who banged to tell you they were there. I wished, then, that we had a door knocker like the ones I'd seen in catalogs: a brass lion with a ring through its nose, or a lady's long hand cupping an iron ball.

"Who could that be?" said my mother, looking up from chopping carrots.

I stared down at a bright chip of carrot peel in the crack between the floor planks. My mother went to the door. From where I sat, I could hear him: The Boott Mills . . . getting to know some families . . . just a moment of your time.

Harriet, too, was listening hard. I picked up my brother from his little box crib, dipped my finger in honey and gave it to him to suck on so he would keep quiet.

"I don't know," I heard my mother say. "We're right in the middle of cooking, and my husband is out in the fields, and our youngest, the baby, has been feeling poorly—"

He told her the pictures he had brought would cheer up any little baby. He told her that for farm folks working their fingers to the bone, sending just one person to the mills could be a real help. None of this would have been enough to get past my mother if she had made up her mind not to let him in. From where I sat I could not see the way he looked at her, but I knew how tricky he was, how deft. He must have gotten past her with his eyes.

When she showed him into the kitchen I did not look up for a good half-minute. My mother pulled out a chair, said she hoped he didn't mind sitting in here, but like she said, we were right in the middle of preparing a stew for the folks out in the fields, who had been out since sunup.

"My daughter Harriet," she said, and Harriet nodded.

"The little one is Luke," said my mother, "and my other daughter, Aimee."

Only then did I look up. He had not sat down. He was holding a hat with a smudge of dust on it. He carried the selfsame case. His voice said, "Aimee. Yes, I do believe we met—where was it?—down the road at the girl Eliza's, the one who's doing so fine down at the mills, is that it?"

His eyes said: I remember I remember you.

"How do you do?" I said.

"Mighty fine, mighty fine. Nice to get out of the chill. This sure is a nice kitchen range you have here—awful handsome nickeling and gingerbread work. Is that a soft- or hard-coal stove?"

My mother's eyes narrowed. I wondered if she were about to change her mind and ask him to leave. It was, though, a stove she was proud of, not even a year old. She blackened it carefully, more often than she needed to, rubbing its stout belly until it gleamed.

"Hard," she said. "Tea?"

"Don't mind if I do, if it's no trouble."

"No trouble," she said.

"Don't mind," the agent said, and his eyes sought mine, "if I do."

As he took out the pictures, Harriet and my mother craned their necks and gathered round. I dandled Luke on my knee. He, too, must have felt a change in the room, something worth watching, for he stayed quiet. Because I had heard it all before, I did not have to listen. I watched. What I saw was a man from the city, two women from the country. His hair combed back from his forehead; their hair wound at the napes of their necks, coming loose. Sweat gleaming on their foreheads from the cooking, the excitement of an unexpected guest. And something else—I caught it, studied it, a new thing, like a second guest who had crept into the house.

They were leaning toward him, my mother and my sister, one on each side. They were arching their necks so the skin stretched, tilting their heads and leaning. Both of them, seeking out his space. They could not help themselves.

"Oh yes," said their voices. And "Interesting," "Such tall buildings," "You don't say, it's amazing, what will they come up with next?"

Something new, said their eyes. Something from outside. A change in the stale kitchen air.

Double-tongued, I thought. A snake in the grass.

They would see through him. Especially my mother would see through. I did not know what I wanted. If she saw through him, she would not believe his speeches and would forbid me from going to the mills. It wasn't that I thought he was lying about what was there, exactly, just that I thought his way of telling it was false. But if she bought him hook, crook and barrel, my mother—wise, all-knowing, eyes in the back of her head—would show herself to be a woman who could be swayed by a city man's smooth tongue.

As he took out picture after picture and gave his little speech, I could see how they, like myself, were concentrating not on his words, but on his person—how the arm leaned, brushed against the table. How the silver cuff links flirted with the light. The dark hair on his knuckles; the blunt square borders of his rosy fingernails and their pale half-moons. But while I watched him and them at the same time, they watched neither each other nor me; the kitchen had become this traveling man. I felt, then, a sickness at the beauty of my mother and sister—each of them so different. Harriet with her face cast in the roundest, gentlest terms, always looking sleepy, her moist eyes staring out at nothing like a cat's. My mother with her clear, bright eyes, her forehead with each of her children written on it in a line, her hands damp with potato and carrot juice.

Get away, I wanted to shout out to them. He came to see me. Me. Leave well enough alone!

He was not looking at me anymore, but between me and them, caught in the current of the three of us, set off balance by us all.

He looked at my mother, leaned toward Harriet, turned and cast a quick, uncertain glance at me.

The girls save a bundle . . . impeccable lodgings . . . industrialists from England . . . a modern miracle . . . the City of Spindles . . . Nothing like it anywhere.

"And you, miss," he said, turning to Harriet. "If I may be so bold to inquire, what are your plans?"

Tell him about the man who wants to marry you, I thought nastily. How each Sunday he comes with flowers or a pie his mother made. Each Sunday they walked, and I watched them start down the road with a sour turning in my stomach, not because I wanted him—he was a miller's son, a dull, tall boy with raw knuckles—but because I knew that with him clutching her elbow, she could turn the bend and find herself in a whole new place.

"I—I don't think I'm cut out for it," she said, leaning to get a closer look at a picture.

"She's planning to settle down and raise a family before long," my mother said.

The agent backed up a few steps, away from the table. I leaned over my baby brother and kissed the side of his warm head. I could picture my small, sweet mouth, how it was shaped like a rose blossom pearled with morning dew. I was a girl in one of the romance stories in my magazines: *It was as if, when she opened her mouth to sing, a nightingale flew from a pink blossom and burst into bright song.* The agent watched me—my leaning, my mouth coming to rest on the downy head.

I began to chant in a whisper to my brother, jiggling him up and down on my knee: "Trot trot to Boston to buy a loaf of bread. Trot trot home again, the old trot's dead."

I could feel the agent's eyes on my hands, which were locked across the baby's middle. Luke let out a crowing noise, and I looked up.

"But Aimee's a little younger, not so ready to settle down just yet, eh?" he said.

Again I kissed the baby, and felt as I lowered my head how the agent had once again come into my circle. My mother must have felt it, too, for she moved away from the table and stood between the visitor and me. My sister took some potatoes to peel and sat down by the hearth.

"We don't think it's a good idea," my mother said. "We talked it over already, me and her father, when Eliza from down the way went over there."

She coughed. "It looks like a nice place—" Then she smiled, met his eyes, polite, and something more. "But not for her. Thank you kindly all the same."

Kahndly. My mother, my *mother* said it the way a southerner would, drawing out the middle, making it soft and open—like the traveling preacher who had held services once under a white tent and drawn out the words of the Bible in a way that had made my bones ache and my insides stretch so that I'd thought I might be about to let the Spirit in. This was not how my mother usually talked. I had never seen her this way before, not with my father, not with his friend Samuel Plain or her own children or the people at church. She was watching the agent carefully, and though she would not give him what he wanted, would not let me go, still she wanted to see if she could sway him with the music of her voice.

We're all the same, I thought then. She's as bad as I am, honey dripping from her lips. It was a good thought, for it meant I was not alone. And a terrible thought, for it made my mother grow smaller before my eyes.

"So you've thought it over and decided against it, Aimee?" the agent said to me.

"She's training to be a schoolteacher," my mother said, and now her voice was hers again, clipped and certain, on the edge of anger: *This is my child you're dancing around. Training to be a schoolteacher. What I could have been and only was for six short months.*

Stay back.

"Plenty of time for that," said the agent.

"I—" My own voice sounded, surprising me.

"She's just barely fifteen. Bit young to be away from home," said my mother.

This time I jumped in before anyone could stop me. "I've read Eliza's letters. I've read all sorts of things about the mills. There's lots of girls my age and younger."

"But you'd only go if your mother and father came round to seeing how it was a fine idea," said the agent.

I glared at him, and he gave me a quick, confiding smile.

"Can't say that'll happen anytime soon," said my mother.

"I'd be mighty happy if I could get a chance to have a word with your husband," the agent said. "I reckon he's working hard—not a good year for the farmers. Are you expecting him back for some of that fine stew?"

"Not for a good two hours yet. They have a full day's work out there."

"I sure would like to meet him."

My mother was growing impatient. I could tell by how she had returned to chopping vegetables, cubes of squash piling up by her hand. "I'll tell him you came by."

"Why, I'd appreciate that," said the agent, looking into her eyes. "And I'll leave you some information so he can see what it's like for himself."

Like a spell, those pictures—the way he could leave them lying about in a kitchen, and the next thing you knew they had printed themselves on the inside flap of your eyelids so that they flashed by at every blink and would settle in for good when you closed your eyes at night. Amazing, the way they took on color. Blue sash, white dress, honey dripping yellow from the hive.

I am quiet, dull and well-behaved, said the girl in the picture to my mother. Your daughter will follow in my steps.

I earn money, walk among throngs of people, see things you cannot even imagine, said the girl in the picture to me. You will follow in my steps.

Harriet and my mother showed the agent to the door, but not until he had stood over me, extended his arm, taken my hand in his, pressed down on my fingers for the briefest moment and said Until We Meet Again. I gave him a broad smile, then felt it curl into a sneer. He brushed the baby's cheek with the crook of his finger, and Luke began to cry.

That evening it all came out.

"I know things about those mills," said my mother as we sat down to supper.

"So do I," I said.

"Yes, but I know different things."

"What different things?"

"Things you don't say at the dinner table. Who does he think he is to come knocking on our door without so much as a warning?"

"What different things?" asked my brother John.

"You should've seen this man," said my mother to my father. "Enough polish to shine the candlesticks. He should've been a play actor, not a factory man."

"You liked him," I muttered.

"What did you say, missy?" snapped my mother.

"Nothing." I poked at the carrots in my stew. They had lost their brightness in the cooking and turned soft and ugly as droppings.

"You answer your mother when she speaks to you," my father said.

"I said . . . I just said I thought you liked him all right, is all. You made him nice and welcome, you and Harriet."

"When someone comes to your door," said my mother, "you offer them tea. That's Christian charity. Your sister knows so too."

I thought of the sampler she had taught me to embroider, which welcomed the tired stranger to our home. As I had sewn it, I had laughed to myself at how, before I stitched the "R," it had read "WELCOME TIRED STRANGE." I would have liked to leave it that way. The agent was a stranger, and strange perhaps, but he did not seem tired, and yet she welcomed him. Did my mother like the saying because it talked of charity, or because a stranger brought newness inside her door?

"Anyway," I said, "Eliza's doing fine, I read her letter."

"Since when did anyone take one letter by a child as the whole gospel truth?" my mother asked, but she was flushed from what I'd said about her liking him, and for once, it was she who would not meet my eyes. I looked at my father to see if he had noticed how she blushed, but he was bent over his food, his wide shoulders sagging. The year before had been a terrible time for wheat prices, and this fall did not promise to be better. My father came in from the fields each day looking dazed and spoke even fewer words than usual.

"I thought that agent was all right," said Harriet. "He's only working at his job, that's all."

"There are jobs and then there are jobs," said my mother. "Running all over the countryside trying to pluck young girls from their homes is not my notion of a job. If my children end up like—"

"If the girl wants to go," I said, "it's not exactly being plucked."

I thought of the Bible: *She seeks wool and flax, and worketh willingly with her hands. She is like the merchants' ships; she bringeth her food from afar.* For months I had been saving up these lines, trying to find a moment to set them forth in my defense. I could point out that farming wasn't the best of lives either. Look how tired you are, I could tell my parents. Year after year, at the mercy of the weather and the insects. Look at the accidents that can happen on the farm.

In his crib, Luke began to fret, and my mother got up and brought him to the table. "What have you heard about those mills?" she asked my father, but he looked at her dully, as if his mind were someplace very far away.

"Who cares, anyway?" said Jeremiah softly. Then, a little louder, "I say just let her go."

I felt a sharp jab in my calf under the table—his foot, striking me the way his voice did not dare to, in a hard, swift kick.

And before I could stop myself, I had reached across the steaming plate of vegetables in the middle of the table and slapped my brother hard across the face.

"Aimee!" my mother cried, and my father rose as if he might strike me.

I pushed back my chair and ran to the sleeping-loft ladder, up and away from them, rung by rung. My name followed me, sharp on my mother's tongue, but my father did not pursue me; he would never strike me now that I bathed behind a curtain. My leg throbbed from where Jeremiah had kicked me. Perhaps I would get a deep blue bruise. I wanted it— something to see, tangible and sore. It had been nearly a year since we had touched in the hayloft. I had known he did not want to wander about together as we used to, but I had not known how sharp his anger was, how pointed. Now I felt its mark upon my leg.

Thank you, I thought, then, to my brother, for he gave me a reason—an excuse, something—to go.

Later that night, after the younger children were asleep, my parents called me down into the front room and shut the door.

"Sit down," said my mother, and I perched on the edge of the wooden bench and knocked quietly on it for luck. She stood over me and shut her eyes for a moment as if she were too tired to hold them open. Then she looked at me.

"Tell me, did you make amends to your brother?"

I shrugged.

"You will. As soon as you leave this room. We do not strike other people in this home."

I swallowed, a foul taste in my mouth, and thought of my father slapping me when I was small. I wanted to say that Jeremiah had kicked me first, to let out a long list of every time I had been pinched and slapped, but I did not dare. They looked large, both of them: my mother folding her arms over her chest, my father standing behind her.

"Aimee, Aimee. You have this . . . temper in you, like a sickness, a fever," she said. "I don't know what's come over you. You used to be so different, off playing by yourself and doing your schoolwork. The schoolmistress tells me you're not yourself lately, losing patience with the children and letting your work fall behind." She sighed. "I wasn't supposed to say anything—she hoped you were going through a spell, but Lord help me, I just don't know. What's come over you? Can't you tell your own parents that?"

I shook my head.

"I can't hear you," said my mother.

"Nothing."

"Oh no?"

"Nothing's come over me. Lots of girls want to go work there—"

"Lots of girls would drive a horse off a cliff if it was the week's fashion. I hoped you had more sense. I guess I should tell you the things I've heard. If, after all that—"

"Heard from who?"

"People at the church, or who've been there. Friends. People with good ears and eyes who aren't trying to sell something. It's not all in those magazines of yours, I can tell you that, with their fancy pictures."

"Eliza's a friend, and she's been there. I read her letters. She says it's just fine."

"What I heard," said my mother, "is that those girls dip snuff to keep the lint out of their throats. And it's so hot in there, in those sealed-off rooms where they make that negro cloth, that the women work naked to the waist."

I shook my head.

"Naked to the waist, did you hear what I just said to you? Like savages." She hunched over and shuddered.

"You can't believe everything you hear," I said, quoting her, and she breathed in sharply, lost her balance for a moment, then strode on.

"One girl—I heard this from Lily and Helen Perkin's mother, who heard it straight from her own daughter's mouth, and you yourself know Helen's a steady girl—one girl, she got in the way of one of those flying shuttles they have in those looms, and it pierced right through her like an arrow and came clean out the other side."

I pictured not the girl's pain, but the perfect roundness of the hole—through cloth, through flesh and bone—pictured bending down and being able to peer right through her, like looking through a keyhole to the room beyond. I would have loved to be able to look clear inside myself, through myself. My mother was speaking in her storytelling voice. *"The shuttle was magic,"* I almost expected her to say. *"And out of the hole grew poppies and tulips, and the tulips opened their red mouths and said 'take me,' and the girl was bad and so she did."*

"All the money those girls make they spend on trifles," she went on. My father nodded hard, standing behind her with his eye on the door. "Fabrics and lace and whatnot from those mills. You have a weakness for all that. Harriet I would send with a cleaner conscience. She'd tire of it soon enough."

Under her words I detected something else. It was the smallest, stingiest sliver of understanding—of "I know what you long for because I, too, have longed." Lace would not bore my mother, who pressed plants into the Bible—lilies where it said Lilies of the Field, vines for the Keeper of the Vineyards— and sewed triangles of tin into our quilts so they would catch the light.

"But Harriet doesn't want to go," I said.

She told me about sickness and tardiness and how the girls were punished and how they fell from grace and lost their pews at the church and how even though the Irish and the Yankees fought, the girls still ended up marrying dirty Irish ditchdiggers if they were lucky, and many weren't even so lucky as that.

"They never come home after that, those girls," said my mother, and I heard a raw spot in her voice.

Then I looked deep into her eyes, which I did love more than any other eyes in the world, the irises rimmed with the thinnest band of pondwater dark brown-green. When I was younger, I had stared into those eyes for long moments, my height placing me level with her gaze while she sat sewing by the fire, until she'd laugh and tell me to go do something, instead of hanging about like a soul bewitched.

"I'll come home," I said.

When I have worked like the women in the Bible and brought my food from afar. When Jeremiah will allow himself to love me again, and my mother will look straight inside me and see nothing but her girl: a clean field, a bright plate, a sky.

When (for I could feel my life hardening like a piece of old, dry bread, crumbling smaller and smaller) I have seen the world.

"You say that now," my mother said.

"I will. Where else would I go? It's just for a year or two, and all the girls go home in the spring for a while, when the freshets come. I can earn two hundred dollars, enough for a dowry. I'm tired of this pla—"

This time my father interrupted. "It's not such a bad place, this town you hate so much, these people—" He waved into the air as if they were all around us and grunted. "You on your high horse."

"So just go right ahead and let me fall."

They both stared at me.

I shook my head in frustration. "So let me fall off my high horse."

"Too clever for your own good, little girl, with all your big jokes. I don't know what to do with you anymore," said my mother. "You don't go hitting your brother at supper—you don't—" Her voice broke, and I thought, please don't cry; you're too old.

When she spoke again, her voice was calmer. "With the baby running a fever, and the trouble with the harvest, and you with your work at school falling off . . . I—to tell you the truth, I just don't know what to do with you anymore. Tell me what to do, why don't you? Tell me. Do you understand? Do you know how tired I am? If you were your own mother, what would you do?"

I shrugged, and her voice grew angry. "Tell me, what would you do?"

"I guess I'd let me go."

"You want this?" she asked quietly.

I nodded. The word *want* did not sound strange and vulgar in her mouth, but a word like any other. What did my mother want, the way she had made her voice dip for the agent? Her voice was careful now, the voice of a good mother, tired but good. I nodded again: I want this, I do. I want.

"After all we've told you?"

"But you don't know—"

She slapped her hands together. "I know a girl shouldn't go running off by herself when she's barely grown, I know what I've heard, which is more than you've heard, but if it's what you persist in wanting—"

She looked at my father. Don't worry; he doesn't care, I wanted to tell her. He cares about the crops and one more mouth to feed.

"I just can't have them hitting each other," she said to him. "I can't have even the grown ones acting like babies. This one and her brother . . . I don't know what's come over them." She turned to me. "Why do you want to go?"

My words came out much surer and clearer than my thoughts. "To send home some money to help here, with the wheat prices so bad, and, I don't know, to save something for my dowry later on, and take all those classes he talked about."

"That's why?"

"And I guess to see somewhere else. It's not so far."

She paused, and I pictured her imagining tall buildings and new people, looms run by water, lessons in languages we had never even heard of—all those things she had never seen or done.

"All right," she said, finally. "You go then, if you persist in wanting to, but don't you start taking work in one of those closed-off hot rooms. I never could do right by you, since the beginning. I never could manage you like the others. Go, if you're so set on it." She turned to my father. "Maybe it will quiet her down a little, let her see that it's not so bad here. Lord knows, she's been in a bad enough humor lately. Of course, it's your decision, in the end."

"Can't hurt, I reckon," said my father doubtfully, "to give it a try. It'd help her put away a nice dowry, anyhow. With the barn roof going, and wheat prices how they are, and Harriet and her fellow carrying on, money won't be stacking up in corners. Not that we couldn't scrape something together, always do, but she can always come home if it don't suit her. It's what girls do nowadays, I figure—the way the men go West. She seems set on going, and we all know that girl has a mule's will."

It was more words than I'd heard him say in months.

My mother nodded. "And if she earns anything, she'll keep it for herself, like you said. I don't hold with taking it from her, like the Cummisks. We don't need it like they do. I don't want folks saying we're putting our own to work for pay. As long as it's clear she's doing it to put away for her own family when she has one." She breathed in deeply. "Girls didn't go off like that on their own when I was young, but it's not the same times, and people do know that."

"Eliza seems to be doing all right," said my father uncertainly.

"They need the money, crowded into that little shack," said my mother. "We don't need to set our own to work. If she goes, it's not because of that."

In her voice I could hear her family pride—how she stepped down in marrying my father. I thought it must be why she was usually the one to decide what her children should do, for my father walked around with a slight air of shame and only burst out every once in a while with his own erratic will. I did not know if most mothers and fathers were like this, or only mine—his temper so strange and violent when it came, and yet so rare; her will staring at me from every corner, every wall I climbed over, each spoon I lifted to my mouth.

I could imagine them at the beginning, how my father brought wheat in to be ground and she stood in the door of her father's mill with the tally sheet, marking figures down in an important hand, still just a girl. That was on Saturdays. Weekdays she was working at the school—to better herself, she said. Not because she had to. I know how she looked back then, can picture it—how level her brown gaze must have been, how calmly and knowingly she looked up at him, this tall, wide young man with the wheat. I picture him courting her by bringing it to be ground in drips and drabs so he would always have an excuse to come back.

Much of this I have had to invent. My father did not talk to me, and I could not turn the rough, silent man I knew into a suitor of any sort. I have had to piece him together from the bits of stories my mother told me when she thought I was too young to remember. Even then, they were stories; I never knew—I'll never know—how much was true. Beneath me, the scuffed toes of my boots stared up at me. "Stepped down," I thought. I did not know why she had married him, if there had been no better prospects, or if somehow he had really won her heart. I placed one foot on top of the other, pressing hard until my toes hurt.

Doesn't my mother care for anything, I found myself thinking, except the neighbors' prying eyes and her own tiredness? How easily they let go, how little convincing, finally, it took for them to let me go away, as if the ghastly stories my mother had heard had been replaced, in a matter of seconds, by new stories about how today, girls went off on their own. Or maybe she remembered the agent, felt his pull. Or perhaps things were worse off than I realized on our farm, even if my parents would not say so out loud.

Their lives, I realized, would fill in without me. For the first time I saw how sturdy, and at the same time, how much composed by chance my family was—and how inessential, really, my own self was to it. I could slip into a well and drown, and for a time they would cry and wring their hands, but then the crops would need tending, the baby would be crying, and though they would not forget me, my spot would fill in with something else, perhaps a new daughter before long.

My baby sister Anna had died at four months old, six years before. Already that was what she was—the one who had died. For a short while I had seen her everywhere I looked—the folds of her wrists, knees and neck, her pink tongue, her eyes—brown like our mother's, gentle and long-lashed as a calf's. Then I had seen her now and then—when I saw another baby at church, or when Luke was born, so much hardier, his head perfectly round where hers had been pinched, his eyes blue and darting. I had loved my baby sister Anna's eyes; I used to get so close to her that our lashes brushed and stare into them, wondering what such a solemn baby thought before words.

Later I hardly ever pictured her, except as Anna The One We Lost, a headstone in the church. Like a bruise that turns purple one day, yellow the next, only to disappear into the skin, she left us. Now we had just a silhouette of her, traced by a peddler a few weeks before she died—a shadow even then, the edges of her face so soft that even on that stiff, black paper they looked blurred. I had been both impressed and troubled by how quickly we had all moved on. Supper, we had eaten, on the very day of her death. We had combed our hair and climbed under the covers. When darkness fell, we slept, to wake again. Even as I swallowed my potatoes and licked the pork gravy from my lips at supper, I had thought how the world should stop for an instant when a life went out of it— how my heart should stop for my sister, if only for a beat. But my heart was strong as an ox, clenched as a fist.

When I got up from the bench I felt weightless, as if I had been leaning my whole body against a heavy rock, trying to move it, and suddenly the rock had disappeared, leaving me tipping into air.

"That's all you have to say?" asked my mother.

"Thank you."

She nodded. "You'll need underthings, a dress, a trunk. We'll have to re-oil my old calfskin trunk. It's cold over there, by the sea."

"It's not by the sea. I think it's a full thirty miles from there to Boston. There's a railroad train." My voice couldn't help lifting with excitement. *The world*, I was thinking, *the world, the world*, as if it were a place I'd never been.

"Near enough to the sea for a sharp wind," my mother said.

I shrugged.

"You'll see—when you start to shiver. Then you'll thank me."

"All right."

"You will. You'll need woolen underthings. Packed in camphor."

She leaned over and brushed a strand of hair from my forehead.

No, I thought. I was afraid that if she acted tender with me, I would begin to cry and beg her to take me back and nestle me like a baby. What if the world turned out to be a bad place? What if a flying shuttle pierced a hole through my bones?

"Aimee, Aimee," my mother said. "Born with a lucky streak. How do you always manage to get what you want? They'll say we let you run wild."

My father was staring at me as if he had never seen me before.

"A factory girl," he said. "Nobody in the family ever went that way."

"Thank goodness there's no more girls to follow," my mother said. "The boys'll need to stay behind to run the farm. All we need now is for one of them to get a yearning to run off out West like those two Nordstrom boys." She rubbed her temples. "If everybody goes out West, there'll be nobody left back home."

I shook my head. "Anyway, I don't."

"Don't what?"

"Always get what I want."

If you only knew what I wanted, I thought—how much, how badly. Then I realized it was more muddled than that. If I only knew what I wanted.

"I just hope for your sake you don't lose that lucky streak," said my mother. "Better never to have one at all than to lose it partway through."

It's no lucky streak, I thought, standing there before her. It's watching the way people move, the things they say and do not say. It's using your head, and your eyes, and the eyes in the back of your head—and who but my mother had taught me that?

It's remembering things people think you can't possibly remember and storing them up in wooden button trays inside your mind.

I was fifteen and thought I knew everything.

My brother Jeremiah would not watch me go. As my mother aired the bandbox, and Harriet and I whitened my underclothes, and my father oiled the calfskin trunk until the hinges moved voiceless and smooth, Jeremiah walked the edges of our land, coming home after supper with the cuffs of his trousers muddy and wet and scratches rising red upon his hands. Nights, he slept out in the toolshed, saying the fresh air helped his cough, for it was early fall and the loft still held the summer air, thick and difficult to breathe.

My mother filled the trunk, fastening a careful list to the inside of the lid so I would know what I had, and so the

other girls would know to leave my things alone. *2 pr gloves.*
1 Luce cape, 1 browncambrick Gown, 1 straw bonet . . . Her
handwriting stumbled around the words, and I winced
when I saw her spelling. I was sure I must be quite smart,
for I had not been to school for any longer than she had,
and still I could tell which words were wrong. Once the decision was made, she stopped telling me horrible stories
about the mills. Just the way her mouth tightened into a
puckered line when she thought I wasn't watching showed
she was thinking anything at all.

Only Harriet and I grew closer in the two weeks before
my departure.

"You'll need this," she whispered late one night, coming with her lantern to where I lay sleepless on my pallet
and pressing a tiny sewing basket into my hand. Inside was
a thimble, some buttons, different-sized needles lined up
like a family on a piece of black cloth. Harriet would never
have gone away herself, but she loved the excitement of it,
the planning. She had never wanted me to be a schoolteacher, had always sulked quietly when I did better than
she at school. This was better—"That Aimee," they could
say in town. "She and that Eliza, running off to who knows
where."

Harriet would gaze down at the picture of the girl by
the beehive—not the way I gazed, not as a way to leave the
room and wedge myself in between the black lines of the
drawing, but as an observer looking at someone from another world. *Go away*, would say the smallest, deepest voice
inside her. Part of her knew she could love me better if I
were not in front of her all the time. Though I think I understood this even then, I still appreciated the way she drew
nearer to me as everyone else in my family drew back. I

would look up from my packing to see her standing silently
behind me, a pale yellow sunbonnet in her hand.

"You'll have to write us all about the bonnets there,"
she'd say, just the slightest edge to her voice. "And send on
a scrap of that cloth made by those machines you work on."

My father talked to me even less than before, for I was
not in the farmyard now, but folding a life for myself inside
a little trunk. When his eyes skimmed over me at dinner I
wondered if he recognized me. Already I felt like a stranger,
the grown daughter, the one who had left. Gone, like Anna.
Sometimes it made me want to open my mouth and let out a
loud and plaintive wail, lean forward and let loose, childish
tears drip down into my plate. *I'm only fifteen*, I wanted to
say then. It did not sound like many years to me, just three
more than once around a clock. If they would only sing to
me and hold me the way they used to, I would stop being
so sullen, look straight at them. Stay. Sitting there, I tried to
remember the blue of my father's lap, but instead his hands
came to me, shoving me away from him. I would have gone
backwards if I could, but I knew I could not, and so instead
I decided I had better grow up in one great burst.

My mother packed my trunk, and I watched from my
mattress.

"You'll need this," she said, "and this," holding up a
shawl, some gloves, wool stockings, before she folded them.
She gave me a Bible, not the one from the kitchen, but another, smaller one that had been hers as a girl, her name
written in the front in pale brown ink. When I picked it up
after she climbed down the ladder, pressed flowers fell
from it like bits of yellowing skin. She gave me a bottle of
ink and a fountain pen, a bundle of coarse paper, a seal and
a piece of red wax, a packet of herbs for if I was feeling
poorly.

"Steep it for two hours in water," she said, and I knew how it would be sweet and bitter, like drinking home.

The night before I was to take the coach at dawn, I went out to the toolshed after Jeremiah had gone to sleep. It was mid-September, the kind of night when the wind comes up from the ground and lifts the leaves from below, exposing their underbellies streaked with yellow and red. I stood outside the toolshed and listened for my brother's breathing. I heard him mutter something; he kept cats in there with him—for company, I supposed. I could feel how he would turn away if I walked into the shed. His skin would tighten around him, his fingers curl into his palms. He would close himself to me.

By the side of the big oak door I stood and thought *I'm sorry I'm sorry I'm sorry*. I thought it hard enough so that I hoped he could feel it, hear it, somehow, but I was not brave enough to go in. My lips moved, but no sound came out. Still, he stopped talking to the cats. Maybe he was listening to my thoughts; perhaps he simply slept.

I prayed for my brother, that he might grow strong in his body, that he might move back into the family after I was gone. I prayed (O Lord I am selfish and undeserving, but please in Thy heart grant me this) that he might love me just a little, somewhere hidden and tiny in the dark red middle of his heart.

I knew it was not right to pray, not when I did it so rarely in a way I thought the Lord could truly hear. Still, I stood outside the toolshed and prayed.

In the morning, my father carried my trunk outside; Harriet kissed me lightly on the cheek; Thomas and John patted me on the shoulder; Luke cried because he was hungry. Nobody mentioned Jeremiah's absence.

Just before I left, my mother held me at arm's length

and looked at me long and hard. I tried to say good-bye, but my voice was somewhere else.

"Write," she said, and wiped a loose strand of hair from my forehead. "And be careful. Make sure they keep the bedclothes clean."

When I look back, I picture the journey marked by a long trail of white thread. It is not fancy thread, but the thinnest, cheapest, factory kind, the sort that breaks if you pull on it too hard. It begins in my mother's hand, and then it trails down the road and through the town and out by the field and into the next town, and on and on until the city, and still it does not stop. It follows the coach the whole way, and when the coach stops by the boardinghouse and I get out, the string follows me into the building, up to the attic room where I will sleep next to five other girls.

I picture it following me for days, going everywhere I go—unwinding longer and longer, its other end still tight in my mother's fist.

This is how I picture it now. I could not, at the time, have imagined so much thread. My mother's hand was empty when I left. I got into a coach filled with girls like me, mute and staring, and though the coach on the outside was red with dark green trim, on the inside it was barn-wood—plain plank boards with narrow benches lining each side. The covered baggage wagon lurched after us like a calf. I had brought the newest catalog to show Eliza, though I was afraid she would scoff now, used to city life. I had come with a pot of honey from her mother's hives.

We were jolted on that trip, bumped and shaken. Nobody spoke much, but our shoulders pressed and banged against each other. So many girls, all of us dressed more or less the same in our brown or gray cloaks. Every so often someone would ask a question of the group: "Do you know where to go to find work?"; "Do you think they ever turn girls away?" Ten or so heads would shake in ignorance. We had all been told that once we arrived there would be work for us, but none of us knew exactly how or where. Each of us had been told by an agent when to get the coach, but that seemed to be as much as they did. I wanted to find out the names of my fellow travelers, where they had come from, if their stomachs felt as watery as mine. Once I looked up, about to ask, but the girl across from me gave me a nervous, weak smile and fastened her gaze upon her shoes. Eliza, I told myself. Eliza will be there.

I had never been more than an hour from my home. We got to the city at sunset, but still I could see the trolley lines, the tall brick buildings, the sun winking on the high glass windows. It was just like in the pictures, and at first I felt a sparkling in my throat: nobody had lied to me—there were window boxes, sidewalks, real city curbs. But then I realized that it still *looked* like a picture—that kind of smallness and flatness, everything too neatly in its place. There were people on the streets, but not many. The buildings were tall, but not, somehow, as tall as I had expected. Only the bank looked as fine as I had hoped, with its sign written in gold, and brass trim curled around its door.

I would put my money in that bank, grow rich, go to Paris and send for my mother, that she might see a new world.

Darkness was beginning to fall when the coachman dropped me in front of the boardinghouse where Eliza was living. "Mrs. Ladd's, number thirty on the Lawrence," I had told him, reading from the card I'd taped to the top of my bandbox, though I did not know what the Lawrence was—a street or a river or something else. The baggageman deposited my trunk on the ground. I thought I would be the only girl to get out, but when I looked behind me, there were four others climbing down, clutching their bandboxes.

"Who do you know at Mrs. Ladd's?" I whispered to the girl closest to me, but she shook her head as if she couldn't understand.

"I asked if you knew someone there," I repeated, a bit louder, standing rigid at her side. She had to speak English, didn't she? We were all just girls from the farms. My legs were stiff from the journey, and I was afraid if I moved too quickly, I would fall.

She turned to me, her face set and determined in the faltering light. "It seems as good a place to begin as anyplace. I don't have folks in this town." Then she looked down, and her voice dipped. "You have people here?"

"Eliza Cummisk," I said. "My friend Eliza, she's no relation. My best friend from home."

"I had a friend Eliza who moved away," she said, frowning. "But then I guess it's the commonest of names."

"Go ahead and knock, misses," the coachman broke in. "I've got to be on my way."

The five of us only stared at the black iron knocker at the center of the door.

"Well, go on," he said. "She won't bite. I leave girls with her all the time."

I could feel how their feet were glued to the cobblestones, and so I leaned over, put my bandbox on the ground and climbed the steps. My legs felt heavy, stuffed with sawdust, but I did not trip or fall.

The iron knocker in my hand was still warm from taking in the sun all day. I let it drop once against the wood—gently, its own free fall—and a tiny knock tried to sound against the door. I lifted the knocker up again, stood there feeling the eyes of those girls and that coachman and baggageman on my back.

I knew that once I went in, everything would change. I could feel, from outside, the life in that house, roomfuls of activity held between its walls. Inside someone called out, and feet sounded quickly, perhaps a child clattering up the stairs. This was a home of sorts to Eliza; now it would be a home of sorts to me. I stood by the door and pulled the knocker back toward me as far as it would go. Then I let it drop.

It was a firm knock—the knock of a girl who knows where she has come from and where she is going. I knew, then, that even my knock could lie for me.

My bandbox, I thought suddenly, since this was the city, where things disappeared. When I turned around it was still there, mocking me with its battered rim.

She opened the door—a tiny, pointed woman with a wide mouth on the edge of a scowl or a laugh.

"More girls," she said, looking at us skeptically. "And so late in the day."

I was hovering outside myself looking down at the slightly crooked part in her hair, her ears—small as a child's—her neat apron and the lantern in her hand, but still somehow my voice came out of me, how my friend Eliza was staying there and had said there might be a place.

"Eliza." She sighed deeply. "There are so many Elizas."

"Eliza Cummisk," I said. She peered at me for a moment, as if she were trying to locate my Eliza in my face.

"Cummisk, Cummisk. Ah," she said. "Little slip of a girl with big eyes and a stubborn streak? That the one you mean?"

Eliza passed before my eyes in all her brightness, and I nodded.

"That one . . . where did she go off to? That Eliza . . . yes, she went off, I think she went to Fall River when they came looking for girls. She and that Mary Guild, and another one. Must have been near ten days ago."

I felt my breath leave me, but still my voice said thank you, ma'am. For a moment I thought I should turn and go—run if I had to, into the city, into the night, anywhere where I might find something familiar, though I had no idea where to begin looking, or what to look for. Then I glanced down off the stoop and saw the four girls and the coachman staring at me, and my bandbox still on the curb. Of course I could not go. I would be murdered near a canal or pulled by my hair into a dark cellar full of city rats as big as dogs. I could hear my mother's voice describing them.

"The girls, they come and go," the woman said. "How many are you?"

"Five of them wanting to stay, Mrs. Ladd," said the coachman. "Five more in the coach. Picked them up all over the south part of New Hampshire and one clear from Maine."

"I can take two," said the woman. "If they're willing to put up in the garret room with the ones already there till some space clears out below. I'm more than full—near thirty-five girls under my roof, plus my own lot."

I felt her hand under my chin, tilting my face down so she could see it better. She lifted her lantern up and pooled me in its light.

"Tall and handsome, aren't you, but mighty pale," she said. "Are you feeling poorly, any troubles of the heart or lungs? Influenza? Sick headaches?"

"No, ma'am."

"They'll give you vaccinations over at the corporation before they take you on. You can stomach a vaccination?"

I nodded, though I did not know what she meant.

She let go of my chin, stepped out onto the stoop and peered at the other girls.

"The one in the blue bonnet," she said. "No, the other

one, you—the big, tall, strapping girl. Are you feeling strong lately, no trouble?"

"No, ma'am," said the girl. "I'm feeling fine."

"You're a good worker?"

The girl nodded.

"I expect the best behavior from my girls, and I give them the best," the woman said. "The best food, the cleanest linen, no vermin, everything in its place. And from you, no running around, no wandering off to the Acre to talk to the canal diggers and whatnot. My girls look out for each other. This is a Christian home, do you understand?"

We nodded.

"We'll be going with the others," said the coachman. "You think at Mrs. Alter's?"

"Maggie Alter always fills up after me," said the woman. "Not that she's not a good keeper, she runs a decent place, full of Boott Mill girls like my own, but her bread sits inside you like a rock and working girls need better than that to get them through."

She looked down, and seeing the expressions on the three girls' faces, caught herself, so that I found a note of kindness in her voice. "But she treats them like her own, Maggie. You'll all be well-off there." She looked down at the coachman and sighed. "If she's all full up, bring them back and we'll find them a corner for one night."

She clapped her hands together, as if she suddenly realized she was wasting time.

"Come on, you two there, if you're coming," she said to me and the blue-bonneted girl, and told the baggageman to leave our trunks in the front hall.

I counted—one, two, three—inside my head. Then I stepped inside the house.

"Your box, there," said Mrs. Ladd. As I turned to see it

sitting alone in the street, the coach disappeared around a corner.

"Run on down and get it," she said, pushing lightly at the small of my back. "Can't leave it lying there. Go on now— all the cold night air is coming in."

The box was heavy when I picked it up; something shifted inside it, rattling. I clutched it to me, the weight of home.

Mrs. Ladd wrote our names in a big blue ledger book and started up the stairs, the light of her lantern wavering as she climbed. As we followed, I counted. We went up and up, one flight of eighteen stairs, two flights, three, then up a narrow staircase almost like a ladder, but not quite, that led to the garret room. The walls were so slanted up there that I could not stand up except in the very center. This will be fine, I thought, since it was like where I had slept at home. Then Mrs. Ladd gestured toward a bed off the ground. It was a string bed like my parents', the mattress resting on a tight rope grid a good two feet off the floor. I had only slept so high when I was very ill and my mother let my fever crest in her own bed. On a bed like that, I would have to knock on the wooden frame to ward off evil thoughts; the plank floor would be too far away.

"We're a little full right now," she said, "but it'll give you a chance to know the other girls. You'll have to both sleep in that bed—it'll make six of you." She pointed to a marble chamber pot. "For the middle of the night," she said. "But no one cleans up after you. Privy's out back, next to the laundry and storeroom.

"You can pay after you find work at the Boott Mill," she said, "but in no more than five days. One dollar and twenty-five cents per week. One of the girls will take you over to the overseer tomorrow. They're sure to need you somewhere or other, even if it's just as loose hands for a bit, till you learn your way. The door locks here at ten o'clock each night. You come in by then, or you spend the night on the street, and Lord knows we don't want that. You'll pick out the church where you'll rent your pew space this Sunday, no use waiting longer. Understand?"

She peered at us, not at all breathless, though it seemed she should be, and I nodded as calmly as I could. Then she pulled two rolled-up pieces of paper from her apron pocket and smiled. "This is the regulations, all put in writing. You can read, can't you, smart girls like yourselves? You'll soon learn this is a home to you. I expect nothing but the best from all my girls, but they're always a good lot."

Then she asked us to come down for cornbread, jam and tea. I was curious if it would taste the same as country bread, but my stomach was tied around itself. I could not imagine coming up with so much money, or why anyone would want to give me work, or how I would know how to pick a church and rent a pew space. I did not want to go into a church again, since there the Lord would make me think about my sins. I wanted to shut my eyes and see only black.

"I think I'd better rest a minute, ma'am," I said.

She frowned at me. "You have to eat, or you get ill. I can't have a houseful of sickly girls. You did tell me you were in good health. The others are all down there."

"Tomorrow I'll eat," I promised. "I'm not sick, I'm just a little funny from the coach."

The tall, silent girl with the blue bonnet followed Mrs. Ladd downstairs, and I was left alone.

Outside, the street was lit by gaslights like in the pictures. The sky was a deep blue falling into black. I lit a tallow candle, partly for the oily comfort of its smell, and then, like a dog in a new place, I sniffed out my surroundings. The girls had hung lines on the wall; their nightclothes were draped there like neatly folded bodies, white and starched. Two beds took up the center of the room. Around them, set like guards, stood four squat calfskin trunks. When I leaned over to put my bandbox under the bed, I saw four other bandboxes crouched in the half-dark. Down below, dim as the sound of mice in walls, I could hear voices, girls talking—like a family, a brood of many sisters. I heard a laugh, high-pitched, then a moment of silence until the steady murmur of voices began again.

Please may they like me, I thought. *Please may I find a place in the mills tomorrow and be able to learn how to work the machines.* I unrolled the piece of paper Mrs. Ladd had given me: "Regulations for the Boardinghouses of the Boott Corporation." "The Keepers of the Boardinghouse," I read, halfway down the page, "Must give an Account of the Names, Numbers and Employment of their Boarders, when Required; and Report the Names of such as are Guilty of any Improper Conduct, or Not in the Habit of attending Public Worship." Although I was alone in the room, I could feel eyes watching me like the eyes of my mother: "All Persons should be Vaccinated who have not been . . . the Yards and Building Must be kept Clean . . . the Doors must be Closed at Ten O'clock . . ."

Again, that word, *vaccinated*. I did not know what it meant. It was only eight o'clock, the front door still open to the world, but I lay my head down on a pillow smelling of bleach and lye. The names of my brothers and sisters began to run through my head like a familiar chant, and I held onto the sounds as if they were solid objects: Harriet Luke Thomas Jeremiah John—and Anna who was gone. Anna was the softest, saddest name, and so I said it over and over to myself, picturing the sewing basket Harriet had given me before I left, the family of needles arranged by size in their strip of black felt.

Anna, Anna, and I could feel her watching me from where she sat in heaven, for though she was only a baby, she was wiser than the rest of us, since she knew what it was like on the other side.

Anna, Anna, Anna, and I slept.

It felt as if I slept for days that first night, though in fact we were woken by a bell at dawn. I was so tired from looking at everything, taking it all in. In my sleep I moved through familiar worlds, even if strange things happened there, like in the dream I had where I shot all the pigs in the sty with my father's gun when he was not home. Even when I shut my eyes I could feel how high up I was, how many floors were stretching out beneath me, even my bed two feet from the floor. Later that first evening, I became half-aware of someone pushing me by the shoulder, making me move toward one corner of the bed. That first night, the bodies next to me could have been my brothers and sisters. But when the bell sounded in my dreams (a familiar sound, I had imagined it so many times; a startling sound, so deep and full it seemed to come from somewhere inside my own head), I woke to find myself cradled into the back of a strange girl, our legs entwined.

I pulled back, away from her, jolted from my sleep.

"Pardon me," I whispered, and leapt up from the bed. She turned toward me, her eyes half-open.

"Morning," she said, yawning so wide I could see the pink cave of her throat.

"Morning."

"You were talking a blue streak in the night," she said.

I wanted to explain, to tell her how I had always talked in the night, and it didn't mean anything. Even more, I wanted to ask her exactly what I had said. One night there, and already I was letting pieces of myself fly out into the night.

But she was up and gone from me, leaning her head over

to comb the snarls from her hair, rushing into her clothes, moving through the flurry of others who were all dressing, too—girls everywhere, talking and yawning, stretching and gesturing, and then they were gone down the stairs, and I and the girl from the coach were left sitting still and panicked, one of us on each side of the wide bed.

8

This morning when I went to feed the rabbits in their lean-to, I found that one of the does had kindled. I leaned over the box, parted the hay and fur and tried to count the babies, but the doe grunted at me and snapped at my hand.

"Hello chicken. It's all right," I told her, backing away. This is when their meanness comes out. Around her sides, straining toward her underbelly, were her children—pink and hairless, blind and deaf, squirming with life.

"Oh! They're beautiful. How many?" I said to her. She is a big, strong rabbit, three years old by now, this her second litter of the year. I knew these were coming. A month ago I let her into the buck's hutch. Last week she started to fill her nesting box with straw and bits of her own fur. She worked steadily, gathering fodder, pulling fluff from her belly with her teeth to work into a nest. Each time I came in, she would turn and glare at me.

I wanted to pull her from them for a moment, hold her up and warn her: Some of them will die; it happens every time. Sometimes I find them right away, lying in the nest with the others. Other times I find them later, stiff and small, or rotting, buried under hay in a corner of the shed. Every once in a while a mother eats her children. I do not know quite what makes this happen. Once a fox had been lurking outside for days, the winter cold and hard. He did not get inside, but the doe must have smelled him. I came in to find her with her front teeth bared, her paws pushing down the kit's head. At her sides were bits of another one—a piece of flesh; a sliver, like a toothpick, of fine bone. The rest of the litter nursed from her teats as she swallowed down the kit.

That day I hurried to get Amos, who was patching holes in the chicken house.

"Oh Lord," he said when he looked down into the nest. Then he pinned the mother against the side of her box, grabbed the dead kit, scooped up all the others in his shirt and hobbled with them to the house. I brought over another nursing doe for them, but she would not feed them, and though we tried to give them drips of milk, they screwed their mouths shut. One by one, they died. Later I told Amos I thought we should have let the mother keep them, eat them if need be.

"She knew something was wrong, or she wouldn't have tried to kill them. We should have left her alone."

He shook his head. "It's not natural. Maybe she's a crazy one and just got the wrong notion. Animals go funny in the head, just like people. I had a cow once who turned into a she-devil overnight. Never turned back, either, just plain lost her mind. I had to shoot her.''

''The rabbit wasn't funny in the head. We should have let them stay with her.''

''And watch her swallow them whole?''

''I don't know. They couldn't live without her.''

''They might have. I've seen it happen before.''

''I still think we should have let them stay,'' I said.

Back to her blood, they would have gone, inside her where they came from. Instead, we were left with six stiff carcasses covered with the finest down, eyes like black stitches, bodies so pale you could see the blue inside, the spidery lines of red.

''Could you take them away?'' I asked Amos. ''Please?''

He gave them to the bog.

Though I am careful, I know it might happen again. Each time I leave the lean-to, I bolt the door so the weasels and foxes can't get in. When I cut Amos's hair, or my own, I save the ends and hang them in bags to make the place smell like people, the way my mother used to hang our hair from poles in the garden to keep the deer away. When a cold snap comes or when I want the company, I bring the rabbits inside and warm them near my stove. If these kits live past three months, the doe will wean them. Then I will give most of them to Amos to sell for their pelts and meat.

Is this strange, to long for their lives this way, then send them to their deaths? When I was a girl my mother said I could play with the lambs and piglets, but I should never name them. ''If they have names,'' she said, ''you'll see their faces after they're dead.'' Anna, I remember thinking, Anna my dead baby sister. My mother was right; even now, when I say my sister's name, her brown eyes open in my mind. I have not named my rabbits, not even the blind one, though I will keep her with me for as long as we both draw breath.

Though I cannot keep them all—they would overrun me—I do not like to stop them from kindling, for I love to watch the busyness in a doe when she begins to prepare her nest. The fur they give me when I shear them is not the fancy kind, not for the rim of a lady's cape or a rich child's sweater, but still I spin it into soft, brown-gray yarn and knit it into stockings and mittens that bring a good price when Amos takes them into town.

Amos brings me back other goods, and news: which wife hurled a frying pan through a window, whose cows got loose and trammeled the village green. The names mean little to me now, but I am hungry for news. He tells me when a child is born, injured or dies, and when there is a railroad accident or turn-out. Sometimes he brings me a newspaper, and I read it slowly, saving each page for a new day; at the end I begin again.

Once, in the years before the war, he came to me and asked if I could spare a pair of the gloves I had knitted. For what, I asked, but Amos would not say. Tell me, I pressed. For someone who needs them. But who? Never mind. But who? Someone cold, I can't say more. In the end, he told me—how slaves were passing through our town, sleeping by day and running toward Canada by night, cold in our weather, carrying their children on their backs. Bring them here, I remember saying, my voice taut with excitement. I pictured a young mother and her baby, how I would feed them and knit the baby mittens. When I told Amos, he grew sharp with me. It's not a game, he said. People are hanging from trees. Some gloves is all they need from you.

I remember the thud I felt, then, at my own uselessness and how little I knew of the world. I handed him the gloves, and a small wooden toy I had carved. Amos took the gloves, but not the toy, saying it would weigh them down. My mouth was full of silent questions: Are you hiding them, have you met them, what do they look like, what language do they speak? I remembered the negro cloth we used to weave for the slaves' trousers, how the girls who ran those machines were seen as the lowest in the mills. That night I dreamed of a slave girl carrying her life to Canada through swamps and thickets. Her skin was dark, but I knew that really she was me, and I woke sick at my own selfishness and told Amos nothing of the dream.

Later he told me when the boys and men in our town went to war, and who came home missing a limb, or didn't come home at all. He told me when the slaves were set free. Now they're coming North, buying land. Now there are no farmgirls at the mills. It was Amos, too, who told me when my father died, and who went with me at dawn a few days later to leave flowers on the grave. Over the years he has come to me with news of inventions: a continuous-feed sewing machine with a metal foot, telegraph lines all the way to St. Louis, a giant bridge crossing the river at Niagara Falls.

He brought me word last June when my brother Luke and his wife had another daughter, Abigail Susan, and yesterday, as if in passing, he mentioned he'd seen my mother leaving the church. I do not ask him for this kind of news, but nor do I stop him. I nodded, my head full of questions: Who was she with? What was the expression on her face? Did she see you? And me in you? Did she look bent with grief or quick with pleasure? Has she grown softer or harder with age?

I pictured her looking up, seeing Amos in the distance,

looking down. Amos—the man who has sinned with the daughter she has forgotten, or wants to have forgotten, or thinks of sometimes, the daughter—I could feel her thinking—who brought trouble on us all. Three children and a husband dead. Aimee as good as dead. Thomas and John moved out West, their letters scarce and saying little. Only Luke with his wife and children left. Abigail Susan, plump and healthy, but just at the beginning of her road. A girl, so bound for some kind of trouble. Sometimes my mother must look down at the baby, see her three girls in her, and find she needs to thrust her away. *Take her*, she says to her daughter-in-law, who knows by the sharp voice to hurry. *Take her, can't you see I'm tired*? Other times, she must sing to the baby or tell her stories.

Leaving the church, my mother would hold her head up high, her hair neatly coiled in its braided bun, her collar starched. Good day, she would nod to the other churchgoers. Poor woman, they might think, though she would not want them to. She might have bread for the poor in her arms, or a blanket for somebody's ill baby. I tried to picture her old and stooped, but found I could not; tried to see her laughing, but could not. Instead she came to me as she was when I was nine or ten, children everywhere around her—me like a shadow at her heels. Her palm cupping my chin as she scrubbed my face with a rag, tilting me to her. Then, she could not see into the future to where we would end up. *The children are well*, she might have written to her mother, who had moved away. *They have good health and good form and keep me running*. In church she would pray to God to keep us well and look with pride over what she had created, a whole family trying to sit up straight. And if her mind wandered in the silence meant for prayers? Where would it go? I saw her, then, old and tired, her hair grown finer and whiter, her clothes hanging on her frame, her hands clenched and knotty at her sides.

Walking down the path, she might see Amos and curse him, and me, in her thoughts. Or perhaps she'd stop and think, for just a second, about how there on the road, looking in her direction, stood the man who smoothed her daughter's hair, brought her coal and grain, kept her living with his love. *How is she?* she might wonder about me, as I wonder about her. *Does she think about me sometimes? Has she found anything like happiness out there?*

Speak to her when you see her again, I almost wanted to say to Amos yesterday. Tell her a joke or a piece of the Bible, let her see the way your whole frame shakes with pleasure when you laugh. Let her see your kind hands, or sit down with her, unpin the cloth and show her how clean your scar is where I've washed it. *If this is sin*, you might say to her. *If this is sin . . .* Or you might shake her by the shoulders and ask *How could you have? . . . Why?*

Why? she'd echo back.

Plumey does not bring me news, but I do not mind; just being with her pleases me. Usually she is calm, but since she has started coming every day, something has seemed to grind upon her nerves. Perhaps it is the leaves from the sugar maples—falling everywhere, violent in their reds. Today, the day the new litter is born, she arrives looking as if she has been rolling down a hill, scraps of leaves stuck to her dress and clinging like moths to her wool stockings. She must be eleven or twelve by now, her body showing the faint, clumsy beginnings of womanhood beneath her frock.

She comes while I am kneeling by the water, scrubbing my butternut and acorn squash and dipping them in vinegar so they will last through the winter. I first see her shape, pale and dotted with bright leaves, in the black water of the bog. I nod to her and straighten up.

"Hello," I say.

She squints down at me.

"It's getting colder," I say. "Why didn't you wear your shawl?"

She throws some leaves down into the water and wraps her arms around herself, as if my words have made her chilly.

"I have a shawl inside," I tell her. "It's hanging on the hook, you know where."

But she is staring at the leaves as they sink a bit below the surface of the water, then rise again, beaded. I can almost see thoughts passing beneath her brow; there is something inside this girl that cannot get out. Like Amos she leaves me even when she is with me. Sometimes I do the same thing to them, turning inside myself in the middle of a visit. But with myself and Amos I know, more or less, where the mind goes. With Plumey I have no idea.

As she crouches and pokes at the leaves with a cattail stem, I wash my store of winter food. I will have parsnips, onions, turnips and beets in my cellar; potatoes, carrots and garlic. Plumey strips off her shoes and stockings and sits with her plump legs dangling in the black water of the bog pond.

"It's cold, isn't it?" I say, and she dips her finger in, reaches over and touches it to my bare wrist.

"Oh yes, it's very cold," I repeat.

She smiles, showing the gap between her two front teeth, and I see a flicker of tongue. Plumey seems to love water; perhaps it is the water, not myself, she comes to see. Partly I think she loves it for the way it lets her see herself, her face mixed in with trees and rushes, my own hands washing vegetables, her own feet dangling. I am the same way and often go to water, not my mirror, when I want to see my face.

At first she pushed the leaves gently, but now, as I pretend not to watch, she jabs them with sticks and sends them down. Still, they keep floating up. Each autumn, silt and leaves rise from the bottom of the bog, as if reaching for the last pockets of warm air. Plumey pushes the leaves down, leans back, waits. When they float back up, she pushes them again, but they will not stay. In the back of her throat she makes a low whimpering noise. I picture animals caught in a burning barn, stomping, turning in their stalls.

"One of the rabbits kindled last night," I tell her. "When they get a little bigger you can have one."

Sometimes I think a small creature to hold might do her good, but though she'll stroke my rabbits absently if I put one in her lap, she does not show much interest.

"Look, Plumey."

I fish a leaf out of the water, reach for a pebble and fold the leaf around it, as if I were wrapping a gift. The wet leaf plasters itself against the stone. Then I send it out into the water where it sinks, down to the chocolate, the kits, the doll she threw in there herself.

Plumey smiles and whispers "yes"—the only word I will get from her today, but it is a fine one and I store it in the back of my mind. Though her hands look bloated, she can move quickly, and she imitates my action. A few of the leaves will wrap around stones, most will not, but she does her best, sending one clumsy package after another into the water until many of the leaves by her side are gone. Then she begins to pluck leaf-bits from her dress and stockings and send them down, only most are too small and will not wrap around a stone. Some of the leaves she has sunk are already coming back up. The water is littered with her scraps.

When she has finished with her game, she sits staring down at her hands. I would like to hold her, to wrap my arms around her and cradle her in my lap, sing, "I had a little nut tree and nothing did it bear, but a silver nutmeg and a golden pear," in the deep voice of my mother. Plumey is too big for that, already becoming a woman and large for her age. She is too spooked for that—probably she would pull away if I tried, or worse, sit still and hard.

I do not wrap her in my arms. Instead I dip my hand in the pond and paint the underside of her wrist with water. I make the letters: ABC. "PLUMEY," I write, then, saying each letter aloud as I paint it, invisible, on her arm. I would like to tell her how quick I was in school, how I still read sometimes, books Amos finds me, mostly about farm tools and the weather, but a few about people in far-off lands. "A" I paint on her arm. "I" "M" "E" "E," and the little line over the "E," the mark that I learned about in Improvement Circle when they told me my name was French. My mother never wrote it that way, did not know to, so mostly I think of it plain. I wipe my name off her wrist and write "RED." Plumey points to a maple leaf. "You're a quick one," I say. "But don't worry, I won't tell."

Later she pulls two heels of bread, two chunks of hard cheese and two apples from her pocket, and we eat, sitting on the two stumps outside my door in the cool afternoon air. I have gotten her to wrap herself in the gray shawl I knitted from my rabbits' wool, and she looks, now, like a plump, molting dove. I do not know if the Doctor and his wife know she comes to see me, but often Plumey has food enough for two. I wonder, if they know she comes, how they think of me. They must not think of me too badly, or they would not let her come. I like to think that the food is meant for me—not as charity, but as a meal to eat with Plumey.

She devours her bread and cheese in two or three deep gulps. I will save half my bread for tomorrow, boil the apple and mash it into sauce. While I am still nibbling, she gets up and walks out onto the peat, where she stands among the rushes and peers through them as if through a slatted window. I think, from where I am sitting, that she might be talking to herself out there, saying not just one word, but a whole string. I lean toward her, straining to hear, but she looks over at me and then turns her back, and I know she will not speak.

As I am shaking crumbs from my skirt, Amos comes—a rare thing, my two visitors at once. He frowns when he sees Plumey staring down at the water.

"What's she staring at so hard?" he asks.

I shrug.

"She comes out here near every day now, doesn't she? They don't know what to do with her, over where she lives. I was just listening to them talk about how she's touched." He jabs at his temple with a long finger.

I tell him to shush. I can feel Plumey listening. My mother would have called her a little pitcher with big ears.

"All right," he says, "but it's not good for a child to spend so much time alone out in a swamp. Don't mind if she hears it."

"She's not alone."

Amos snorts. "You know what I mean."

I turn from him, for he has hurt me and I intend to let him see it. If my company is the same as the company of stumps and owls, then he may as well not come see me. I shake my head as if I have just remembered something I need to get and rise to go into the house. I can feel Amos's eyes on me, but he does not speak.

Inside, I am blinded for a moment by the change of light. My wall has one glass window, but I have covered the bottom half with clippings from magazines the way the girls at the factory did—to give myself things to read when I am passing by and keep the boys from town from peering in. There is nothing in here I need to get, so instead I lower myself down to the bed, and find, to my surprise, that I am crying.

It happens to me sometimes, at the slightest change in the air or a rough word. My tears come up through thick skin, the most careful of ways. I never expect them, and yet they come. When I am not crying I am the most regular of women, each day the same, each moment part of a rhythm that I like because I know it: I tend each corner of my world. But when these moments come I become the girl I used to be, and I cannot stop the liquid rising out of me, the shaking that makes me clutch at my knees through the fabric of my dress.

Is she alone when she is with me, I wonder as I rock myself. If she is, does that make me a Nothing, a Not-To-Be-Considered-Company, not only to Plumey but to Amos, too, since the words came from his mouth? I am not vain the way I once was, but I would like for them to like—I need for them to love me, in at least some crooked, silent way.

I do not want them to hear me, not Amos, especially not Plumey. For her I must be a still place to hold onto, not a trembling, nervous girl. In the darkness of my house I breathe in until my tears sink down. For a few minutes I drink the air of the place I live, until it fills me up. Then I close my face the best I can, rise, and walk out into the sun. When my eyes adjust to the light again I see that Plumey is gone, my shawl left folded neatly by the door, and Amos is cutting rushes for my baskets.

"You don't need to do that," I say.

He grunts.

"Where did she go?"

"She ran off the minute you went inside. Scared of me, I reckon."

"Not Plumey."

"Sure, all the young ones are scared. They think I prop up the devil with my crutches. Their parents tell them." He holds a rush up to his head for horns.

"No, Plumey doesn't set store with all that."

"Did she tell you that? Does she talk to you? Can she talk? Have you worked a spell on her? Seems you can get anyone to talk."

"She didn't tell me, but I know from how she is."

"Huh. I guess she's good company, better than me with all my complaining."

He wants me to see that he is jealous and so forgive him for what he said before. I tighten my mouth.

"I guess," he tries again, "it's good for her too, having someone to show her how to make baskets and spin. The Doctor might not take care of her forever. She should know ways to get by."

"I don't show her anything."

"You do, even if she just watches. You have a way with your hands."

I shake my head.

"Look," he says, "I *will* attract the devil if my leg gets any dirtier. How about some of your bog wine and a bath?"

I bring out two gourds and a jug of my wine, and he sits on the log and rolls his trouser leg up. I have been cleaning for five minutes, the old familiar skin, when I feel his hands on my shoulders, resting lightly, not the palms, but his ten fingertips.

"Hello you," he says.

I look up at him, then to the ground.

"I—I mean, don't go taking it wrong, what I said," he tells me. "It was just, you know, seeing her standing out there by herself. I only meant—I was just saying that she should have real family, and some people her own age."

She has me, I think, but do not say. I scrub hard at his leg, but Amos must feel how, deep inside me, my bones are trembling, for he lowers his hands so that my shoulders are pressed beneath his palms. He bears down.

"All right?" he says, and I nod.

I cannot be nothing, for I feel my shoulders pressing up against his palms.

Later, when we have drunk half a jug of my bittersweet bog wine and the air is blurred with dusk, we move inside and stoke the fire in the stove. Sometimes with drink, Amos grows sentimental. Sometimes—tonight—he grows ornery. I would not give him the wine if I knew he was going to turn that way, but I never know. I sit on the edge of my bed, and he leans back against the wall on a bench he made himself. Earlier I found the blind rabbit huddled in a corner of the lean-to and brought her in with us, since she seems to feel the cold more than the rest.

"Their graves are all overgrown," he says. He is talking about my family.

"One whole corner of the churchyard. For a time your mother was taking care of it. Now it's a pile of crabgrass."

I say nothing.

"I suppose," he says, "that Luke could do it, but I reckon they're busy over there with the new baby and the farming. And your mother's not well these days. I know you don't want to hear about it, but she's not going to li—"

"Please," I beg him. "Don't." And I hum a tuneless song.

"Never mind your mother, then," he says. "But the

graves are something else. You should weed your family's plot. It's not right, letting a holy place go like that."

He knows I will not pluck at the base of stones that mark my family gone from me. Still he goes on. "It would only take an hour. You could even go at night."

"You weed," I say. "You do it, if it matters so much to you."

He snorts. "I don't walk through the gates of the Lord, remember? I don't walk through the door of that old church. *Lo, the days shall come upon you, that He will take you away with hooks, and your posterity with fishhooks.* That's Amos. Didn't know you were visiting with a prophet, did you? I'll go fishing to get my posterity back, but not in that churchyard—"

He laughs, low in his throat, a grunting sound like the ones my rabbit makes, and she lifts her ears. I want to tell him that if it is so hard for him to be away, he should go back to the Lord. The words of the Bible seem to move through Amos's head the way other words move through mine, and though he will not walk into the church, still it is a holy place to him. For me, those words never inched deep into my heart, although I knew they were supposed to. The Lord was always the one who saw when I did wrong, and I was not good enough to love Him more for this. Instead I kept Him out, and His words mostly reminded me of slaps. But Amos was born with a deep voice and a bigger faith than mine, a wider circle in his bitterness and hope, for though I was a wildly hopeful girl, over the years I have learned—most of the time—to keep both bitterness and hope in check.

If he weren't flushed with drink, I would tell him that I don't mind the thought of my family lying in a plot among weeds that are green in summer, hollowed into husks in fall and winter, pushing their tips through the ground in spring. Milkweed for Jeremiah, the pods pale and fluffy like his hair.

Brown-eyed Susans for Anna. For my father, wheat, though it is not a weed. Plain grass for Harriet. See how it can be woven into a basket, made into a bookmark, or used to hold your braid?

I talk to them, I'd tell him. *I don't weed at their graves but I speak to them. I may stay here, but from here I tend.*

And what about his own parents, buried a few towns over, his mother who died when he was still a boy, his father a preacher who died later, a stern and bookish man? Sometimes in his sleep Amos calls out for his mother, a boy's longing in a man's voice. Other times he tells me pieces of what he recalls of her: she sang the Bible, she was afraid of high places, she wanted a daughter and cried when she cut off Amos's baby curls. This remembering, I'd like to think, is itself a kind of tending. But is it tending if it only happens in the mind?

"I need some more wine, Aimee," Amos tells me, his voice already thick with it.

"No more," I answer. I touch my mouth to his palm, put my lips to his wrist and feel his pulse. He reaches for me, groping, the touch of a drunken man. It will be dark soon, and I want him to leave now, to stumble home while he can still see. Otherwise he will stay, and tonight I do not want him in my bed, drunk and telling me to weed my family's grave.

"All gone, hah!" he says. "You have enough wine for a wedding party under those planks, you crafty woman. What are you thinking? Do you have plans for us? Or are you drinking your life away alone out here? Hmm?"

"No more, Amos. You've had enough. Go before it gets dark. In the dark you could fall." I start to unbutton my dress and reach for my nightdress on its hook. Amos stands behind me, encircling my waist.

"I've fallen already," he says. "Oh, how you cut me to the quick, you want me gone from here."

He is right. I am tired and want to think of Plumey sleeping and children sleeping everywhere, to sleep myself. I turn and rest my head against his chest for a moment. Then I put on my nightdress, stoke the fire, and climb into bed.

"Come back tomorrow. Tomorrow come and stay the night. Tonight my bones need rest." I send one hand combing through the dark and find my rabbit, who will sleep on the end of my bed, breathing her quick, shallow breaths.

"Rest," Amos echoes, leaning over me. I kiss him and taste wine on his lips.

"Be careful walking back, all right?"

"Why do you need *rest*?" he asks, straightening up and blowing out the candles. "Don't you know that rest is for the lazy and the dead?"

"Tomorrow," I murmur. I shut my eyes, but I can hear him tugging at something, loosening my floorboard to get at another jug of wine. Then I feel a blanket being pulled up over me and the edges smoothed.

First you heard the first bell ringing in the belltower and it was time to rise. Then you heard the second bell ringing and it was time to eat. Then you heard the third bell ringing and it was time to work. Fourth bell, eat. Fifth bell, prayers. Sixth bell, sleep. First bell. I had never heard such ringing in my ears, never seen so many rooms and buildings lined up like honeycomb. First floor, carding. Second floor, spinning. Third and fourth floors, weaving. And down below, the waterworks grinding their teeth, turning the wheels which moved the straps which pulled the looms.

My first morning, after the girls had all gone off to work, Mrs. Ladd sent the other new girl, Constance, and me to look for a place in the corporation, with her oldest daughter as a guide. We went to the Boott Mill since all the girls at Mrs. Ladd's worked there. In a low brick building they called the Counting Room, a woman sat me down on a stool, kneeled down and came at my leg with what looked like a little silver knife.

"No!" I found myself yelling, my leg springing out so that I nearly kicked her. I stood up and backed toward the wall, smoothing down my skirts.

"It's for your own good, so you don't get ill," she said flatly. "All our girls get vaccinations. Now sit down and let me see your leg if you want to find work here."

I thought it must be a cure, like the herbal remedies my mother used, but my mother had never cut me open. In my mind I saw the girl who had been pierced with a shuttle. At the time, I had thought my mother was making up stories; now I was not so sure.

"I don't get ill, ever," I told the woman. "My legs are fine. I'll be just fine without—"

"Sit." She pointed to a stool. "It's to put medicine into your blood. Good. Now shut your eyes. Go on now."

The pain was brief. When I opened my eyes she was pouring liquid into my wound and covering it with a strip of cotton.

Then a red-faced man came in, looked me over, and asked was I healthy, fast, and quick of mind?

"Yes," I said quickly, and a bit too loud, wondering if he had seen me with my skirt raised up. Then I added "sir," because it seemed from his expression that perhaps I should have said it in the first place. He laughed, deep in his round belly, looked at me closely and said, "This one knows what she's about. What's your name?"

"Aimee Slater, sir."

"Are you from these parts?"

"New Hampshire, sir."

"Born there?"

I nodded.

"Farm?"

Again I bobbed my head.

"Well, all right," he said. "They sure do pick funny names out there. You have good eyesight?"

I nodded.

"Any dizzy spells, fainting?"

I shook my head.

"Are you a patient girl? Can you concentrate for more than two seconds at a time? Think on your feet?"

"Yes, sir."

"Six times twelve?"

I stared at him.

"Six times twelve equals a barrel of apples? Did they send you to school in the fine state of New Hampshire?"

"Seventy-two, sir."

"Seventy-two divided by eight?"

"Nine."

"Nine times one hundred and ten?"

I hesitated, tried to see it in my mind. "It's . . . nine hundred and ninety."

He stared at me still more closely, and I felt the air tighten the way it had when the agent had looked at me. This man was round, red and ugly. Old. He was wearing a fancy gray suit, but it was smudged on both the cuffs as if he had been working on the machines.

"One of my best girls just left to get married," he said. "Shame. We need a girl with good eyesight and a head for figures, one who can follow the plan for the beam. How'd you like to be a drawing-in girl? I believe you're tall enough."

"That'd be fine, sir," I said, not knowing what he meant, but happy that he wanted me for something.

"Fine?" he echoed, laughing.

"Ha!" said the woman who had cut my leg, though I hadn't thought she was listening. "You start out that good and soon you'll be running the place."

What I didn't know was that I was starting out at the best job, the one all the girls coveted, and that because of this, they would dislike me before I even opened my mouth. I could not know, then, that there were only twelve of us in the whole corporation with that job, and that we had the reputation for being the prettiest, quickest and most-favored girls.

"We'll start you in the dressing room," said the man, "and see if you're as fine as you say."

When I turned around, hoping Constance was still behind me and would be sent to the same place, I saw that she was gone. I stood there waiting for more instructions, my leg stinging from where they had stuck me. What had they put in my blood, these people with their needles and their laughs?

You can leave, a voice inside me said. You can walk out the door and leave.

Did I almost do it? I do not think so. I had my curiosity and pride. I had passed the first test, gotten the numbers right. I wanted to see what was next. Besides, I knew how Jeremiah would smirk if I came back to the farm the next day, and how smug my mother would look. Stay, I told myself, and I leaned against the doorway and knocked on its wood casing behind my back where they could not see. As soon as my knuckles touched wood, I settled.

"This way," the man said, and I followed him up the stairs.

A girl showed me how to do the drawing-in, her hands as quick as barn swallows darting in and out of the walls of thread that hung from a giant spool on the ceiling. This is the warp beam, she said, wound somewhere else and brought here for drawing-in; then they would take the whole frame upstairs and put it on the loom. In three hours I was to thread two thousand warp threads through the harness and the reed—one by one.

She gave me directions, showing me which part was which—things called heddles, eyes and reeds—leaning in close to me: "You'll see, it's easy, once you get a feel for it."

I still didn't understand how anything worked, or what I was making happen when I drew a thread through a tiny hole with a metal hook. The machine was full of layers and grids, wood and metal, forest greens and dulled silvers, dark oil gleaming. Iron weights swung down from each side like donkey's ears. Did it really take something this big, this full of parts, to make a piece of cloth like the fabric my mother wove at home? I concentrated: the heddles were the long metal sticks with eyelets at the top. The reeds were close together like the teeth of a lice comb. If the pattern said #1 through harness #3, you poked the hook back behind the heddle, snagged the thread, and pulled it through the correct little eye, then through the space between the teeth.

I nodded. I could do that; I was sure I could. I smiled weakly at the girl and said it looked like she knew how to do it fine.

She jerked her chin toward the overseer. "One mistake and there'll be a big run in the fabric, or else a stripe down the middle. Then they dock you. You just have to go about it nice and slow, pull the thread through gentle, but not *too* slow or they'll be after you for that.''

Threads hanging like a steady sheet of rain before my face, to be coaxed through the tiniest of holes. My task sounded as if it came out of the stories my mother used to tell me, of princesses locked up in towers and told to make golden cloaks out of piles of flax. But the place—the place was worlds apart from the still, stone rooms of those old tales. I had never seen so many machines—beams like the one I was to draw-in hanging from the ceiling on enormous wooden spools, and on the other side of the long room, huge frames with great, groaning joints and turning leather belts.

There were girls everywhere, hands flying, heads bowed so you could see how neatly they had parted their hair. The one who had shown me what to do left after ten minutes to work on her own beam. My mother was right, it was hot in there, steamy and moist, but none of the girls were nude to the waist. The air was hard to breathe, smelling, I learned later, of the sizing they used to stiffen the unwoven webs, but I hardly noticed at first. My throat, I thought, was tight with newness; my eyes stung from the strangeness of the scene.

Even my own skin looked different in this place, glowing slightly, the whole room cast in a greenish light from the hundreds of plants lined up on the windowsills and the overseer's desk. I couldn't understand why anyone would grow ordinary ivy inside, but it didn't matter; my mind wakened to the motion, my body hummed. I could even hear it, as if a factory were running inside myself—a high pitch, just a little painful in my ears. This must have been what they meant by the city. What amazed me was how, in what looked like so much muddle, everyone seemed to know just what to do. My own hands felt clumsy and stiff, the hook slippery. All the other hands in the room moved so quickly and easily, and I could not stop watching them, so many fingers threading or tending, fixing things I would not have known were broken.

Stop watching, fool, I had to tell myself. Work. I liked the name of my job—*drawing-in*—and I said it softly to myself, a bit sad that my frame was not in motion, that I was apart from the clank and clatter, my beast silent and still. I knew that upstairs, on the weaving floor, everything was moving. I could hear echoes, clankings in the ceiling, mixed in with the whirrings of belts on my floor. Somewhere in the belly of the building, water churned through a wheel.

"Draw-in," I whispered to myself. "Draw-in draw-in."

It took me five hours to thread the beam. By the time I had finished I had rows of white lines floating before my eyes, and my fingers were blistered and swollen from where they had pressed against the hook. Still, I had grown fond of the frame, so big and sturdy and *there*, letting me weave things through it as if I were braiding its mane before a fair. I wanted to talk to someone, show off my work ("See?" the square of quilt held up, the mother squinting, nodding). I turned to look for the girl who had instructed me so I could ask her if I had done all right, but I couldn't pick her out from all the other girls, so many blue, brown or gray dresses and aprons, so many bent heads. Anyway, I didn't know her name.

Then the bell rang. Everything stopped.

The belts on the ceiling stopped moving, the clankings from above us turned to silence. The whole building tensed. And then, from the stillness, noise—girls' voices, calling, crying out, clamoring. Names crisscrossing in the air. And a new kind of motion—arms retrieving cloaks and bonnets from hooks on the far brick wall, repinning hair into buns, stretching up into the air to work out cricks. Bodies moving toward the stairs swiftly, almost desperately, like hogs toward a trough of slop. I thought a thought—*somebody could get crushed in all that rush*—then realized it was my mother's.

I stood still and apart, watching as they disappeared in a surge through the door. I knew it was time for noon dinner back at the boardinghouse, but I was afraid of getting caught in that wave of people, and anyway I was not hungry, wanted to show that I could work more, grow quicker, better, my hands an asset here, so far from home. My job didn't depend on the wheels turning and the belts moving. I could start another beam, toughen the sore spots on my hands. Then I remembered Mrs. Ladd saying she wouldn't let sickly girls stay on with her and pictured my mother chiding me to keep up my health by eating well. I was the last one down and did not have to push through anyone. I followed the wave of girls.

If Eliza had been there, we would have left the mill together, gone for our dinner arm in arm, talking about what we had seen. Her eyes would brighten as she leaned over to whisper bits of gossip about the girls she had met, the bonnets they wore, the towns they came from, the stories they told. She would have known everything about everybody by now. But Eliza had disappeared without a word to me, and I did not know how far off she was, or if she would ever come back. Even the sight of Constance, the other new girl, would have made me happy, but she had been sent to some other pocket of the vast building, and anyway I was not sure I'd be able to recognize her among so many girls.

What amazed me was how they all looked the same, and I wondered if I, too, blended in like one ant in an anthill, just another Operative, which was what they called us. I was vain and used to standing out and did not like to think of it. I did not yet know I had a treasured job. I vowed I would find something new and bright to wind into my hair.

Dinner at the boardinghouse that first day was pea soup,

corned beef, turnips and parsnips, baked Indian pudding. I remember each thing, how it sat thick and heavy on my plate, each plate different from all the others, my own with a windmill in its center and a stout green girl with wooden shoes and a winged hat. I scraped my food around, pretending to eat, until I had seen the whole picture, but I could not really eat, my mind and belly stretched taut with lines of thread and rows of girls. I did find Constance back at the boardinghouse. They had put her in carding, down on the first floor.

"It's all right, I think," she said, and I saw how she gobbled her food down and even took a second helping. But just as I was thinking I should really try to eat, the bell rang outside somewhere and it was time to go, forks dropping, girls rising, everybody rushing out the door. Constance pulled on my arm, and we followed, almost at a run. From other doors, other boardinghouses, girls streamed out, blue and brown and gray. What would happen, I wondered, if the bell ever broke?

Only when we were walking back together did Constance stop for a second and ask me if I thought I was quick enough at the work.

"No," I said. I showed her my hands with their raw edges. "It took me five hours to do what they mean us to do in three."

"I don't know if I can get quick enough," she said. Her hands flew over her dark blue dress as she spoke, picking at specks of cotton lint. "All those bells make me crazy. I keep waiting for them to start up."

As I watched her trying not to cry, I remembered my brother, the way his hands always fluttered for a minute before the tears came on. I wanted to sit her down and rock her, the way I used to rock Jeremiah, the way my mother used to rock me. I put my hand on her shoulder.

"You'll get faster, they don't expect us to know everything right away," I said, and she nodded and swallowed hard.

"You better start eating, Aimee. You hardly touched anything. Here, I saved you this." From her pocket she pulled a small, round roll.

Constance, I said in my mind. It was a beautiful name, a name about staying.

"Thank you," I said and took it, though I was sure I would not eat it.

She tugged on my arm. "Come on, we need to hurry or the gate will close."

Later, hunger working at my insides because the next bell took so much longer than I expected to ring, I did eat the roll, biting off quick nibbles between threads, then shoving it back in my pocket. A girl next to me saw me eating and shook her head, pointing to the overseer, who was in the far corner leaning over a frame. I popped the rest of the roll into my mouth and swallowed.

"All gone," I mouthed to her, and she smiled wide, showing a place where a tooth was gone.

Walking back later, seven o'clock already and a chill in the air, I found myself surrounded in the street by a cluster of girls.

"New drawing-in girl, right?" one of them said.

I nodded. I wanted to talk to them, but I was so tired that my head felt empty of words.

"How do you like it?"

"Fine, I mean I'm awfully tired. I'm not so quick at it yet. I have to get faster, that's all."

"What'd they move you from?"

"Nowhere. I mean, I came myself from New Hampshire."

"You went straight to it? Right in from the country?" she said, and again I nodded.

"You have family in the corporation?" another girl asked.

"No."

"Lucky you, somebody likes you. Must be him—" She jerked her chin toward a large stone house by the river, with six glass windows on each story along the front, and a fountain in the garden. From where we stood on the sidewalk we could see a woman's bent head in a window, and the glow of an astral lamp, though it was not yet dark. I had noticed the house as I walked by that morning. It was so beautiful, the grounds so finely kept, that I had ached to look at it.

"Is it the owner's?" I asked.

"The agent's," she said, and I wondered if it were my agent, the one with green eyes, the snaky song-and-dance man. Perhaps he had known, somehow, that I was coming and had talked to the man in the counting house, gotten me a favor. But I hadn't ever spoken to the agent again after the day he had come to the house. Another agent, an old man, had signed me up in Mr. Curtis's store and had not looked twice at me.

"I don't know him," I said to the girl. "I guess I don't know anybody here. My friend Eliza was supposed to be here, but she left just before I got here. What about you?"

But she seemed already to have made up her mind about me, for as we walked along the group of girls was steered, somehow, into a tight circle away from me, and I found myself walking alone.

Now, when I look back, my aloneness of those first few weeks seems like nothing. Some girls were not friendly, but Constance was gentle and kind and Mrs. Ladd worried after me and made sure I ate. Still, there was a panic opening and shutting inside me all the time, like nothing I'd ever known. At home I had wanted, for the past year, to get away and be by myself. But it was an easy want, since I always knew that each night would find me lying near my brothers and sisters, and each morning I would sit across from my mother and eat at the table my father had cut from our trees.

At the mill, although I was surrounded by more company than I had ever seen in my life, there *was* no familiar, nothing to return to. I had never seen so many people, so much motion, and while I loved to watch it all, I did not feel part of it. I knew I should be grateful for the job I had been assigned, but I wanted to work on a loom, where thread turned to cloth before your eyes, and I did not like the way my job made the other girls act with me. In a little while, I decided, when I could thread a beam in less than three hours and show how quick I was, I would ask to be switched to the weaving room.

I joined a church; they told us to join so I did. The first Sunday, as I sat wedged between two other girls waiting for the sermon to begin, I felt how young and well-behaved I must look, my forehead smooth as a clean slate. Would my teeth begin to fall out as I sat there, until I had lost a tooth for every lie? My mother had once told me a story like that. The preacher talked about industry and perseverance, the value of thrift and truthfulness. It was a good sermon in that it left me little room for my own thoughts.

I joined an Improvement Circle, where we were supposed to read French and study History. I went for a while, but I was always so tired when I got home from work, and so many of the girls knew so much about everything that I could not keep up. I had always been quick at school, but here were girls who spoke other languages and knew the names of all the men who came to speak at the Lyceum, and all about how the mills were built and who built them.

I learned that a man had gone to England and memorized the plans for the power loom in his own head after one look at them during a factory tour. I learned that the year before, the girls had organized turn-outs protesting the length of the work day. I loved the thought of that, all those girls marching and chanting, singing songs they had made up. Perhaps I could have held a sign. I learned that the mill was a place of secrets, with a Print Works no one could enter because the inventions might be stolen away. I began to stare at the closed doors along the staircase in the mill, wanting to get inside to where small, secret prints were hatching like insects on the cloth.

Every time I got inside one place, I found a new place to want. My name should have meant Want, but in Improvement Circle, I learned how in French it meant Loved.

Once a week the stagecoach brought a letter from my mother:

> *My dear Daughter, The first of October Father hurt his foot was not abel to work for two weeks. Stil he has a very lame side but is abel to be up most of the time. Luke has grown a toothe Annie Sandborn is to be married to John Bell he has bought half a lot of land and built her a house four good rooms on the ground & paid for it. Old Mr Sibley is Dead did you hear. Life to you seems long & old age so far off as neither to be dreded nor provided for yet a few years will place you far along lifes road as your grandparents now are & they can easily see to the naturel end of their journey without glasses. Try to live at all times & in all things so that in after years you may not have remorse. Spend your time wiseley now and you need not dread wrincles white hair or old age.*
>
> > *Your loving mother*

And the next week:

My Aimee I went with your sister Harriet to a Laydies Public meeting last night. They had a very good one and very good Dialog. They had an old fashiond quilting party they were fiting out a girl to be married. It was Mary C. Clements. She acted her part very well they all did When the time came for her to be married she was all dressed. The brides maids wer there, everything was redy when they found out the gentleman she was to marry had married another. And so it came out that Thare is Many a Slip Between the Cup and the Lip. Be a good girl. Try to do right everything you do. Take care of your health, save your ernings. Write once a week when convenent but be sure to write once a fortnight unless prevented by Illness Your mother who Loves You

I wanted these letters from my mother because, as I read them, I could feel her hand moving over the page as over my brow, the paper marked, sometimes, by a grease spot so that I could tell she had been writing at the kitchen table, or by a small rip that must have been where Luke had grabbed at the page. I wanted the news she sent, though it was never enough, and almost always concerned people other than my family. I wanted the way my name was written on the outside in a firmer hand than the rest of the letter, loved to picture how the paper had traveled from her to me, a bridge. Each week I waited for it to come, with its dark red seal like a drop of family blood.

At the same time, I did not want the letters. I did not like to see how my mother made spelling mistakes, for all her big talk. I could not match her smooth, clear speaking voice with the jagged roughness of these words. In the new world of the city, I found myself growing more and more ashamed of her, so that I would hide the letters away, not because I was afraid someone would see what they said, but because I feared the smart girls in the Improvement Circle would shun me when they learned my mother could not spell. Then I hated myself for that, knowing that their mothers probably could not spell either, and it was not a good reason for shame.

More than that, I did not want the letters because they were full of warnings. Everything she wrote I read in ten different ways: she knew, she did not know, she halfway knew; she knew in her heart but not in her head, in her head but not her heart. He had told her. No, not Jeremiah, who sat on his secrets like a brooding hen. She never gave me news of him, and his absence wedged the words apart and made me search for my brother in between. In her letters, my mother warned me about slipping; she told me to live well now so I would not have remorse later. She could not spell perfectly, but she was not a stupid woman.

There's many a slip between the cup and the lip.

I wrote her back careful, neat letters about Improvement Circle even after I stopped going, using my bandbox as a desk because our room had no table and I did not want to write downstairs where everyone could see me. I did not tell her that I had bought a new Scotch gingham with my first week's pay, or how I could feel men's eyes on me when I walked along the street. She would tell me to bow my head, when instead I was holding it high. I told her I was a drawing-in girl, but I did not tell her it was the best job. My mother would not want me to be singled out that way so early on. Nor did I tell her that, best job or not, my hands were covered with calluses like warts, and my throat felt choked with lint.

I sent my love, in a neat row of words according to age, to my father, my mother, Harriet, John, Jeremiah, Thomas and Luke. When I wrote Jeremiah's name I wondered if he would even read the letter. Sometimes Harriet wrote a few words on the end of my mother's notes. My father did not write to me, nor did Jeremiah, and for months and months, I heard no news of him.

One night I dreamed of Jeremiah and myself grown old together, past the age of touching, past everything but a gentle hollowing out. In my dream we lived together in the farmhouse, and we were more like ghosts than people; a hand could pass right through us, a gust of wind carry us away. With skin like that, it was impossible to touch or be touched. All day we would sit together shucking corn or stringing beans, tossing peas into a tin pot and listening to them clink. There was no barn outside the house, no garden, though we had plenty of food. That was a good dream, where my brother and I were friends.

Other times I dreamed of what had happened in the barn, and sometimes I was my mother watching, and sometimes I was myself watching myself, and often I was simply something above or outside which could see everything—the girl with her legs undone. Then I would wake wondering if the Lord were showing me what He had seen.

A phrenologist came to town and Constance asked me to go. At first I did not know what she meant, and even when I found out what he was, a reader of heads, the word *phrenologist* still scared me. I knew that if he read my skull he would tell me I was bad. I told myself that in not wanting to go, I was trying to obey my mother and stay on the narrow path. Really I was scared of what I'd find out. But then Constance said fine, she'd go with some other girls, and I saw that I might lose her if I wasn't careful.

"All right, I'll go with you," I told her, "but I'll only watch."

We went on a Thursday night after work, tightening our shawls around us in the cold air, waiting in a long line of girls which snaked around the side of the building and up some narrow stairs. It appeared he was a famous man, this phrenologist, come all the way from England. Stories passed down the line: he could read the future, past and present; he carried the skull of a baby in his bag and wore a necklace of human teeth beneath his collar; he had touched the head of the Queen of England, and his own head was covered with scars where other doctors had cut windows to peer at his remarkable brain.

It took hours for us to get to the top of the stairs and inside the small, dark room. My arms were exhausted from working all day, my legs stiff and tired. Still, we waited, barely moving forward, step by tiny step. Constance and I whispered to each other while we stood there.

"What if he finds out we're dunces from the bumps on our heads?" she asked. She let her mouth hang slack and gave me a vacant stare.

I giggled and lifted my chin high. "Or queens."

"I think your head is noble." She put her hand lightly on my forehead as if she were checking for a fever, then took it back.

I put my hand on the back of her neck where it met her head.

"Ow, cold," she said.

I made my voice deep. "Your head shows you'll marry a mill owner, little miss."

"Ha!"

"No, it does. Can I be your maid? Can I have your old shoes?"

"Of course. And some diamonds."

We moved up a few steps. "What do you think he'll tell?" asked Constance.

I shrugged. "He'll tell you you're sweet, kind, good and smart. I'm not doing it."

"But why? After waiting in line for so long?"

"It's bad luck to be told the future by a stranger."

And worse for him to uncover pieces of the past.

"He won't tell you what's going to happen. He'll just read your character."

"It's a waste of money."

"Don't be scared," said Constance, and I wondered how far inside me she could see. Standing close to her, smelling her clean, blond hair, I thought how lucky I was to have made a new friend. I reached over and took her hand.

"We're almost there," she said.

When we got to the room we started to walk in together, but a woman at the door said we had to go one at a time.

"You go first," I said to Constance, forgetting that I had said I wasn't going to go at all.

"No, you," she whispered.

"One of you go, there's a crowd if you didn't notice," said the woman, her voice raspy and sour, and she took my arm and steered me inside.

In the middle of the room was a big plaster skull divided into parts, each with a number written on it, and a chart sitting underneath. A pointer lay next to it like a spear. All around, propped on shelves and leaning against walls, were terrible pictures that looked like ink drawings of the leavings in a slaughteryard: *The Base of the Brain, The Upper Surface of the Brain, The Nervous System*—a drawing of a headless man with pine needles springing from his bones.

"Sit," said the Doctor, and the woman leaned in from the doorway and pulled me out a chair. Then she reached for the door and closed it, standing like a guard in the shadows. Outside I could hear the jagged chatter of girls.

The Doctor wore a somber black city suit with a gold watch chain peeking out, but his hands were huge and red like a farmer's, and all I could think, watching him peer at his chart and shuffle a piece of paper around, was that he was about to touch me. My mother was the only person who had ever really covered my skull with her hands, combing my hair, parting it to look for ticks after I had been lying in the fields, stroking it when I was feverish or had a headache. Never, ever, had my head been touched all over by a man, except by my brother when he braided my hair. The thought made my throat close up.

Then he came and stood behind my chair.

"Oh, no thank you, sir," I said, swiveling around. "I just came to see."

"Oh?" he said. "I'm afraid my bottled brain collection doesn't travel well. This is all there is to see—a few dusty pictures. Good day, then, miss."

"I came—I mean, really I came to be with my friend."

But already he had lowered his wide palms onto my head, as I knew he would—as I was, in fact, willing him to do. His hands felt wide and cupping, the hands of my father, if my father had been the sort to cup my head. This was nothing like my brother, these hands too big, too sure. He pressed on my neck. He put two fingers on each of my temples, stood still for a moment with his palm pressed up against my forehead.

He was a man who had probably touched hundreds, thousands of heads. I *was* my head as I sat there, as if my body below had disappeared in all its tiredness and aches, all its misplaced longings. I liked that, wanted to fall into the cups of those hands for a long while, to rest there, simply a head. He did not seem to think I was pretty or feel anything at all about me, and for this I was immensely grateful. He touched me as if I were a piece of marble he was examining for flaws before deciding whether to carve it into a headstone. When he had run his fingers over every part of my head, he came around in front of me and peered into my face.

"Miss, you have a nervous temperament," he told me. "I could see it in your complexion, and here—" He touched above my temple with an outstretched finger. "Is this not so?"

"I don't know," I said. I had an urge to tell him that anyone could have seen my nervous temperament in the way I hesitated while coming into the room, but I did not want to stop him from telling me more.

He cleared his throat. "If your head were smooth and evenly developed, you would be of a uniform, even character, but like most people with your temperament, you have a large development of the organs in the upper and lateral portions of the head. This means you will feel strongly the reverses of feeling and fortune. Do you like to read?"

"Yes, sir."

"I thought so. You also, I would venture, like to cook. Your domestic propensities, here"—he touched the base of my neck—"are strongly developed, as is your organ of inhabitiveness. You are a girl who likes her hearth."

I did not like to cook, and I preferred being outdoors to sitting by the fire. He was probably another charlatan, the kind my mother warned me about. But still I wondered if he had felt anything else, anything truly bad on my head. If he could find a bump to stand for my sins, I might give up their burden. It could not be my fault to have been born with a certain kind of head. Carefully, I formulated the words.

"Is there anything really, I don't know . . . *bad*, sir, that you see?"

He peered over me. "Bad? How do you mean?"

"I don't know—anything I should be careful of . . ."

Again his hands moved over my head and stopped around my ears.

"Your—yes, your selfish propensities are a bit . . . over-developed," he said, but his tone was questioning. This time he was right; I was a selfish girl, could often see only myself, but that did not interest me just then. I could not ask him about touching; it was not a word a girl was supposed to say. I could not ask him how much a mother could see.

He coughed and said, "Very well, good day, miss. Pay Mrs. O'Connor at the door."

I wanted to stay there in a room where I was all head. "But there are so many numbers on the skull, Doctor," I said. "Couldn't you tell me just a little more?"

"Humph," he said. "Selfish propensities, indeed. You're not the only little factory girl who wants a turn."

Though I told myself I did not believe the phrenologist, I lay in bed at night for a week after my visit with my hands traveling over my own head, trying to see what I could find. I was looking for something dramatic—a bump the size of a robin's egg, or a strange, protruding ridge. Or to be able, some-how, through feeling, to see inside. I remembered the drawing of the Upper Surface of the Brain—the twisting channels, plump and round as worms, the gash down the center like a cut.

Outside, my head was smooth, hard and unyielding, but I knew how to make it pretty. During the day I wove my braid with an indigo ribbon before I pinned it up. I could thread a beam in a little over three hours by now. I knew girls to say hello to, the overseer seemed to like me, and Constance was becoming a good friend. Each day I walked home adding up how much money I had made: fifty-two cents a day before I paid for board and lodging. It was hard to save much after all the expenses, but still I loved the thought of even the smallest bits of money piling up in the bank—the first thing I had ever owned.

What would I do with my savings? I did not know. Part of me wanted to save enough to buy a ticket on a ship and see the world. Red pomegranates, I would see, and green parrots. But then I pictured the wide, blank ocean, and myself, small as a matchstick, shivering on the deck. My parents had told me to save for a dowry. I would need sheets—starched, bleached and folded small—and some iron pans for cooking, and some dishes, perhaps the ones with bluebirds over a bridge. That would be all right, saving for a dowry, as soon as I met the perfect husband to save for. In my mind they stood side by side, the husband and the ship, each one as dim as the future, moving toward me across the sea.

On December 3, 1844, I learned in a letter from my mother that my brother Jeremiah was dead. She sent a band of black crepe for me to wind around my arm; she sealed the letter in black wax. She enclosed a memorial picture—an engraving of a tall gravestone with my brother's name written on it in her hand, and a lady, gentleman and little girl praying nearby, clutching calla lilies. On the back she wrote: *Consumption, Fourteen Years and Three Months, Peace and Heaven, Blessed be Thy Name.*

"The fare is more than we can do and Winter is coming on," she wrote in the letter, though she must have known I could have paid the fare myself. She told me not to come home.

10

Before I received the letter from my mother, my insides were a dark, thick mass of brambles. When I read that Jeremiah had died and that I was not to come home for the funeral, something died inside me too. What was left was a hole so vast I could not tell where it began or ended. Except sometimes—wedged between two girls at night, or jammed, during the day, between a stool and a machine. Then, as the world pressed up, I would feel the edges of the hole flapping around inside me like loose sheets in the wind, or hanging stiff and bloody like pieces of hide hung out to dry.

When that happened, I froze and concentrated on the flapping—on that bit of movement or the stiff, stale edge that might show me the borders of the hole and let me climb out, or at least hold on for a moment and catch my breath. Most of the time, the minute I tried to picture my brother, to remember the texture of his hair or see him sitting on the stone wall at dawn, I would get a picture for a second, and then the edges would fall away and I would be left with nothing but a hole without color or edge.

Then I would reach for my mother: *Catch me, let me rest.* But she was not there, and sometimes I felt as if she had died too. I was sure that the reason she had told me not to come home was that the whole thing was my fault. I could see, looking back, a long chain leading to my brother's death. The touching, yes, but that was only one thing, for there was also the way I had lied to my mother, pretending nothing had happened; the times I had thought Jeremiah was fake-coughing; the slap in the face; the way I stood in the wind outside the toolshed and did not have the courage to go in.

Lord help me, I thought, and I prayed hard on Sunday and every other day. I could not make up my own prayers, could not find any words except for Sorry, and so I chanted prayers from my earliest childhood, ones I had said before I knew what the words meant. *Jesus beacon of the night bathe me in Thy holy light Lord God with Thy radiant love spirit me to worlds above.* But God would not help me, for He had lived with me in my thoughts.

I stopped eating much, and most of the time I felt nothing, but sometimes a burning would tear through my stomach. I had already swallowed the herbs my mother sent with me, early on when I needed a taste of home. Now I could not write her to send me a special mixture of her stomach herbs, for I believed I was meant to feel such pain, and she would know that to help me was wrong. Instead I bought a small amber bottle of Ayer's Sarsaparilla. It tasted like tree sap, woody and bitter, but also like city medicine, with an edge like metal shavings. At first I hoped it would give me inner resources like Eliza's, but it only seemed to make me tired, and eventually I decided that was all right, too. Each evening when I got back to the boardinghouse, I took twice as much as the label recommended. At night I slept gratefully, and for a gentle moment each morning when I woke, I did not remember who I was.

After I got that letter from my mother, I got switched to the weaving room by telling the overseer that the extra steam piped into the dressing room was making me ill. I was pale, thin and tired, so he believed me. Really I wanted the noise and angry clatter of the power looms. I was the perfect worker: swift, accurate, obsessed. Within a week I was tending two looms.

In spare moments when the shuttles were full and no threads were broken or tangled, the other girls went to the windowsills to tend their plants. In the moist heat the ivy spread its trails up along the windowpanes, and the geraniums flared into bloom. The girls would have contests: whose flower was the biggest, whose ivy would reach the upper window first.

At first I had loved those plants—how they tinted the rooms with a still, green light, so that it seemed as if our crashing-loud machines had been placed in the middle of a forest glade. Now the vines began to look caught. They could climb and climb, but they would never get to where the air was fresh. If the plants were placed too close together, they choked each other, winding their way into tight snarls until the leaves turned yellow at the edges and hung limp. Some plants went on for months this way, half-living. When an ivy finally died, the overseer whisked it off the way he sent sick girls home; everything had to look healthy in case someone came through on a tour.

Sometimes I hoped I would get sent home. "White lung," they called the disease that brought girls back to the farm. I wanted my lungs to be pure white and wrapped. Or perhaps I would grow ill changing the bobbin. We all saved time by using our mouths to suck the tail end of the thread through the hole in the shuttle, rather than using our fingers or a hook. Everyone called this the Kiss of Death because the shuttle was dirty with other girls' mouths and lint, but we did it anyway because it was fast. Sometimes, after my brother died, I breathed in for an extra second, drinking in the dirty oil of the wood. At home, I thought, my mother would bathe me, lie me down in the bed where I was born, nurse me back to health with bitter herbs and the strength of her hands.

I grew pale, but I was not feverish. Faster, I worked. Better. The praise from the overseer felt like the only words I could hear: Fine, good, speedy, good, fine. My body would not turn sick on me. Crazy girl, I thought, for I remembered how I had begged my parents to send me to the mills, and now all I could think about was how to leave, and yet still I worked harder every day.

Do not come home, she had written. Because of money, because of winter, but I became sure that Jeremiah had asked, in his last moments, that I not be there. And if he had asked, then I was sure that my mother, eyes in the back of her head, knew how I had sinned and lied, and then used my sinning as an excuse to go away.

Before, in the drawing-in room, I had listened to the voices of the other girls, tried to sort out their words from the whirring of the fans. Sometimes I had joined in. In the weaving room, you could open your mouth and not hear your own words come out. It sounded like a waterfall in there, rushing, constant, with a steady heartbeat pulsing— thum-*thump*, thum-*thump*—so that I imagined myself crashing over Niagara Falls with my heart sounding loud in my ears. My bones would slam down on the rocks the way the flying shuttle slammed against the metal of the frame.

Over and over, my face set calm and rigid, my hands capable, I pushed my mind over this edge.

Sometimes one of the leather belts that ran the looms burst into flames from the friction, or the waterwheel got stuck, and then they would shut the whole place down. It took a while for the quiet to enter my ears, but then an enormous, tense silence would come, everything gone still. It was not like the bell ringing, gonging out our freedom. At a breakdown, everyone had to stay put.

We girls always stood with our hands at our sides, close in to the looms, then, because a breakdown meant a whole line of overseers and loom-fixers coming through, pressing past us, breathing close to us, sometimes; other times scolding us, as if the fact that a stick had floated down the canal and gotten caught in the waterwheel were our fault. Still, most girls loved a breakdown, saw it as a chance to catch their breath or send sidelong glances to the loom-fixer. If the trouble went on long enough, sometimes we were sent outside to walk by the canals or huddle together in the cold until the bell rang again, calling us back in.

In the beginning, when it was all new to me, I had loved a breakdown, too, if only to get that sound out of my ears. I knew the men looked at me. When visitors came through to see how the mill was run, often the overseer would stop at my beam or loom. I knew I was a good worker, and so perhaps they were watching the way I changed the bobbin, or tied my weaver's knots in the broken warp, or set the caught shuttle free. But I also knew the men didn't look much at the machines; I could feel their eyes on my neck and chest and face. I didn't know how to think about that. Part of me was flattered, part of me shy. Part of me was hot, tired and breathless and wanted to spring forward like a wild colt and kick those men who strolled in and out of the mill with their undented top hats and shiny shoes, their hands clasped behind their backs. Still, it was a break in the routine.

After Jeremiah died, I wanted nothing so much as for the rhythm to go on, steady as a trance or lullaby. They moved me from two looms to four, then five when the girl beside me grew ill and was sent back to Maine. They used my bolts as examples: No runs here, no snags, no ladders. Aimee will make a nice little bundle the way she works so smooth. The more the overseer praised me, the less the other girls on my floor would speak to me. Already they disliked me because I had started with drawing-in, and because I'd gotten so quiet, so bent over my work, when they were always pressed to the windows whenever they had a free moment.

But outside the window was just another big, brick mill. I wanted to step barefoot across the rocks in the creek at home and find my brother standing on the other side. My feet had grown pale over the months, and swollen from standing in front of the looms. I had to spend four dollars on a pair of new black shoes, a size bigger than my old ones, and still I had to leave the laces loose. The spots on my feet that had been rough and thick peeled off as winter came. Soon, I thought, I will have no skin left from the days when I lived with my family. Soon I will be a whole new person.

I knew this should have made me feel relieved: a new person—I might come up with a new name, a new family. I

knew I should be happy because I was losing my skin like
the witch in my mother's story. I had wanted that. Perhaps
I would be free to fly into the night. But even as I peeled
flakes of skin from my heel, I missed what I tore away. To
see it flaking made me feel as if I, too, were dying. Also I
knew how raw the witch had been without her skin, and
how she had burned and ached when she tried to get back
into it after her husband filled it with pepper and coarse
salt.

Sometimes the answers seemed simple: She should
never have gone back home, that witch. She should have left
her skin where it was and lived a life without edges, mixing
with air. Only I also knew how empty air could be, apart
from everything. Her cabin was home to her. She couldn't
get away from that.

Tell me a different story, I pleaded to my mother, who
was lying miles and miles away, grieving for her son. *Give
me a different ending.* I wanted to see the witch slide into her
skin with ease each dawn, and still get to leave it in a pile
every night.

One night I dreamed of the animals on the farm—
milking the cows, stretching and then letting up on each
udder; calming the bay mare by taking her long face between my hands and blowing air into her nostrils until I
could taste her hot, green breath. All those living things I
used to touch. I dreamed of feathers and milk, and then the
dream split down the middle like the phrenologist's picture
of a brain, and I saw raw things—the stillborn bloody calf,
the bright burn on Eliza's arm when she touched the blacksmith's iron, the slaughter corner of the barn where my father stuffed the chickens into tin cones and took their heads.
I dreamed of the blood from my body that I stopped each

month with rags, only in my dream it would not stop, but filled the canals and waterworks and ran the power looms.

I was emptied out, but I could not leave myself.

My mother stopped writing me real letters after that, except tiny notes here and there, clipped bits of news written in a tense hand, always ending with Be a Good Girl. When I look back now, I see that she was probably beaten down with grief, bone-tired from how she had brought seven children into the world, only to have two taken away. I probably seemed like another one partly gone from her. Now I can see that the line in my head leading from my own bad thoughts to my brother's death was itself a false and selfish one: I could not see how small I was in the world. Then, I thought my mother filled her days with angry thoughts of me. Now I think that in those months following my brother's death, she began to give up and grow old.

Why did she tell me not to come to the funeral? I am still not sure, but perhaps it was as simple as her words: *The fare is more than we can do and Winter is coming on.*

A few weeks after Jeremiah died, Constance met me after work with a small, wrapped packet in her hand. I had hardly spoken to her since I had found out, since I could not begin to explain the strange, stepless place I found myself. I had told her my brother had died, then said no more. At night when she was sleeping I had pressed my palm against her back or touched a clump of her hair, and in this way she had unknowingly comforted me, but by day I had moved far into myself.

"Aimee, don't walk so fast, I need to give you something," she said as we passed out of the gates.

No, I thought. A present wrapped in calico could only mean good-bye.

"I made you this," she said, "so you'll remember me."
She thrust out the packet. "I've decided to go back home."

"Constance, it'll get better, you'll see," I said, trying to
keep the panic from my voice.

"I'm tired, I miss my family. I want to go." She cupped
the packet between her hands and looked at me, a simple,
childlike missing in her eyes, and I felt all old and twisted
up. Something must have shown on my face, for she put her
hand on my sleeve.

"Why don't you go back, too? It'll be easier there, you
can be near the others, even if your brother's gone."

"It'll get better here," I repeated. "No one likes it at
first. It just takes a little while to get used to it. Try for a few
more months, you'll see."

She sighed. "I don't know. I wanted to make money
for them, so my brother could go to college, but I'm not
quick on the machines, I get too nervous, and I'm all tired
out. I think they'll be glad to have me back, it was me that
thought of going in the first place. I can do piecework at
home, maybe, like my mother. I'm going home for Christmas anyway, so I'll just stay."

"I'm sorry," I burst out. "I know I haven't been talking
to you much—"

"No," said Constance, "it's not you. Not at all."

"We can get put in the same room at the mill. I'm sure
we can."

"Here." She tried to hand me the present, but I shook
my head. Standing there, I felt my body start to shake.

"Oh don't, Aimee," said Constance.

I turned from her, cut down to a canal path and started
half-running along it.

"Wait!" she called, running after me, but I could not
stop—my legs pounding the dirt, my eyes tearing, the dusty

path before me blurred. She must have followed me for a mile, always a few steps behind. Finally, by the locks, I found I could hardly breathe, and I lowered myself to the ground, my back against the gatehouse wall. My breath came short and fast now, but I was no longer crying. I looked up at Constance through the dusk and tried to smile.

"Here," she said. "Please take it."

She held out the packet again, and I opened it to find a brooch pin woven with a lock of her hair, blond like my brother's, with her name and mine scratched into the brass on the back.

"I'll keep it always," I said. "Help me put it on?"

She kneeled and pinned it to my cloak, then stood back up. "Probably I'll get there and be bored and come back, and you can save a place for me."

I nodded.

"But I think maybe you should go home, too. You're too thin, you know, and awful pale."

"I'm fine."

She looked down at me as I sat there on the ground. "*Why* do you want to stay?"

"Things will get better here. It's not so bad. I'm sorry I've been so—"

"It's not you, I'm not cut out for it. I don't know why I came in the first place, for the money, I guess."

"You'll be happier back home," I said, knowing, despite myself, that it was true.

"Before I go, will you give me a lock of your hair?"

I nodded. Stay, I wanted to beg her, but I knew I could not.

"Come on," she said. "If you get any more dusty, Mrs. Ladd won't let you through the door."

She put out her hand and pulled me up. When I felt

her warm hand closing around mine, it all began again, my sobs rattling me. Constance stood with her hand on my shoulder until my breath smoothed out.

"All right?" she said.

I shrugged, then nodded.

"He's with his maker," she said. "You know that."

"I didn't even get to—" My throat shut hard around my words.

"You should go back where you belong, where they'll look after you."

I shook my head.

"Come on," said Constance, and I took her hand and let her lead me back.

Later, at the boardinghouse, I cut a long, fat curl from my head and braided it around one of the metal hooks we used in the factory. I kissed it for luck and knocked it against wood for more luck. Then I wrapped it in a piece of lace and tucked it under Constance's pillow. I wished for a world where something, anything, stayed constant.

A week later she was gone.

I am sitting outside with Plumey when three boys come. I hear them before I see them, sending out yells that echo off the hills. When they appear on the other side of the pond, I think perhaps they are about to go hunting. They look bigger than the boys who sometimes come. Two hounds snap at their heels.

Go away, I think. Off my land.

Each time they come and let off shots in the distance, my rabbits grow skittish. And I do not want Plumey to hear the way the boys sometimes shout things at me: *There was a woman and what do you think?*

She straightens up and peers at them.

"It's all right," I tell her. "It's only boys from town. They won't hurt us."

I'm not sure I really mean this. My garden has been trampled in the past by boys like these, my chickens stolen. But there is always my rifle hanging above the door, which I might use to scare them off, and anyway there is no use worrying her.

"Here," I say.

I am trying to teach her how to carve. I hand her a piece of wood that I have half-made into a cow. With its nose too sharp and its back too curved, it looks more like a sick dog.

"You do the rest," I tell her, but she is staring across the pond, and though her hand closes around the carving, she does not seem to see it.

I wonder, do these boys remind her of her brothers? I try to picture Plumey skipping down the road with her brothers and sisters, or going to sleep next to them at night. I am so used to seeing her alone that it is hard to see. Or perhaps she knows these boys from town. When I look up again I see that they have moved closer to us, near the big tree where I hang my stockings out.

I watch as they kneel by the water; one of them leans over a thick glass cider bottle while another stirs up the mud with a stick. The third boy bends over, something in his hand.

Oh! I am a child again, all expectation, my throat tight with the thought of it.

The swamp gas, when they light it inside the bottle, explodes in a purple blueness, a dense cloud of flame. I can only think how beautiful it is, how briefly blue and shimmering in the middle of the gray, autumn day. I can only think of all the colors hidden in the thick mud layers of my bog.

I do not think of Plumey, but then she is gone from my side, flinging down the carving. She runs toward my garden, a pale blur, crouches down among my pole beans as if she might hide there. From her mouth comes a terrible whimpering noise.

"Plumey!" I call out to her, but she does not seem to hear, her own noises louder now—sharp, rhythmic cries as if someone were poking her with a stick. The pole beans are black with frost, limp on their poles; the poles themselves are weathered and flimsy, poked at crazy angles in the dirt. Plumey holds onto the thin pole as if it could save her life and presses her face against it. I cannot quite tell from where I am sitting, but she might even be filling her mouth with leaves.

Oh no, I think, oh no, oh no.

Perhaps she really is crazy, a girl possessed. I know I must get up and go to her, pull her away from the garden and lead her away from their eyes. But the noise she is making keeps me hunched over myself, it is so raw.

Stop, little one, I think to her, stop stop stop, but still I do not move.

"Crazy girl," calls the boy who lit the bottle, and he looks at his friends and laughs in a short bark. "You courting a pile of beans? Wish it was me, ha!"

Something in his voice must reach her, for Plumey stops her cries, straightens up and looks around—for me? It is not until her eyes come to rest on me, perhaps with a kind of hope, that I manage to speak.

"You—you leave her be," I call to the boys, who turn to me as if they have not seen me sitting there all along.

"She's the one making all the noise," says one of the boys. Then he makes chicken sounds under his breath. The other two sputter with laughter.

"She's only a child," I say. "You scared her. Now go on home."

The middle boy sneers at me, showing his pink gums. "You're all crazy out here, just like they say. You saw that girl stuffing her mouth with leaves. She's the one we should put a match to. Pouff!"

He blows into the air, then turns to go.

After they leave, Plumey comes back to me and sits on the ground by my feet. A long time passes. The air grows colder, but we do not move; it is as if we are waiting for a guest who never comes. Finally, when it is almost dark and both of us are shivering, she gets up and trudges home.

The next afternoon she is back, and the next. Each afternoon we sit patiently.

The minute she begins to talk, I think *but of course.*

It has been five days since the boys played with the bog gas; the air is gray again, the bog water smooth and black. For hours we've been sitting outside in silence, wrapped in tattered shawls. Her words seem to be tugged from deep inside her stomach, taut and reluctant.

"They. Wanted—" she says. She does not look at me, but stares out at the distance, her knees pulled tight against her chest.

"What, Plumey? What did you say?"

I am half-expecting one of her chants about feather renovators or Doctor Wilson's Pain Curing Remedies.

"To burn us. Down. They wanted . . ." Her words are clear as spring water.

"Plumey," I say. I am so proud of her for speaking real words that I must remind myself to listen to what she says. I touch her hand, but she does not seem to notice.

"To burn—burn us. To—"

"Who?" I ask. "Those boys last week?"

She nods.

"No," I tell her. "They were playing with the bubbles in the bog, the gas it makes—you've never seen that before?—but they didn't want to hurt us."

I do not tell her that Jeremiah, Harriet and I once played the same game, stirring the mud on the bottom of the bog until the bubbles rose; capturing them in a bottle; lighting them into the briefest, deepest gasp of blue. Jeremiah, his hand shielding his eyes, his breath sucked in at the colors. Harriet worried someone would see. Myself, the one who lit the match.

"It's all right," I tell her. "You're all right."

She lets out a long groan that is not the sound of a child, but of a woman who has seen too much.

"Oh goose," I say. "What? Tell me? You can tell me."

And then Plumey begins to talk, clasping her knees, her eyes fixed, the whole time, on the place where the boys played with the bottle. She does not begin with small talk, or nonsense, or ways of getting there. She begins. She tells me how one brother was sleeping on one side, the other brother on the other. She had eaten twelve apples that day, her brothers had dared her, that morning she had eaten on and on.

"I had—" she says. "I had to go—" She makes a vomiting gesture with her mouth. "In the grass. The apples." She rubs her belly as if they were still souring inside her.

When she looked up, she must have thought a ghost was trailing from one corner of the house, thin wispiness rising into air. She must have thought it was her dead grandfather come back. She watched, moving backward into the bushes. Then the corner of the ghost turned orange, and as Plumey stood among the twigs, the whole place swelled with light.

Hours might have passed, or minutes. As the fire moved up and the roof caved in, she sank onto her knees and watched.

"A little house," she said, and she made a box with her hands as if to show me just how small.

Inside was her family. Plumey ran. Through thickets and brush, through daylight, then darkness. A long time, she spent in the woods. Days and nights and days; she is not sure how many. She does not tell me what she did there, a girl of five or six, what she thought about or ate, how she knew the way back home. Her words as she tells me what happened are not new words, not groping; they are careful and rehearsed. She has been talking to herself about this for a long time. She does not list the people she lost inside that house.

"All gone," she says and blows into the air.

She has been looking over at the bog, at the place where the flame was, but now she turns to look at me, her face puzzled.

"What, Plumey?"

She lets out a deep sigh, as if she is too tired to go on. Then she begins again. "Those boys—"

"They're gone now."

She shrugs. "Why?"

"They went back to where they live, they don't come out here often."

"Why?" she says again, shaking her head in frustration.

I try to help her. "Why what? Why don't they come here often? Why did they do that, with the bottle? Is that it?"

She nods.

"It's just a game. Children play that game sometimes, that's all. Nobody wants to hurt you. Just leave them alone and they'll leave you be."

I want to comfort her, but also warn her: nobody wants to hurt you, but beware.

"Why did I eat all those apples?"

"Somebody was watching over you."

She shakes her head, almost angrily, and I see how stupid it is of me to suggest that she might find providence in such a loss. She turns away and curls back up inside herself, lying in the grass at my feet.

"Shhh," I say and bend to stroke her back. I do not know what to do with such sadness in a girl not even grown yet. Her questions are like nuggets, hard and difficult; I can see why she has saved them for so long. After a few minutes she sleeps, and then her fists open and her eyelids grow smooth, a child's.

I see her covered with dirt, coming back into the town, her eyes revealing nothing, her knees locked straight as she stood in a metal tub while someone washed away her layers, leaving her with just her unprotected skin.

I cover her with a blanket, then sit and keep watch over her. It is almost dusk when she begins to stir, and she opens her eyes to see me sitting nearby.

"You slept," I tell her. She nods, and I wonder if she has moved back into silence.

"They'll be worrying about you, little one. You should go."

She sits up, clears the sleep from her eyes and yawns.

"Did they— Will they come back?" she asks.

"No," I say, then realize I am making false promises. "I don't think so. If they do I'll make them leave, I have my rifle. But they weren't going to hurt you."

She nods, and I think her face looks looser now, easier.

"I did not like those boys," she says, and she smiles slightly, as if she realizes how funny it sounds.

"I know."

She lies back down, curls inside the blanket.

"Plumey?"

She looks up at me.

"Why were you gobbling up the leaves of my pole beans?"

Again she smiles, a shy, lopsided grin.

"Did they taste good? Should I make a soup?"

She shakes her head, then burrows it in her arms, and I realize I have gone too far.

"It's getting dark. You'd better get up and go home," I tell her. "They'll worry if you're gone too long."

But she does not seem to hear me, already covered by sleep, which must bring her back to the places she'd like to leave, or forward, to places she'd like to go. I sing to her as she sleeps: *"Bye-a-baby bunting, Papa's gone a hunting, to catch a little rabbit skin, to wrap his baby bunting in . . ."*

I will let her rest for a few more minutes. Then, though I'd like nothing more than to keep her as my own, I will send her home.

12

Something had to happen. This is what I tell myself, looking back—that I could not have gone on the way I was, that I would have fallen through myself until I hit a bottom. Then, like my brother, I would have died, but where he still had, I thought, a chance of making it to heaven, I might have gone the other way, and I began to picture hell not as a fiery place where the skin can feel, but as Nothing multiplied. I did not die, of course. Christmas came and went; New Year's, too. I heard nothing from my family to mark the holidays, but I hardly noticed, lost (as they must have been) in my own grief-filled, clockless time. Then one morning—it must have been early January—the shuttle in one of my looms stopped in midflight, and a man came to fix it, the youngest mechanician, the one with laughing eyes and a careful, serious mouth.

I watched as he set down two whale oil lanterns near the base, leaned and peered. I watched as he reached his hand into the workings of my loom, the parts I did not know about. I saw him pull out a metal disc, bent and blackened, and replace it with a new, shiny one that he pulled from a battered wooden box at his feet. As he stared hard at the machine, I stared hard at him. In his forearms I could see the soft snakings of blue veins, like the arms of my father's friend Samuel Plain. He leaned, and a lock of hair fell over his forehead. He pushed it back, and I watched how his fingers wove through the strands, then left them. He had a long, handsome face, the face of a gentle horse.

From the empty space that was my brother dead, something rose up. It could have taken other channels: A letter from my mother telling me to come home, Eliza returning, Constance staying—any of these things might have given me something to hold onto, and then he would have passed through my life in a matter of minutes. The church, too, might have helped me if I had been able to ask.

I could not ask in the church, and my mother did not tell me to come home. I knew I was a pretty girl. I had seen how I could change the texture of the air around me simply by using my eyes. I willed for the loom to stay broken, and when he went to start up the machine again my wish was answered, for my loom still did not work. I willed for him to turn and look at me, ask me a question about my loom.

He looked at me and asked me a question, but his voice got lost among the banging of the other looms. I smiled and shook my head, and he pointed toward the doorway of the weaving room. I pictured my mother standing there, hands

on hips: *Do not go over there with everyone watching you, and
you with your bold eyes.* But then the mechanician was picking up his toolbox and walking toward the door, and the
overseer was motioning for me to follow. I could feel the
eyes of the other girls on me as I walked, my arms tight at
my sides.

Outside the massive, wooden doors, a stillness. We
stood in the hallway, where dusty sunlight filtered down in
sheets.

"That's better," he said. "Can't even hear yourself
think in there. I thought it was a gear. That one was bent
some, but I changed it and it's still not working. Can you
tell me what happened when it stopped, miss?"

"I don't know," I said, surprised that I could hear my
own voice. "It was going along fine, and then I guess the
shuttle just got off track, and then the reed smashed into it
and ripped the warp, and—I don't know—it just stopped."

He nodded and smiled, as if I were a child who had
said her lesson well. That could have been the end of it, but
I wanted to stay just a minute longer in this hall where noise
was muffled and dust specks floated, sleepy, in the sun. I
remembered the girl on the mill money: her curly hair, her
loom and the man beside her—the way the light poured in.

I looked at him. I said I had always wondered how a
power loom actually worked. The man nodded eagerly. He
walked over to the wide doors with their glass windows
and peered through, and I followed. He pointed at the shed
of a machine and started to tell me about the loom's insides—a lot of words I didn't really care about, but I nodded and peered.

Then our arms brushed, and I felt the world as a place
with ledges and rims again.

I wanted to grip his arm with all my ten fingers and not

let go. Instead, I acted like the girls in the romance stories I had read. I made my every gesture speak, but softly. I tilted my head and leaned toward the window. I asked simple questions.

"Oh really," I said. "You don't say."

I acted like my mother and Harriet had when the agent came to the house, only with me I think there was a certain glint in the words I said, in the way I said them. Someone watching might have thought I had done it many times before—that it was a game to me. I had not done it many times before, not the whole thing, although I had practiced parts of it in the mirror and on the street.

Far inside me a voice was calling *help help*—not the way a beautiful maiden caught on the edge of a cliff would call down to her prince, but in a dull, steely stutter that could not stop itself.

He did not hear that part. If he had heard it, he would have turned and left. He saw the indigo ribbon in my hair, my gray eyes, the way I looked at him, part boldness, part shyness. He said he thought maybe he still needed to adjust something called the pick cam and bent down to rummage in his toolbox.

"What's your name, miss?" he asked softly from where he knelt. For a moment I panicked. Had I done something wrong? Would he report me? I hadn't even been touching the loom when it broke. But then I looked down at him and saw how he was blushing, looking too hard at the wrenches in the box. I must have been silent for too long, for he spoke again.

"I asked you what's your name?"

This time his voice came out louder, harsher. I looked through the window in the door. The overseer was nowhere in sight.

"I'm not in trouble, am I?" I asked. "It just happened, by itself—"

"Of course not. I need to write it on the log sheet, not to blame anyone, but so they'll know not to dock you for the breaks in the bolt. Don't worry, I'll tell them it wasn't your fault." He straightened up and looked at me, almost tenderly. "Anyway, all that aside, we were never properly introduced."

"Aimee Slater," I said. "Aimee."

Then he leaned closer, so close I could feel the eyes of all the other girls boring through the door.

"Curious name. Aimee? Is that it?"

Suddenly, with him leaning next to me that way, I wasn't even sure myself. Aimee—it was a name that lived inside my head and on the tongues of my family, but then what was inside my head and what was Aimee, and where, in the space that had become my insides, might there live a real girl with a real name, someone with substance, solid to the touch?

I shook my head, so tired suddenly. It was too much trouble for me to act like the girls in the stories. I wanted to lie down inside his coat on the floor and sleep. *Take me home and care for me*, I wanted to say to this man who fixed things. I stopped fluttering my eyelashes and gave him a real look, straight into his eyes and filled, I imagine, with my own tired grief.

He leaned so close that I could feel the breath of his words. "Well, it's a pretty name, Aimee. I'm William. William Tanning. Nothing fancy about that name. Same name my father has, and his father. Look, I'm going to adjust the pick cam and I think that'll take care of it, probably just needs to be timed a little different. If you have any more

problems, you'll let me know? They can always find me in
the machine shop or out on the floor.''

Help help, stuttered the voice, but I could not say that.
Still, I did not let him go, nor did I lie down on the wooden
floor and sleep. I asked him if he liked it there, working in
the machine shop. I made our conversation go on just five
more seconds. It was enough. Would I like to go out walking that Saturday along the towpath and take tea in town,
if it wasn't too forward to ask?

''Yes,'' I whispered, but I had backed away, and he
could not hear me.

''All right,'' I said, louder, nodding. ''Yes.''

And there in the hall outside the weaving room, he
made a small, stiff bow.

I did not want him to court me. I wanted him to swallow
me whole and spit me out as someone new. I wanted him to
erase and replace my brother, to comfort me like my mother.
Too many things, I wanted, but he did not know that; I'm not
even sure I knew it myself. I imagined how he would bring me
presents, how we'd walk bundled in the cold along the towpath by the canal, watching the locks move up and down.
Other girls did this sort of walking. My mother might not
mind, if she could see; it could mean a husband for me, a man
of good station, one who might make something of himself. I
pictured her meeting him, such a tall, strong gentleman:
''Hello, ma'am, it surely is a pleasure.'' My mother would look
him up and down, inside and out, to see if he were fit for me.

William. He had wide shoulders and nostrils which
tensed like an animal sensing something. He knew how to
read the insides of those machines. In bed the night my loom
broke, I wondered if he could take me apart like a broken loom

and pull out the bad parts, filling me back up with gleaming silver workings. Part of me knew to be careful—not of him, necessarily, for so far he had behaved like a gentleman, but of my own untethered self. I remembered the way I had felt in the barn, the throbbing in my veins and head. But that seemed so far off. Since then I'd felt more like I was wrapped in a ball of cotton.

He came to the door of the boardinghouse, and all the girls saw how he brought me chocolates: *Bon-Bons de Paris.* I opened the box right there, handed out the sweets wrapped in crinkled silver. The girls crowded round me. I ate a chocolate, but I could not taste it, seeing him standing there watching. I could tell the small smile on his lips was aching to spread into a loose, boyish grin.

"Save a few for later," he said, and I gave the box to Mrs. Ladd and asked her to keep it for me until I got back. She squinted at him and asked his name.

"It's cold out there and you've been feeling poorly," she told me. "Don't stay out too long."

That first day, I did not stay out too long. I walked with my hands pressed together inside the muff I had bought with my own money, and as he walked beside me in strides I had to strain to match, he told me about drill presses, planers, drop hammers, screw augers, named all the machines in the shop where he worked as if they were prize horses he had raised himself, and his arms began to circle with the excitement of it, and his voice went up in pitch. He told me he wanted to invent something. He didn't know just what yet, but he had a project in mind, something about a way to improve a lathe.

"That's the way this whole place got started," he said. "Just a few inventions by fellows like me."

If I could invent something, I thought, I would invent my brother back, still only ten.

"In Philadelphia," he said, "they're inventing looms that run three times as fast as these."

I listened and did not listen to his talk. I liked how bright his voice got, how happy he seemed around wheels, pulleys and tethers. I could understand that; I, too, liked the way the looms made me feel when I lost myself in their movement. Fixing them would be even better; you would know what went on inside. I liked the sound of his voice, but his words meant little to me. I listened, nodded and smiled, and finally he stopped by a frost-covered bush, all out of breath, and said, "But I'm sorry; I'm talking too much. You talk to me."

I could have told him about coming to the mill and not finding Eliza, about my brother dying while I was there and Constance leaving, about starting as a drawing-in girl and how that made all the other girls dislike me. I could have shown him how, if he stared hard enough into my eyes, he would have found a panic under all their careful shine.

Instead, I talked about the money I had saved, the lectures I had gone to, how happy I was to be in a big town like this, so much to see, how much faster I was getting at my work. I did not tell him how I only worked so hard so I did not have to think. I listed my brothers and sisters but left out Anna and Jeremiah. Something halted in my voice when I went through the names, but he did not seem to notice.

When I had finished, he said, "Oh, but you're shivering."

I was not shivering, or not from the cold anyway. Something in me was still stuttering to get out. He took me to a place that served linden flower tea and sugar cookies shaped like crescent moons. He was wearing a deep blue silk cravat and had a billfold full of money. He was, he told me, twenty-two years old, and I thought how seven was supposed to be a lucky number, and he was seven years older than myself. Sitting there on a high, red, velvet chair sipping tea, my feet dangling off the ground, I felt myself dissolving. Once, as we reached for a cookie at the same time, our hands brushed and I looked up to see him staring at me, almost studiously, his head tilted to one side.

"What?" I asked, giggling, worried I had sugar on my nose, but he shook his head. I looked down to see his hands covered with powdered sugar and pictured myself leaning over his hand, tasting the crannies between his fingers. Then I might hide there, in the dark, sure spaces.

No, I told myself. If I did not watch out, I would tell him everything.

For months I had been keeping my thoughts from even the Lord, from even myself, as best I could. When I thought of his name, William, I thought of William Tell, and the words *tell William* started moving through my head. I wondered what he would do if I told him about touching my brother. I imagined his face twisting up, how he might push the ivory teacups off the table and rise to go, crunching on the shards. I couldn't tell him about the touching, but instead, walking back to the boardinghouse drowsy and filled with warm tea, I told him my brother had died.

I didn't mean to tell him; it just came out. I said I had left something out earlier, when I was naming my family. Jeremiah was another brother, I said, and my throat closed up so that I had to stop by a gas lamp and suck in draughts of winter air.

I told him because I had to tell someone. I had not worn the band of crepe my mother sent on my arm because I did not want people asking questions: Why didn't you go home for the funeral, how old was he, was he ill for long? Instead, I had tied it around my leg under my skirt, where no one could see. In the gray late afternoon light by the post office, I told him of my brother's death, hoping that somehow once I had said the words, I would be free to move on to other things.

For a minute it worked. He said he was sorry, and then he reached over and touched my face with his gloved hand, and I felt how there were still living creatures on this earth. After a moment he backed away, and we were at my door, and he was saying good-bye, he hoped he would see me again the next Sunday, and then he was gone, and again I was alone.

I was alone, but not in the way I had been before. There are so many different kinds of aloneness. When I was a small girl, my aloneness was of the precious kind. I sought it, treasured time apart from my family when I might wander the fields listening to the uncurling of my own thoughts, the way you can hear corn grow on summer nights. Somebody was always nearby. After Jeremiah died, my aloneness turned into something that had nothing to do with who was around me. I was always alone—at work, in the boardinghouse at night— and although I was not happy, I did not seek the company of people. I had nothing to say to anyone, too many secrets, a sorrow too wide to name.

But in the week after William and I walked along the towpath, I wanted nothing but to see him again. I was alone *from* him. In the days apart from him he grew in my mind. His hair became glossier, his words more interesting. I nibbled on the chocolate he had given me, taking tiny, careful bites, until soon the taste of chocolate stopped being a slap from my father and became the taste of wanting to see him again, and the flattened silver labels that I saved in the bottom of my bandbox became pieces of his soul reflecting my own face back to me—my eyes distorted, as big as saucers and stretched with longing. His name half-replaced the name of Jeremiah in my mind. It was with great relief that I felt my brother dim.

I thought this was all right, this kind of wanting. Girls

were supposed to want to walk with suitors along the tow-path. In a week I invented a life for us. We would move to a city I had only heard of—Philadelphia, perhaps, where there was an institute for mechanicians where he said he wanted to study. We would live in a city house with pane windows, carpets, and doilies like perfect spiderwebs on the sofa arms. When we shut the windows it would be so quiet inside, just the sound of our two voices speaking half-words. I'd be *in* love—love like a house, a place to live in. On a big feather bed in a white room, I'd sleep for days and wake to find him sitting by my side.

Nothing was enough for me, and it is because of this that I crossed with trouble. The second week we had tea again. The following Wednesday he met me after work, and I missed supper at the boardinghouse, causing Mrs. Ladd to frown at me as I tried to slip past her up to my room. I found that I could talk to him. I did not tell him anything important after telling him about Jeremiah, but I chattered about the girls I shared a room with, and the way I imagined things inside the closed parts of the mill, and the places I wanted to go when I saved enough money to get passage on a ship.

"To the pyramids in Egypt," I told him. "Or Paris, where they made that chocolate. Or somewhere with elephants to ride. Like India, I read about it there. They sleep under big veils."

I did not tell him that I had already imagined a life for us together in Philadelphia. He liked it when I talked of voyaging, leaned over me and called me his pirate. He brought me ribbons, a bracelet, a pincushion shaped like an apple and stabbed with hundreds of shiny silver pins. Loom-fixers, like drawing-in girls, were favored at the mill. Some of them did go on to be inventors, even owners. The girls at the boarding-house told me I was lucky and should hold onto him, and I pictured myself clinging to him as if he were a raft.

Hold on.

Nothing was ever enough. Tea and walks and more talk, and I began to feel the emptiness again, as if there were a great hand in my insides pushing out whatever managed to find its way between my ribs. I could not tell him about this, and his own talk was so full of pulleys and cranks that sometimes it seemed to take off on its own accord, like a machine where the start lever is stuck. I began to feel the world turning flat and gray again, and so I started to play with things in order to keep the colors bright.

One day, walking down by the canal, I saw a sheet of ice on the path in front of me, and rather than sidestep it, I slid onto it, and rather than catch my balance, I fell. I did not mean to, exactly, but somewhere I knew I might walk on, listening dimly to his talk, or I might feel my cheek rub against the burning cold of ice and feel his gloved hands slide under my armpits and lift me up.

I fell and his hands came down around my waist, and for a long instant I did not want to rise from there and be shep-herded back into the warm cafe to drink tea. I knew freezing to death was supposed to be a gentle passage. I wanted him to crouch over me as I lay on the ice, to hold me as I went to meet my brother.

Get up, a voice inside me said. *Don't lie on the ground like a dead horse. Make use of your own two legs.* But something stronger in me than my own two legs did not want to move.

He pulled me up, swifter than swift, all concern. I told him I had felt faint, had not seen the ice. I'm fine, I said, I'm fine, but in fact my legs did feel weak, and I wished he would open up his thick, gray overcoat and squirrel me inside. He held my arm, but too carefully, as if I were a lady. Inside the boardinghouse, drinking tea in the front parlor, I realized that my hair had fallen halfway down, unpinned, and I did not pin it up. I thanked him for his help, and when I lay my hand over his, I kept it there for an instant too long. He watched me with surprise. He thought I was too young to know anything.

I knew that the world looked dull and flat and that I wanted him to take me away. And so I cannot say he started it. I did not know what I was starting, exactly, but I started it. I couldn't see him; instead I saw something of my own making. Sometimes he would break through with a surprising remark or a sharp word. Once he listed some of the girls from my boardinghouse in order of their prettiness.

"You first, of course," he said. "Then Polly, Olive, Mary Laura, Helen, Anna, and the red-haired one who's always singing out of tune . . ."

I had not known he was looking, each time he came to pick me up. Polly was as smug and stiff as a wax doll. I tried not to hear him, to ignore the stains on the picture I had drawn. Mostly he talked and talked and didn't seem to care if I really listened, or else I talked and didn't care if he really listened. This passed for love to me then—this and the tautness of the air when he leaned close.

In January we walked and walked along the towpath, and he kissed me, kisses quick and brief as pecks.

In February I took sick from the cold and the long work hours, and he visited me in my room with Mrs. Ladd hovering in the doorway. I felt how our eyes were tugging on each other, how the bedcovers outlined my shape. When he left I dove into my fever, and then it was March and I began eating again, and working, and I had never been so hungry, something changed inside me. Once, when he kissed me at the end of one of our walks, I leaned into him and tasted him and felt the silky lining of his cheek.

I knew very little about William, really, except that he wanted me somehow and for some reason. He wanted to walk with me, bring me things, talk to me, pull me from my sickness. I could back away and his face would fall in pain. I backed away, stepped forward, backed away. Early on, when we had begun our walks, he had said that someday he wanted me to marry him. Each week I thought he would ask me. Each week he did not.

I stepped forward. We stepped forward. It happened the first time in the finishing room one night after the mill had closed, cloth everywhere—strewn on the floor, stacked in piles, making up the layers of my skirts. He told me he had been there after hours to fix something and had left some doors unlocked. He must have planned the whole thing. I had no idea where we were going when he led me to the mills, through the side gate which opened quietly before his hand, but I did not question him. I loved the mystery of it, walking through the dark with my hand in his, not knowing where we would end up. Perhaps, I thought, he would kneel in the hallway where we had spoken our first words and ask me to be his wife.

The room was long and dark, stacked with bolts of fabric waiting to be shipped to Boston and Philadelphia, and down South. How strange, I thought, to be here with no people. I remembered an abandoned wasps' nest I had found once—how, when you shook it, it rattled with the carcasses of wasps. I would not have been surprised if girls had appeared like ghosts from behind the cloth, watching. And myself watching myself.

"What if they find us here?" I asked him.

He put his finger to my lips. I had an answer, but I did

not tell him: *Maybe then you will marry me. Or maybe then they will send me home.*

I sat on the edge of a bolt of cloth two feet off the ground, and he sat beside me. I knew something would change that night, and for this, if for nothing else, I thanked the Lord.

A ring? A proclamation? I do not know if I really expected these things. I may have done stupid things, but I was not a stupid girl. One by one my skirts were lifted. Nothing in my life had ever seemed quite so strange to me as this—to be here far from home, in this room, with this man unwrapping me until my skin touched air. I was not afraid, not exactly. I did not think *stop* to myself, nor *go*. I thought how nice it was that I could make him tremble and his breath go fast. I thought, unwrap me, hold me, and for a moment he made me feel sleepy and safe, and then the pain was sharp and brief and I thought *Oh I am not all dead inside.*

The first time we were together like this, he did not fill my emptiness. He was not like a boy, not like my brother. He smelled full and slightly sour, like a man. He did not cure my ache, but he helped, his hands in the small of my back, pushing in, his mouth on my mouth as if we could help each other breathe. In the silence that was our touching, my mouth could not say help me, but my body could. I felt him press against my stomach and my back, my inside walls, and I knew I had edges again.

I did not bleed, not one drop, nor even know, then, that most women did. Afterwards I clung to him and wept. He smoothed my forehead the way a mother would, told me shush. Even as I cried, I thought how strange and lovely—a grown man saying shush that way. He thought I was crying for what I had just lost. I was crying for my brother who was dead, my mother who would hate me if she saw me lying there on scraps of cloth, who would look at me and say *Of course.*

I was crying because I felt as pink and seeping as a burn. He did not seem to notice the strand of mourning weed I had wrapped around my thigh. In the middle of my tears, two thoughts came to me so small and distant I could not make them seem real: *I could get with child. He will never marry me now.*

I met him again, and again. I went to his rooms when I was supposed to be at church. Outside, bells rang; in the churches, I knew, the girls sat so straight you could balance hymnals on their heads. Hold me, I said to him without saying a word, and he unknotted the tight knots I got in my neck from standing so long at the looms.

"When I'm rich I'll take you to Europe," he told me, nuzzling my neck. "I'll take you to India and buy you an elephant to ride."

"As your wife?"

"Of course."

"Do you mean that?"

"Two elephants and a monkey," he said. "And silk for your dresses. Come here."

One day I brought sugar cookies to his room in a square white box tied with a red string. After he ate them I licked the sweetness from between his fingers, cranny by cranny, the way I had wanted to in the tea shop.

"Hello, pretty cat," he said.

I arched my back and made a deep purring noise.

He smiled down at me. "What a funny girl you are," he said. "Full of surprises."

"What kinds of surprises?"

"Nice ones."

"What kinds of nice ones?"

"Purr again."

I did, and he put his hand against my throat and held it there.

"Is that a surprise, my purring?" I asked.

"Yes."

"Why?"

"Because most girls don't purr. Cats purr."

"And girls?"

"Girls . . . chatter. Walk together. And don't purr."

I could hear my mother in his voice, and I grew panicked. I leaned away from him. "I'm glad you liked the cookies. I had better go."

"No, kitten," he said. "Don't go, don't go."

He brushed his hand along the bottom of the cookie box, then held it out to me, and I couldn't help myself. I tumbled toward him, a happy child again, there in that room where skin was dusted with sugar and I could flick out my tongue and taste.

I gained a reputation and had to move out of the boardinghouse; some girls told on me, I do not know which ones. I took a room in a shabby boardinghouse on the edge of town, with a private family who let me come and go as I liked. As spring came, we found each other by the canal at night and knelt in the bushes by the locks. I began to long for the length of him against my length, like a bandage. After I had been with him I could feel how he had filled me, but never for long enough. Nothing ever stayed.

Sometimes I filled myself with watered-down vinegar after he had been in me, to keep from getting with child. A woman who lived downstairs had told me this would work— the same woman, Cora, who asked me if I bled much the first time. The vinegar was biting and crude and tore up my insides, and I rarely used it. I was not thinking clearly; I only knew that most of the time I did not want to hurt myself that way. My mother would have told me that sometimes you have to do things that push against your want. She would have been right, but at the time I could not have listened. Sometimes I pictured myself walking next to William down a city street, one arm on his arm, the other cradling a blurry white bundle. Often I walked with myself clenched together to keep a part of him from trickling out.

I gained a reputation and the girls from the weaving room whispered about me as I walked by, or looked at me when they thought I couldn't see, their eyes bright and curious as a raccoon's. I knew that any day now, I would be told not to come to work anymore. It was part of our job to tattle on each other. There had been a few other girls like me—one day there, the next day gone.

I wore lace, baubles and bright facepaint, and sin ran after me like a hungry child. I gained a reputation and lay with many other men. That is the story anyway, what I imagine the young women told the old women told the girls after I left the city and came back home. It is not true. I wore one small ribbon in my hair, as I always had. I cannot say I was true to William, because I'm not sure I ever knew him well enough to be true to him, but I did not lie with other men.

First there was monthly blood, and then there was not. For a time I told myself that it was because I was nervous and sad, but when more than three months passed and still there was no blood, I sent a messenger boy with a letter to William—too scared to tell him myself—and when a week passed and he did not answer or come to see me, I wrote a second letter, and when still there was no answer, I went to where he lived and knocked. The boardinghouse keeper peered at me.

"I'm looking for William," I said. "William Tanning."

"Gone to Philadelphia for some sort of instruction," she said.

"Do you know when he'll be back?"

She shook her head and started to shut the door.

"I need—" I couldn't figure out how to end the sentence. "I sent him two letters, do you know if he got them?"

"All the letters go in a basket on the front table, where the boarders pick them up," she said flatly. "I don't guess it's any of my business who they're to or who they're from."

"Could I look?" I craned my neck past her into the house, but she placed her wide girth right in front of me.

"Can't let you do that. One moment." She shut the door and I stood there staring up at his window, thinking I might see a flash of his sleeve or his head as he crossed the room. Philadelphia. I was sure she was lying.

"No letters in the basket for Mr. Tanning," she said when she returned. "Good day, miss."

I sent a letter to my mother. I wrote in the cursive I had learned in Improvement Circle. I wrote beautifully, like someone from the city. Then I remembered my mother could not easily read cursive, and I tore it up and began again, in the ugly block print of the poor.

I wrote to her because I could not think what else to do. Now I know: I should have tried to manage on my own. I was not a girl with foresight, could not see around corners, could hardly see right down the road. I wrote to my mother because she had told me I must, unless I was prevented by ill health. This was not ill health, though I did feel ill; it was a stirring. How many times had she felt it within herself? Seven children, five still moving through the world. Each morning now I woke ill and swollen. I wanted my mother to spread a cool cloth on my head.

My mother wrote back:

> *You Shame shame me if it has not Qickened you must go*
> *fast to a Lady Doctor who will Unblock you you can tell*
> *it has Qickened if you feel it move inside you like a fish*

She did not sign her letter. Inside it were scraps of paper she had torn from her magazines: Madame Drummett's Lunar Pills. Sleeping Lucy—Clairvoyant, Female Maladies and Teeth. French Renovating Pills.

I sat and read her letter with a hand on my belly. I *had* felt it move in me, just like a fish, a tailflop of something slippery inside water, a minnow's turn. I had felt that. For a few minutes I stared at the scraps of paper, the drawings of smiling lady doctors, the edges jagged where my mother had torn them out. How did my mother know about this? I must have read the advertisements, too, before, or passed right by them when I read the magazines. A Lady Doctor who will Unblock you. No, no, I thought, there is nothing to unblock; I am all empty inside. And yet there was that hint of movement. Qickened. *I have*, I wrote back to her. *I have Qickened*. I thought she would write back telling me to get on the next stagecoach. Her letter came quickly:

> *I have found It a Family. They will pay your way until It*
> *comes. Do not come home.*

13

The people were rich and they had no child. They sent me money for my lodging and to buy myself milk, vegetables, meat and fruit. In the tall, peeling boardinghouse on the edge of town where no one asked questions, I waited. Even before I began to show, I was told they did not need me anymore at the mill. Too many girls had known about William, then seen me vomiting and dizzy. I might have told the overseer that I did good work, might have asked why I could not stay on, but I knew it would not do any good. It was written in the agreement that they did not have work for girls like me.

I left silently, secretly glad, and said good-bye to no

one. I did not want to stand aching in the clatter of the mill. The noise there had begun to gnaw at me, no longer something I could hide in. Each time I looked at a loom I pictured William reaching inside. I sent him a third letter, and a fourth, asking him to come see me, and he did not answer. One day I went to his boardinghouse again and stood for a long time by the front door.

You said, I thought, but I no longer believed anything and knew what a fool I had been.

Finally I knocked. The boardinghouse keeper looked me over.

"He's not here, miss. And I do think he's taken up with someone else." She coughed. "I mean, I thought you should know."

I nodded wearily. "Could you tell him I came? Tell him I need—"

Once again I didn't know what I needed, exactly. I was eating like a rich girl. A husband. Could you tell him I need a husband? Remind him that he promised to take me to India and buy me an elephant? That he found me strange and funny in a nice way? That I love him, am *in love* with him, Sweet William like the flower, William Tell. *Foolish girl, didn't I teach you anything?* came my mother's voice. I shook my head. "Never mind."

"Poor girl," the woman said. "There's nothing for you here. Why don't you go home where you came from?"

Once a week a freckled boy delivered money to me in a brown envelope, more than I had ever had before, and notes written in a beautiful curly script: "Please do not eat Pepper or Garlic." "Take a bowl of Duck Broth twice a day. Pray do not get damp." I knew that the notes were from a woman who cared only about what grew inside me, but in my blurred solitude I sometimes convinced myself that they were from my mother, who never wrote me anymore. The woman who wrote the words could make beautiful, graceful letters and wanted to fill me with good things.

At first I was not hungry, and I disobeyed the notes. My hands swelled up, shed the calluses they had gotten at the mills. My palms itched, and I hammered them against the rough wood walls to make them stop. After a time (I do not remember how long, for time itself stopped moving in a straight line and became a twisted, folded thing) a hunger rose up in me, and a superstitious fear, and I began to do everything the notes said, as if they came from a magic source.

Every morning I went out and bought food. I ate clotted cream while I waited. I ate red meat half-cooked by a sullen scullery maid downstairs and still felt a thirsty longing for more blood. I sat in my room like a rich, lazy girl and could not stop the hunger, nor keep my hands from moving to my mouth.

Sometimes, making my way up and down the stairs, I passed the other lodgers. Strange people, all of them—what my mother would have called riffraff. A drunken man who had lost his hand in the waterwheel at the mill; a spinster who walked with her palms pressed together in prayer. Cora, a woman from England who must have been over fifty and dressed like a gypsy with earrings and embroidered shawls. It was said she took callers in her room. Most of the lodgers ignored me so completely that I had to wonder if I even cast a shadow, but Cora took a liking to me.

"Happens to the best of us, love," she said one day when I passed her on the stairs, her gaze resting frankly on my stomach. "Have a licorice?" From somewhere inside her shawl she pulled out a dusty candy stick and handed it to me.

I took it, but I could not imagine eating something that had sat so close to her.

"Did you love him?" she asked sadly, and I felt tears spill from my eyes.

"You did," she said. "Oh, you poor lass, you loved him and now look where he's gone and left you. Was he a gentleman?"

I nodded, my voice too choked with tears for me to speak.

"I thought so," she said. "The worst kind, they swallow you up and spit you out. You loved him with your whole heart, didn't you?"

"Yes," I said, and I think I believed it at that moment: red velvet, white sugar, hands that could take me away. My whole heart.

"What's his name?" She leaned closer. "I might know him, I could get him to help."

"No," I said, the licorice sticky in my fist. She couldn't know him, not this aging woman with her stale candies. Anyway, I still thought he might come help me on his own.

"It's all right, I'm fine," I said, and my voice surprised me, for now it *sounded* fine.

"Oh no you're not," she answered. "You have a broken heart."

"I don't."

"Oh?" said Cora. "Well, then, that's a blessing, since there's plenty more fish in the sea. Time to forget about this one and move on."

"No!" I burst out, hovering on the stairs, my own confusion dizzying me. "I did, I *do* love him, don't you see?"

"Whatever you say, luv." She shrugged and moved on. "Can't nobody know but you."

Looking back, I see that Cora was probably a kind

woman and might have been a sort of friend. But at the time I thought of myself as a mistake in that house, the first normal person ever to live there, not like the others. Up and down the stairs I went, in and out the door, but I did not stop to talk. In the back of my mind, at every moment, was my mother: *How often do they wash, these people? Holes in her ears, like a savage. A Godless house, and that crazy woman whispering her devil's prayers.*

Once, when I was about six months along, William came to see me. He handed me a little money. He said he had no more. From under his jacket he pulled a small black kitten—to keep me company, he said.

"I loved you," he told me, shaking his head.

"You do?" I said, realizing as soon as the words left my mouth that I should have said, "You did."

He nodded.

"Then marry me."

And he said, "Aimee, I'm so sorry," and I knew he was thinking of his profession and the institute in Philadelphia. He rested his head on my knee and cried the racked cries of a grown man, and I looked down at the crown of his head as if from a great distance and watched the kitten wander, sniffing, about the room.

"You have to help me," I said. "Why didn't you answer my letters? I came to see you. Why didn't you let me in?"

A rage began to knot inside me that he could shake and tremble like that and bring me a helpless animal to care for, and then get up and go, for I knew he would go.

"Find me more money," I said, "so I can go somewhere with it."

Anywhere. I was not thinking clearly, did not know what I wanted: William or a child, both or nothing, anything but this. I had to plan something. I knew he had no more money, had nothing but desire, grown tired now, and clever hands, and inventions he wanted to invent.

"Start again," he told me. "Forget about it all. You're still so young. Give it to someone who can care for it better, and then go home."

"Would you marry me, if I gave it away? You said you would. Remember?"

"Please," he said. "You know I would if I could. I wish you had told me earlier, we could have gone away someplace, before anyone knew. Or we could have—you know—brought you to a doctor. It's too late now." He looked at his pocketwatch. "I'm sorry, kitten. I can't stay."

"We could still go away. I did tell you, I wrote you, I came—"

"It's too late," said William. "I have my job here, my reputation, don't you see? Sweet girl. You know I'll always think of you, but you need to do as your mother says and start a new life."

He leaned up toward me, stretched out his hand to touch my cheek, but I stood and backed away. I might have hissed, scratched his cheek. I could feel claws growing from my fingertips. Instead I leaned over my belly and whispered.

"Take that cat," I said, though part of me was longing for something live to nuzzle with my chin.

"I thought you'd like her," he said, but I would not answer, nor even look at him. He scooped up the animal and left.

That much I blame him for—the leaving. I cannot blame him for all of what came before that, for I was, in my way, a girl with her eyes open, but the leaving me there, the running, that I will never forgive. At the time, as I heard his steps grow dimmer on the stairs, I felt only a dull, quiet disappointment that I could have thought I had known and loved this man named William. I wanted, for a moment, to call him back again. He might hold me then, like before. Instead I listened as his footsteps thumped down the stairs, playing out his words: *start again.*

What were they thinking, all those people (William, Cora, later my own mother) who kept telling me to forget and start again? Nothing leaves you; things just shake and tumble and return. How could they not know that, my mother who had lost two children, William who had been alive for over twenty years? Slowly, listening to him go away, an anger began in me that would keep me shut inside myself for years and years. First it was small, that anger, and tired. If I had not been so tired I might have run away, far from my mother's plans. But I found that I could not move, limp within the very marrow of my bones.

Day by day by day I watched my changes, and after a while I stopped being hungry and wanted to make myself small and thin again. When I did want to eat, my longing was not for food, but for chalk or ash, and I pictured myself covered with gray chalkiness, or being eaten into a soft, quiet mound like ash. Sometimes I remembered the schoolroom where I had been an apprentice, the dusty whiteness of my hands at the end of a day. If only I had learned, then, to live inside that dust. Instead I had become a vain girl, so pleased with the outer trappings of my self, always washing my hands. Now that self was swelled and ugly, and my breasts ached and changed color, and a line of pigment striped my belly like a skunk's. It reminded me of earlier times, moving from my quick girl body to the itching skin of a woman. I wanted to be ten again, my chest a plain board, my openings nothing I noticed.

One morning in September, Cora heard me crying in my room and came in without knocking.

"Pennyroyal tea is what you need, love," she said. "Or tansy and featherfew, as much as you can stomach. It'll empty you right out and leave you new. Should have done it a lot earlier, is all, but it's never too late. Put a little honey in, and some gin if you've got some, and some cayenne. Won't feel too good while it's happening, but you're a young, strong girl."

Some mornings, on the days when I woke up feeling tired and dreamy, floating in my own salt sea, I would not have listened. But this morning I had been doubled up with cramps, cursing both the monstrousness inside me, and my mother for wanting to take it away. Yes, I thought, I will take it away myself, before she gets to it. When the messenger boy came, I took the food money from him, went to the chemist's and came back with a large packet of pennyroyal tea. I drank one cup, then another and another. It did not work. Instead I vomited long and hard into the bedpan, then stumbled down the stairs to empty the pan out behind the house. I could not stand straight, the tearing inside me was so sharp. Probably, I thought, hunched on the landing on my way back up, I have not ended its life, only ruined it. Probably it will come out covered with coarse hair or missing some part of itself.

I'm sorry, I thought. I'm sorry, but I could not help it.

But I was not sorry, not really, for I had not begun to think about what was inside me as a being that could live on its own. I knew there was something there, could feel it in my aches, see it in my growing, but I did not think of it as a child. Sometimes, even, I thought of it as a beast, with sharp white teeth and fingernails that scraped. Go away, I'd whisper to it. Stop growing and leave me be.

I made white doilies, in that room, to cover the plump city sofas I would never have. I sang songs to myself. I chewed my nails down to the quick and plucked the hairs from my belly. Often I spoke to my brother Jeremiah.

"Don't cough, it's all right," I told him and pounded on the mattress beside me as if it were his back. "Don't follow me, can't you see"—had it really been, had I really wanted it?—"that I want to be alone? Oh all right, you can come along."

By the eighth month I had spent more time alone than ever before in my life. Something changed then, settled inside me, and I began to feel the weight of a curled presence, a gentle, heavy life. It was then, I think, that I began to talk to what lay within me. Often I thought of it as a small girl doll, naked and made of china and cloth, with jet black hair, round black eyes, a mouth pursed up in red. I pictured painted shoes on the baby inside me, who really looked more like a tiny woman—and a lace collar, but no other clothes. The doll I had never had, had never wanted, really, since dolls had always filled me with fear. This was the doll my parents gave my sister Harriet on her tenth Christmas, the one she had christened Isabel. Now I was sixteen, my birthday come and gone, still not much more than a child myself. When I pictured keeping my baby, I saw myself singing to her (it was always a her) sitting in a wheatfield, telling her stories like the ones my mother told me.

She never cried, the stiff, painted baby in my mind. She never ate, for I could not bear the thought of my own body full of milk like the teats of a bursting cow. She never grew bigger, or old, or away from me, and though she was like a doll, I did not fear her. When I held her against myself she was soft and yielding, but still she somehow never lost her china shape.

That was the child I did not want to give up, the one I

would keep in the room where I lay waiting. Sometimes, in my sleep, another child came to me, and this one was nothing *but* hunger, all aching, howling need, biting at me until I bled, chewing on my fingers and screaming screams that made the mill seem like a quiet place. I knew, in those moments, that I had to rid myself of this creature. In one dream William plucked her away by the scruff of her neck as if she were a kitten, and I was glad.

One day in late January when I was nearing my time, I saw the agent on the street. I saw him first from far away, tipping his hat to a gentleman, and then he was peering into a shop window and walking straight toward me, and I could feel how fat I had become, how ugly in the cloak that I had let out myself and filled with an unmatching fabric from an old dress. If only, I thought, I had passed him on the street when I had first arrived. I remembered the way he had looked at me. I would not have tumbled toward him the way I did with William, because I knew he was a man of tricks. I would have been cautious, and my caution might have brought me safety, a house with many glass windows and rooms full of astral lamps.

But that day on the street, the agent walked right past me, and though his green eyes rested on me for an instant, they did not stay with me. I thought I saw a brief moment of disgust, as if he had seen a child squatting in a courtyard, letting out a yellow stream. I knew I was too ugly for him now, no longer the girl I used to be. I wondered if he recognized me. He might have heard about me; girls like myself were used as a loud lesson in that town. At first I thought he saw me and refused to show he knew me; then I realized I had probably passed by his eyes simply as some anonymous married woman approaching her lying-in.

Would my mother recognize me if I passed her on the

street? This man had stared into my eyes in Eliza's house and in my own. He had given me pictures, remembered my name, and I had convinced myself that he had thought of me when he was riding in the coach. Now he did not know me anymore. Even worse, he had never known me; probably he had noted my name in his ledger and not remembered it at all. Walking there, heavy in my limbs, I knew that none of it had ever really happened—his thoughts in the coach, his wanting. Maybe a glimmer, yes, but I knew now how the world was full of pretty girls like me, girls beneath his station. In the city we were like pigeons, a blur of gray, a blur of blue.

It was as if I had gotten my wish and lost my skin. I could move through the world without making a ripple in the air. That was what stunned me. Back in my room I thought and thought about how you could know and not know people, how you could lose touch. That phrase haunted me—*lose touch*—for I felt I had lost touch with everything and everyone. I had never known the agent, but he had lived for some time in my mind, and I had convinced myself that I had lived in his. I had never known William, not really, except as an opening for my need. Had I known anyone? I wondered. I had known my brother's voice and his white blond hair and his careful, nervous body that rose from sleep with racking coughs. I had known his breath and touched between his legs, but had I ever really known his thoughts? Had I known my mother, who never wrote me anymore, but left me here alone?

You left *us*, my mother interrupted. This was a comfort to me, the way she came to me through backward channels, just a voice. The way she comes to me still. And yet it was only a small comfort, since I did not know if the voice I heard was hers, or my own sharp voice of reason taking on her form.

Everyone, I could hear her say, is born and dies alone.

In the last month of waiting I began to love myself again,

for I could feel motion inside me, everything filling back up. I did not love where I was going, nor the person I had become. I did not love the long silences of my days, nor the way my body swelled. But for two months—the rest of it I cannot count—for the last two months I was not alone. In the last days I began to long for my life to continue like this forever, despite the heavy pressure on my insides. The stairs were too difficult by now; I relieved myself in the chamber pot, more often than I would have ever thought possible, and paid the scullery maid to take it away.

Like a bear in its winter burrow, I felt time blur. If I could only have stayed there in that room as winter fell around me, humming softly to myself.

When the midwife examined me and told me it was time, I prayed she might be wrong. They say children do not want to come into the world; this is why they scream and kick so and arrive wrapped in tangled cords, their faces still bearing the press-marks of the womb. But what about a mother who is really still a child?

I did not want you to come into the world. Everyone is born alone, but until people are born, they are surrounded. Every girl is alone once she is born, but if she becomes a mother she returns to doubleness for a little time. I had never thought of this, watching my mother and aunts grow big with child. Now it seemed to me a miracle, a cure to all my troubles.

I did not want to let you out.

Let us stay this way for a while, I prayed each night. And lying there, I squeezed my body shut.

It is important to know where and how and when you were born.

You were born in a high room in a small bed at the top of four flights of stairs. From between the narrow hips of a narrow girl, the two of you were born. That there were two of you inside me was a secret—one I didn't even know myself until the very end. I could not tell one from two, knew only that I would wake sometimes in the middle of the night with the feeling of a festival inside me, a crowd, all jostling. Now I know it was four feet pressed against my middle, four hands which often felt like more, an army of hands inside me—moving, multiplying, pressing on. With your twenty fingers, your twenty toes, you examined and caressed me, learning the fabric of my womb. No one had ever been so far inside. When I did not please you, you showed your double will, kicking and pinching in the dark.

Four eyes straining to see through blood and skin, cotton and wool, for you were born on the second of February, Eighteen hundred and forty-six.

I do not know the exact hour, minute and second of your birth. I am sorry. It was nighttime, somewhere between midnight and dawn.

You were born in a room with a slanted ceiling and one small window up by where I lay my head. Rough pine floors, rough pine walls, the planks still leaking sap in slow, brown streams. The kind of room reserved for the lowest of the maids, only I liked that room, though I never would have told the widow who kept the house. I liked how dark it was, away from everything, how I could rest there, hearing the noises of the rest of the boardinghouse so far away: wood scraping, voices, a door opening, someone going out or coming in, it didn't matter. We were close to heaven in that room, four stories up, and in a bed off the floor since this was the city, where even girls slept off the floor.

Lying there waiting for you, I sometimes had to remind myself: I was not a girl, I was a woman, enormous now, my belly tight as a drum. Or my flesh was a woman's, for inside my spirit was curled up with you, a third child. Like my mother I was waiting to give birth in a high string bed. White feathers from my pillow pricked my cheek like tiny needles, the sharp touch of an old goose. Stiff black hairs poked their way through the horsehair mattress, an old horse sleeping, far from its farm.

The day you were born, it came to me that there were

two of you. I do not know how I knew, for I could not feel
you both, exactly. Still, looking down at the hugeness of my
belly and up at the ceiling above me, I could sense two other
spirits in the room.

Please let me be right, I thought. One for the rich people my mother found, one for me to keep. Perhaps I could
simply never leave that room. In the far corner, I would put
a cookstove. By the foot of the bed, a cradle. Out the window, a basket on a rope. Someone kind would leave us food.
Only one cradle at the foot of the bed, because that was my
intention—to let go of one of you the way it had been
planned and give birth silently, secretly, to the other.

"The afterbirth," they might whisper if they saw sweat
bead on my brow and a stiffening under the covers. They
would turn their heads, leave the room to get more steaming rags, to wrap the wailing child in a blanket, to catch
their breath and shake their heads at the shame of it all.

Seamlessly, quietly, the hidden one—my second
chance—would slide from me.

Then I would hide you (which one of you? the last one
out, it was the only way to choose) under the covers, my
hand over your mouth. In the warmth and darkness, it
would not be so different from the place you had just left.
You would curl between my legs and sleep. Later, when
they had left me alone, I would wind you in cloth, tie you
to my chest, and run with you. I had fourteen dollars and
would walk the twenty miles to Boston. There I would find
a way for us to live.

I wanted to keep you inside myself, inside a room. I
wanted to take you to the city. I was just a girl with the belly
of a woman and had no idea, really, what I wanted. I told
myself stories the way a girl tells stories to a friend: I'll do

this and this and this. You were not—I am sorry—people to me. You were the brand-new anchors of my soul.

My body shuddered, pushed and shuddered, and after I do not know how long, one of you came ripping from me, all hotness, hitched to me—so briefly—with a long gray rope. After the first of you was born, I was so bone-tired, so wrenched open that once again I thought I would just stop there.

No no

no need to run, I thought. Just never let it out. Then the heavings started, my breath grew quick despite myself. I could not stop from howling at the heat tearing my hips apart, cracking the joints of my bones.

"Lord have mercy!" said the housekeeper, bending into my screams, her hands red from me. "What's this?"

"I thought so," said the midwife. "Such a little girl, and hiding two inside."

I held my breath, pulled myself in and tried to be as still as death, but I could not keep you from the world.

You were born on Merrimack Street, number sixty-three, fourth floor, the room on the left all the way in the back. Perhaps it is still standing.

I did not mean to sleep. I slept. When I woke, the midwife, the kettle, the afterbirths, and you were gone.

Phantom stones, only, left in your place, gray and heavy, round and fixed. Like Amos's phantom leg—always begging to be touched. I love those stones, love their heaviness and difficult weight and how I can feel them shift each time I move. I do not love them because they are good to me, but because they are all I have left of you. Round and stubborn, nicked and waterworn, gray as a full sky about to tear. I am not without food, or drink—not, I don't think, without love—but when I press on my stomach with my hands, I can still feel those stones with me after all these years.

15

First my mother told me to come home with my stomach flat and hide my sin.

"I had a letter from the Family," she wrote. "They say they have been Twice Blessed. Now ends our Corespondents. NoOne here knows a Thing. Come Home, now that It is Over."

I was dulled, flat and stupid in my grief, but I knew that nothing was over. I went home because I did not know where else to go. Looking back, I see how this was my biggest mistake. I should have pulled myself from grief, dragged myself out of the slow, heavy sadness that made me too tired to move, and gone after you. In those first days

I should have said *Stop! I've changed my mind.* If I was old enough to make you, I was old enough to keep you; I see that now. But I was not a wise girl—older than my years in some ways, yes, but not wise or seeing.

My mother, in my mind, was the seeing one. The mere thought of her filled me with a rage so distilled I felt it like a fine-ground powder in the marrow of my bones. At the time, I thought I was angry because she took me from you. Looking back, I see how this was just the final thing, and the easiest to see. There was how Jeremiah had died and she had told me not to come home; how she let me go in the first place; how her words were heavier with warnings than with love. And my grief? I thought it, then, the pure, hot grief of missing babies, but it had a longer thread than that, enough names to fill a sampler, and two blank spots at the bottom for the ones I could not name.

I was angrier at my mother than I had ever been, but I could not resist her pull. Come home, my mother said. I came.

When I arrived like a sleepwalker at the door, she moved as if to embrace me. I stepped back, and she dropped her hands to her sides.

"How was the journey?" she asked. I could only stare at her.

"You must be cold and hungry. There's hot soup," she said. My father would not look at me, and after a few minutes he went outside. Luke was two years old and did not know me. Harriet was married and gone.

My mother put a bowl of soup on the table, and I watched the steam climb up and disappear. "Have a seat," she said, as if I were a guest, but still I stood there watching.

"You're not hungry?" said my mother. "Well, then, thirsty? I have some calming tea."

I felt my breath grow quicker and shallower; the only word I could think of was *why*.

"Please sit," my mother said, impatience crossing her face like a brief shadow. I stood, still in my cloak, arms folded, knees locked. I watched the soup grow cold.

"Well," she said finally. "I reckon you're tired. Maybe you'd like to lie down before you eat."

That was my signal to climb the ladder to my old loft bed, where the same blue quilt was pulled tight enough to bounce a button on. From up there I could hear her voice, talking to Luke. At one point he laughed, and she did too, their laughter as foreign to my ears as the call of a loon or crow. But the quilt was the same worn cotton as before, and I climbed beneath it with my cloak still on, wrapped myself up, and slept.

That evening she tried again to give me things to drink and calm my nerves. For the first time, she spoke of what had happened.

"You're pale as a ghost and much too thin for someone who has just . . . I mean, have you been eating anything at all?" I stared at my knees, and she let out a deep sigh. "I know it's hard now, but in the end you'll see it's the best thing for everyone. Time heals all wounds—"

If I had been able to find any liquid in my wool-dry mouth, I would have spit at her.

That first day, I thought only about how she still had me, her daughter, and I had nothing. I was sure that even if she couldn't see it herself, deep down she meant it as a punishment: two gone from her, and so two gone from me. A schoolroom balance, neat and perfect. I could kill myself, I thought, and make her lose another child. My mother's hair had streaked with gray in the time I had been gone. Her mouth had grown bitter, cracked around the edges like old wax, and though she spoke of time healing wounds, her words sounded wooden, as if she did not believe in them herself.

On the second day, she sat down at the kitchen table and showed me a piece of the Bible:

> When the time of her delivery came, there were twins in her womb. And when she was in labor, one put out a hand; and the midwife took and bound on his hand a scarlet thread, saying, "This came out first." But as he drew back his hand, behold, his brother came out; and she said, "What a breach you have made for yourself!" Therefore his name was called Perez. Afterwards his brother came out with the scarlet thread upon his hand; and his name was called Zerah.

Tamar was the name of the mother. She was thought to be a harlot, for she had covered up her face, and they could not tell who she really was beneath her veil.

My mother watched me, and I sat, numb through the center of myself, with the open book before me and thought only: Who spun that scarlet thread? Was it made on a wooden wheel, turned by the hand of a woman, or spun by a spinning machine? And what dyed it red—a steel vat of dye heated by coal, stirred by a huge metal corkscrew? Or the blood of a woman, the mother of twins? Perhaps the thread was white when it was brought into the birthing room. Perhaps the midwife set it down near the woman, and it rolled over on the mattress down into the slope made by her weight and soaked up the dye of her blood. Or maybe the wrist of the child, soaked from his mother's insides, was what changed the color of that thread.

Who, I wondered, sitting there with my face set in the

expression I had learned to put on in front of people during the past few months—the frozen mouth, the still, calm eyes; nothing enters me, nothing leaves me—who have I become beneath my veil?

I do not know why my mother showed me the page, never understood what lesson she wanted me to take from it. Already we were miles and miles apart, sitting close in the kitchen the way we used to, at right angles by the table my father had cut from an oak tree at the bottom of the hill.

What I took from the story, later, when I was alone in this house with a Bible she had left me and which I keep, still, in the rafters, was this: Maybe Zerah wanted to stay inside her. He put out his hand and felt the coldness, the stinginess of the air, and wanted to go back in. Or maybe Tamar, like me, had decided to give up the first and keep the second child, and knowing this, Zerah wanted to be the second one, but they wouldn't let him cheat, tagging him with that length of scarlet thread.

Which of you came first? I do not know. In that city which spun enough thread to wrap the world inside a ball of yarn, no one leaned down inside my legs and tagged you with a scarlet thread.

Why? I wanted to ask her. Why did you arrange to have them taken?

I remembered begging to keep a sick pony when I was small, promising I would nurse it back to health myself. My mother had told me I was not able, too young, the pony too sick. One morning the animal had simply disappeared. Now I wanted to stand in front of her and scream that I was able, not too young, able! But I could not find the words, my voice and hands grasping for bodies that were not there.

I closed the Bible and pushed it back toward her, then left the kitchen and climbed into the loft. In the old rocking chair up there, I rocked and felt how, though I was still just a girl, my breasts ached and my stomach had an extra, ugly pouch of skin. With my hair knotted and tangled, I knew I must look like a madwoman, and I was glad.

Walked into the brook, she did. Just lay down in the water and held her breath. Stark naked. Jumped into the waterwheel where the falls come over. Nude to the waist. Shot herself between the eyes with her father's hog rifle, a true shot, a hole right through her, you could see clear to the other side.

Did I almost do it? Somewhere past my thoughts, inside my tired veins, I knew I was gathering the strength to look for you. I did not almost do it, but day by day I pictured my mother finding me blue and dead.

Faster, I rocked, more violently.

"All right, now," she kept repeating during the first few days, climbing up to find me rocking, trying to still me with her hand. "Things will get better, you'll see." I steeled my body to her touch and showed no sign of knowing she was there. She could not know how part of me was calling Mama. Each morning I vomited as if it were the beginning and my children were starting to grow, only now the stuff was clear and watery, nothing left inside me to come up.

I came home with my stomach flat enough to pass for flat, but I would not hide my sin. After a few days I decided I could not stay inside any longer, for I felt I might break in two and let her try to mend me. I decided to take a walk. My mother saw me lacing up my boots and said she thought it would do me good, as long as I was not seen.

"Wrap yourself well and stay in the fields," she said. "I worry about you right now, going to town alone."

Shame shame shame on you, her eyes said. Do not let them see you. Do not, whatever you do, tell.

I walked the snowy fields, down to the pond with its thick skin of ice. You're the selfsame girl, I told myself—the one who used to run along this bank, who lay in this field when the corn was high and tried to hear it grow. If I concentrated hard enough, I could stare at the ground as it passed beneath my feet and remind myself that this was the same ground it had always been, same ice, same pond. If I stayed out until my throat grew sore and my feet ached with cold, I found that I could move back inside myself as if I—and somehow as if you—had never left. The next day I also went walking, and the next, going until I could go no more, feet stomping, arms pumping at my sides. Then I came home, stepped around my mother, climbed up to the loft and lay down, the icicles thawing from my hair.

One morning, after I had been home for a week, my mother told me she had decided I should go to town and show myself clean, scrubbed and proper.

"You can get some things for me at the dry goods store," she said. "Just like you used to. What they don't know won't hurt them."

Hurt them? I thought. Her deep voice had started to sound tinny in my head, as one adage after another piled up.

I bathed behind the same old curtain, combed my hair, dabbed vanilla extract behind my temples. I was not in my right mind, but neither was I gone mad. I pulled my hair back so tightly my scalp ached. I scrubbed my face until my cheeks were chapped. Then I put on my long cloak and my mother's Sunday shawl and hat and left the house.

"Oh! Aimee, you're back! You gave me a start, I thought for a minute you were your mother," Eliza's mother said when

I passed her on the icy road, her words a cloud. "When did you get home?"

"Just now," I said, pointing down the road as if I had just then arrived from the city.

"Oh, I didn't know. Welcome." Her eyes searched me. "How was it? Was it all right there? Were the folks there good to you? I heard you were a fine worker—we always knew you'd make a mark. Did you come back with pots of gold?"

I stared at her.

She laughed nervously. "Did you find a nice young man? You know Eliza found one, seems like a good fellow, she always does all right for herself, that one. Did you come back to start up housekeeping?"

"How is Eliza?" I found myself asking. A good man a nice young man housekeeping keeping how is she?

"Oh, too far away, you know, used to be girls stayed closer to home, but I never could keep that one at my side, ever since she learned to walk, she was running, you know what she's like." She shrugged cheerfully. "She's expecting. I'll go down there before it comes."

"Expecting?"

I knew what the word meant, but when she said it, it didn't make sense to me. Nothing made sense as I stood in the cold looking at the puffs of air leave her mouth. I must have stiffened, for she leaned toward me and touched my face with her gloved hand.

"What is it, Aimee?" She took her hand away and looked me over again. "Are you feeling poorly? You're much too pale. Oh, I knew that place was no good—a young girl should stay home with her family. Come to the house and I'll brew you a cup of hot tea."

I turned away.

"Come on, then," she said.

"No, ma'am. I can't."

"For a few minutes, that's all, to warm your feet. I'll send one of the boys to tell your mother."

"I can't." I hugged my mother's shawl closer to me.

Eliza's mother drew in her breath. "Are you all right, child?"

I shook my head.

"What happened, lamb? What on earth did they do to you down there?"

In the city, I know she meant now: What did they do to you down there in the city? But at the time I could not help myself and dropped my hands from the shawl to my empty middle.

"I lost them," I told her, pointing to my belly. My mouth was not mine; my face was wet with someone else's tears. I stood apart from myself, my double watching from the ditch.

"Oh," she said. "Oh, Lord, I didn't even know—I'm sorry. Did he—do you, you know there can be others, I lost one, too, there can be others for you and your—I didn't know. Bless them, poor small souls, may they rest in peace."

"They're not dead," I said. And turned and left her there.

Soon the whole town knew.

Then my mother told me to get down on my knees and beg forgiveness of the town and the Lord, but long ago she had taught me pride, and pride does not unlearn itself, and so I would not beg.

She said, "If you'd only show some shame in your eyes. It's happened to others, you're not the only one. There was April Davis, remember? Now she has a fine family of her own, everybody just forgot. Somebody might have you, still."

She meant Joseph Carter, who had lost his wife to the

fever and had six young children. She meant Karl Smith, slow-witted as an ox, and with an ox's strong back and half his father's land and good hands. You can tell a person by his hands, my mother said, and I stared at mine. The calluses from the mills had disappeared during my months in the attic room. Now, for the first time in my life, I had the soft hands of a lady.

"We can invent something," said my mother, panic in her voice. "A husband who was murdered in the street, or killed in a mill accident. The city is a dangerous place, everybody knows that, I told you that before you went there. We'll have to make something up."

"No."

She did not seem to hear me. "What, exactly, did you tell her? How much? Did you tell her everything? Did you?" She came to me, held me by my shoulders.

Obedient, still—her daughter, still—I shook my head. I knew what she was thinking, how she had started out high, from a good family, and then she had married my father and sunk a little, but it was still all right, they made do, they ran a fine farm, they had good, clean, bright children. People looked up to them. Years and years of wetting the cloth before taking the iron to it, pressing the seams straight as rulers, keeping even the underclothes bleached clean. Years and years, and now this.

"We need to invent a real tragedy," she said.

I wondered, then, what made my tragedy unreal and gave realness to her invented one. And what made my sin so terrible, and her sin of inventing a dead husband all right? As I listened to her, she grew smaller before my eyes.

If you would only hang your head in church.

I thought of Mary and how her son had no earthly father, no father to be seen, and still kings came to offer presents. Of

course no one had ever been inside Mary except her little son.
I prayed that I had borne sons and not daughters, that no one
might get them with child. Not one son and one daughter, for
then, if they were separated at birth, they might meet later and
sin without knowing and make a child with a head like a calf
or withered arms. I had heard of such things. But I knew they
were daughters, both of them, for they were cupped inside me,
two stones, two silver spoons that would turn dark with age.

Every once in a while my mother's face grew young
again—when she was holding Luke, singing to him, running a
wet rag over his face and behind his ears. The rest of us had
been weaned after our first year, but my mother still nursed
him, this boy big enough to ask for his own milk, to tug on her
and begin to unbutton her dress. I was sure she did it out of
cruelty to me, some kind of lesson. If I came across her nursing
him, my own breasts tingled and burned, and I climbed upstairs, eaten with envy—of my mother, that she had a child to
nurse, and of Luke, that he could cry and she would lean over
him and fill him with herself.

I could not so much as look at Luke, this brother I did not
know anymore, could not bear how ready he was to crawl into
my arms, how sturdy he was, or the joy he brought to my
mother's disappointed eyes. Each time he cried, each tumble,
burp, or half-formed word, made me hate him—the wrong
child, hers. A baby just two years older than my own. At night
when he woke crying I plugged my ears so I did not have to
hear my mother calm him or lift him to her. I pictured blankets
smothering his face, a sickness covering him with pox.

Then I hated myself for hating a person so small.

Soon after I met Eliza's mother on the road, I began sleeping in the toolshed in the dead of winter; I could not be near
my mother and her baby and half-wanted to catch my death

of cold. In the toolshed, on the straw where Jeremiah used to lie, I spoke to him.

I'm coming to see you, I told him. In the chattering of my teeth, I thought I could feel what it was like to be all bone.

I'm not going back inside, I said to Jeremiah, knowing he would understand. My mother left a pile of quilts for me, and a bed warmer. I threw the quilts outside, but in the middle of the night the cold defeated me, and I pulled them back in and crawled beneath them.

"I will not—" she said in the morning through the cracks, "I refuse to let you lie down and die."

They made her sleep in the toolshed, can you imagine? Just a girl and she caught her death of cold. A heap of troubles that family's had, from starting out so fine. Three of them gone already. They kept her in the barnyard with the dogs.

One night when I started to leave the kitchen for the shed, she told me I had better stay in the house.

"Don't you go out there," she said to me. "You're taking this too far. There's stubbornness, and then there's downright crazyness. I thought you knew the difference. It's time—it's time to stop." Her voice snagged on itself, and she shut her eyes for a moment. I hoped she was seeing me in there, stone dead. "Do you hear me, child?" she asked.

My father stood up as if to block my way, but I hugged close to the wall and approached the door.

"*Child?* I'm not a child," I said. "Remember?"

"Oh, I remember," my mother said, her voice hard now. "You're a fool, that's what you are."

"I'll sleep where I like."

"The whole town knows it," she said.

My father almost never said anything anymore, so that sometimes I wondered if he still recognized me. Now he leaned over and pounded his hand on the table.

"Go, then," he said. "Sleep in the barn, leave us in peace. You'll be the death of your own mother. Hasn't she had enough trouble?"

"I said I was going."

"Well then, go." His voice was almost taunting.

"No," my mother said. "It's just letting her get her way."

"Always did," said my father. "Reckon she always will."

No, don't you see, they're gone, I wanted to say to her. Jeremiah, and Anna, and now my two. Don't you see what we've lost, both of us, all of us? The white blond strands of my brother's hair came to me suddenly, the blue-branched veins of his arms. How many griefs could one person hold at once? What happened at his burial, I wanted to ask. And in his last days, did he mention me? You, you, you, I could hear her answering. No, I'd try to explain. Him, my brother, Jeremiah, gone. My hands at my sides felt empty, the knuckles swollen; my wrists throbbed with something thicker and less life-giving than blood. I stood in the open doorway, letting in the cold.

"Shut the door," said my father. "And go."

That was the fifth night I spent in the toolshed. After a week there, I found words rising in my throat. The next afternoon I came to my mother in the kitchen when Luke was napping.

"I need to find them," I said to her, and for the first time since I had come home, I looked straight into the green-brown of her eyes. "I need to somehow get them back."

"That love is blind with one eye and sees but poorly with the other is true," said my mother, "but they're gone, you can't have them back, and if you show no shame, the people will hate you for it, and if you try to get them back, you'll ruin their lives and our lives and your own."

"My own?"

"You can still ruin the lives of others." She was sitting at the table drying plates, going over and over them in circles with a piece of flowered cloth.

"Where are they?" I asked her. "Just tell me where they are."

"Happy. And well-cared-for. With a good home, which is more than you could give them, the way things are. Someday you'll have others, when you're married and all this is water under the bridge. You have no idea how hard it is, being a good mother, you just don't kn—"

"Where are they?"

"Far from here, it's best not to think about it."

"Where? In Boston? Portland? Albany? The countryside? Just tell me."

She shrugged, and I imagined the plates shattering against the iron belly of the stove.

"You *do* know, I know you do—where are they?" I felt myself beginning to cry, but I pushed it down; I could not act like a child in front of my mother, or she would never tell me where my children were. "The lady sent me notes, telling me what to eat. They're at the mills, aren't they? They're right where I could find them."

"No," said my mother. "A different lady arranged things; she was in the city—" She stopped herself. "Why do I let you trick me into telling you things? You need to forget. You could do good works for the church, help with the food baskets. It's the way you walk around so proud that leads you into trouble. Eliza's mother told the whole—"

"I'll get a job teaching school and save enough money to get them back. I already have some saved, from the mills."

My mother shook her head. "People here wouldn't take

kindly to having you teach their children, not after you've spread your story all around town.''

"Then I'll go somewhere else—"

She got up and began to stack the dishes on a shelf. "Aimee, you can go to the end of the world, and still they're not yours anymore. You gave them up, for their own good. You did the best thing. You gave them up.''

I gave you up.

At the time, I could not hear my mother. No, I thought, I am just a girl, following her mother's orders. Nothing, nothing is my fault.

Does it matter that now I can see it differently? It is true that my mother was a rigid woman with one eye always on the town, and that her plans were wrong for me, but I swallowed them like bitter herbs, and that is not her fault. Did I take them because I still thought of myself as her little girl? Or because, lying there waiting to give birth, I pictured howling demons tugging at me? I do not know. It was only in the last days before you were born that I realized I could not bear to lose you. It was only after I came back that I realized I was not a little girl anymore. At sixteen, I was a woman with a pouch of skin on her belly, and I was angrier with my mother than I could say.

One day, when she was in town with Luke, I searched her things for a slip of paper with your address. I went through her like she had gone through me, to take from her what she had taken from me. I looked under the mattress, in the sewing box, between the folded layers of her underclothes. I pried up the floorboards by her bed, picked up her Bible from the kitchen shelf and shook it, releasing a shower of old flowers and letters, mostly from me. I looked in the pie safe and the rafters, the rag bin and her apron pockets. Nothing. Not even other secrets; her life was as plain as the pie tins she kept scrubbed clean. I knew she might come back while I was still searching, but I could not care. In my mind's eye I could see the paper, folded in half and covered, on the inside, with her print: A street, a town, a Sir and Madam.

You.

She found me sitting among a pile of her dresses, the whole house tumbled from my search. Luke saw the heap of cloth, clapped his hands, and dove into it. My mother looked around.

"Out!" she screamed. "Out of my house! You ruin everything, you're nothing but trouble, ruining my whole life! Who are you, to go through my house like this? You get out and leave my things alone!"

The few times she had yelled at me when I was a child, I had burst immediately into tears; now, the louder she got, the calmer I felt, watching her face grow red. You're angry, I thought, because you have nothing, no secrets, no chocolate wrappers or trinkets from the city. Your life is a tiny ironed square, and you're trying to make mine the same.

"It's here, then, isn't it?" I said. "It's here someplace."

My brother was whimpering beside me and reached out to touch my arm, but I swatted him away. He did not cry; still my mother bent down and snatched him up.

"It's all right, Luke." She looked at me. "Don't you dare be rough with him."

I stood, taller than my mother now, and watched her smooth Luke's hair. I could see myself as she must see me—dangerous, a wild animal, someone who might bite a child. She had always told us to stay away from mother animals in the woods. They'll do anything, she said, for their young. Only now here I was, her child grown up, and my own two gone. I did not know which was stronger—my need to make my mother yield, or the drumming ache of wanting my children back.

"Just tell me where the address is," I said. "Please?"

Something crumpled in her face, softened for a moment. To this day I will never know if she was about to tell me. Then she looked around the room at the mess I'd made and touched her temple. "It's here. Someplace you can't sneak while I'm out."

"Tell me."

I pictured my mother's brain all twisted around my children, squeezing them by the waist. I could never get inside her head—for my whole life I had been trying. I might beg her, shake her until her teeth clattered, torture her with words or fire, but I would never get inside. The unfairness of it flattened me.

"They're mine," I said, but my voice was dull. "Just tell me where they are."

"I can't," she said. "Don't you see how I can't? It would only lead to trouble."

I shook my head.

"They're happy and healthy in a fine home, but if you can't take solace in that, you have to try to think of them as dead."

"No—" I said, my gut clutching.

"Not to the world," said my mother, "but to you."

That was the day I took two blankets, a box of matches, some tea, a pot, and two loaves of bread and trudged thirty minutes to the hunting shack on the edge of the bog. Someone had been in there recently—charred wood sat in the middle of the crude fireplace; some venison bones were on the floor. For three hours I huddled in my blanket and cried the loose, childish tears I had not allowed myself in front of my mother. I cried until I crouched in the doorway and vomited onto the frozen ground.

Then I got up and built a fire.

Was this luck, this shack on the edge of my father's bog? Was it a kindness, the things my mother brought me later in the week: more blankets, an iron skillet, a blue tin plate with a black chip like a birthmark on its rim? Every girl wants a house of her own, just her size, with windows and a door. As a child, I had invented a family in this house: Harriet, the father; Jeremiah, the baby; myself, the busy mother. I had knelt inside it making soups and stews and howled like a wolf outside its door. I had found quiet here, too, standing in the dark listening to the rise and fall of my own breath. My mother's father had built this place, and although it was small and meant really just for shelter from a storm, a place to catch your breath or clean your rifle, he had built it from good wood and put down a plank floor.

I was not planning to stay, was not planning anything; each day dripped into the next. Over the first few months my parents brought me a stove, a lantern, a spade and hoe, three chickens from their coop. My father put a real glass window into the frame and strengthened the roof and walls. I sat watching, silent, unsure whether to say thank you or ask why they were not inviting me back home. They seemed to think I had made a decision, or perhaps they thought it was theirs. One day, and the next day and the next, until somehow I had made a decision.

Out of our lives, out to the farthest corner of our land. Anything less, and they will think we murder our own. Anything more, and they will think we live in willful sin.

In the beginning my mother visited me with Luke—to bring me milk and flour and see if my head was bowed. She stood in the doorway, thin and tensed, neither in nor out. Her hands trembled with the disappointment of it all. Luke tried to toddle inside, his arms outstretched.

"No," my mother said, grabbing him by the collar.

Baby, I called out inside myself. Baby come here.

Each time I tried to picture my children, I saw my youngest brother's face, until my days became one long image of Luke, only sometimes he was a girl child and sometimes he was a tiny infant, and always he was there and not there, mine and not mine, my mother standing in between. For a week I would not see him, and something would settle in me, calm. Then my mother would come with food, and he would lurch toward me until I was convinced he was really mine, and I needed to snatch him away.

Bye-a-baby bunting, I wanted to sing to him. *Daddy's gone a hunting, to catch a little rabbit skin, to wrap the baby bunting in . . .*

Other times, I prayed he would choke on my mother's milk and die.

Nights, I could not sleep, but kept going back, again and again, to the months I had spent in the attic room waiting to give birth. I had sung to my children, then, so I was sure they knew my voice. Each time I had drawn a breath, their world had risen, fallen; when I sneezed, they had felt a tiny shock. My blood had become their blood, my skin their skin. The goose broth I'd swallowed had made them fit and strong. Now they were in a strange place, growing away from me, and I lay in the hunting shack trying to picture what size they were, how their heads were shaped, what sorts of pictures passed across their minds. The question that plagued me most was whether or not they could remember me. They had spent nine whole months with me, and so I thought it likely that I had left a memory trace inside them, just as they had left a trace in me. But perhaps they were too small, too animal, to remember even a shape, sound, or voice that was an echo of myself. And though I wanted them to know me, I could not bear to think of how, in remembering, they would feel in their bones that I had let them go.

Lying stiff in my bed, I scrubbed their diapers, lifted them from their cradles, felt the soft spots on their heads. I bathed them in warm water and dribbled it down their fronts, making them squeal. I gave them my finger to suck on, burped them on my shoulder, watched while their breaths rose and fell in sleep. When they cried, I offered them a clean rag dipped in honey to suck on. When they coughed, I put a drop of oil in their throats. My mother thought I was still a child and would not be able to care for them, but she was wrong. I knew about babies, had learned it all from her.

Hold on, I told them. Please. Just wait and I'll be there.

When my grief came to me in pictures like this, it fed off hope and so was bearable, but other times I mourned what I had never known and could not begin to picture. Then my sorrow was shapeless, ending in dry heaves that brought up nothing but nothing.

At first when she came, my mother and I said nothing, only Here is some cornmeal (thank you), and Here is some black tea (thank you), and Your father will be up to patch the holes. Each time, she brought my brother, and with every visit it became harder and harder for me to picture my own two children, their faces blotted out by his.

I began to have terrible thoughts about Luke. Dead, I imagined him, like little Anna. *Such a pretty fat boy, dressed in his finest clothes. He got a hole in his heart, just stopped breathing one day. Can you imagine?* Dead, or else living here with me. Each time I saw him and wished him dead, I knocked on wood to undo my curse, then wished him dead again and knocked, and wished and knocked.

For the first time in my life, I was afraid of myself.

One day, when I looked at my brother's laughing face and saw him stiff and blue, I told my mother I could no longer see Luke, could she leave him home?

"He's your brother," she said, standing just outside my door. "Your own flesh and blood."

"I know."

"Only a child."

"I know."

"Just where should I leave him? Your sister is sick, with one of her own on the way, your father is working, John is thirty miles away. I'll leave him playing by the stove, is that what you want? So I can walk all the way over here to give you some bread?"

"I know you can't leave him all alone. I can't—I just can't see him, that's all. Please take him away."

I looked up at my mother, and something in my eyes must have frightened her, for she picked up my brother and turned his face into her shoulder.

"Sometimes I wonder if the devil's in you," she muttered, and I wanted to say yes, let that be it, for then they could take me to the church and tug on me with all their clean spirits, and the devil would fly out. But I knew I had no devil inside me, no stranger. I said nothing, and closed my face.

My mother stopped bringing me things. When, rarely, she came with a pail of milk or seven loaves of bread, she was a woman gray with bitterness, two children dead, Harriet ill from a miscarriage and a thickness of the blood, myself a bringer-on of shame. She left the things outside the door and walked off, holding my brother tightly by the hand. Now I wish I had gone to see my sister as she lay ill or tried to comfort my mother in her grief. But I *was* a large portion of her grief, and at the time I could not feel the weight of any sorrow on top of my own.

Three times I went to her house on Sundays when she was at church and searched again for an address—but carefully now, leaving no traces of myself. Three times I found nothing, just her clothing folded neatly, her Bible emptied out of flowers, her still, still life.

Sometimes people came out to see me: Eliza's mother, who said Eliza had one son, then two sons, then three sons and was too far and too busy to come home much. Karl Smith, slow-witted as an ox, who brought me a tin pail filled with trout, one fish still gasping.

"Did my mother tell you to come?" I asked, squinting up at him in the sun.

He shrugged his enormous shoulders and held out the bucket. For a moment I had a flash of how small I was beside him—how, at the least twitch of his will, his broad weight could push me onto the ground. But then I stared up at his small, blue eyes and remembered the boys I had taught at the school, the way they could not look at me straight on when I asked them questions.

"Why," I asked, in my calmest voice, staring him down, "are you bringing me fish?"

He shrugged.

"Did someone send you here? My mother?"

He shifted his feet.

"Who sent you here?" I tried to make my voice kinder.

"They say—some say . . . there's talk you're looking to marry." Against the bucket, the fish's tail made a steady thudding sound.

I shook my head. "You can tell my mother not to make folks walk all the way out here for nothing."

"Yes, ma'am," said Karl Smith. He looked down uncertainly at the bucket in his big hands.

"Take them back," I said. "Fry them up for dinner."

If I hadn't been so angry at my mother, I might have said I was sorry, I knew it wasn't his fault. He looked at me again, as if he was not sure what I had just told him. Then he turned and left, his bucket sloshing water.

Once a month a woman from the church came, her mouth tight with disapproval, her arms heaped with food. Sometimes I said no thank you, but if I were sick, or hungry, or simply too tired to feed myself, I took the basket, but did not bow my head in shame. Sometimes I walked to town to get things, hoarding the money I had left from the mills, a few pennies for this, a half-penny for that. Slowly I began to make small things to sell and trade: pine baskets, twig brooms, bowls I carved from wood. Most of what I made went for food and coal, but I managed each month to save a tiny bit so I could go back to the mills and look for my children. After I had been home for over a year, I thought I had enough to stay in the city for a few days and place an advertisement in the newspaper.

The day I set out to go was in late April; I washed my hair and put on my best dress. It was a Thursday, the day the traveling peddler came through. I would smile at him, and he would take me in his cart. I remember I gathered my money and put it in my stocking; I wrapped an indigo ribbon in my hair. I walked to town and stood outside the Bennetts' house by the peddler's laden cart and dusty horse while he visited with Mrs. Bennett. When he came out, I smiled at him and said good day; he was a new one and would not know who I was.

I made up a story of an old sick aunt who lay dying in the city. I need to see her, I said. She's dear to me and is not long for this world. Might I come with you, I said, if you're going toward Lowell or Boston? I used my old tricks—the smile, the tilt of the head, but they felt funny to me now, like a dance I had not done in years. He looked at me for a long time, studying me, and I could tell he did not believe my story.

"What's a girl like you need in the city?" he asked. He was a young man, not much older than myself, with a plump and pleasant face. I almost told him the truth, but thought better of it. My aunt, I repeated. A dear old lady. No family near her; I need to be by her side.

Finally he agreed to take me, but said first he had to make his rounds to the other houses. Wait by the church, he said.

At first I did not want to stand there, not where everyone in town could see me, but then I realized it did not matter: I would go to the city and find my children, take them away and never come back to this town. An hour passed, and another. I stood at first, then sat on a low stone wall. People walked by— some I did not know; Eliza's mother, who nodded to me but did not say hello. Finally the peddler returned. I rose to climb into the cart, but he held out his hand to stop me.

"I need to pick up a load of goods halfway there," he said. "Turns out I won't have room."

Something dropped inside me. "Please," I told him. "I can sit up front, I can pay you, please—"

He shook his head, and I knew he had spoken to my mother.

"Please," I said again. "Don't believe—"

"I don't believe you have a dying aunt in the city," he said, and I felt my anger rising.

"Then I don't believe you have a load of goods to pick up halfway there," I returned. "What did she tell you?"

"You *are* a little spitfire. Fair enough about the load of goods. I can't take you, though. Two liars behind one old nag could only lead to trouble. Sorry, miss."

"I've lost—" I started.

But he snapped the reins and left me standing there.

After that, something gave up inside me, something broke, and I fell into a sort of dream. When I had to, I wandered about and found things to eat, or went to town to buy or trade things, but mostly I stayed in the house, for though I would never have told my mother, I found a dulled peace there, a way to sit still with my thoughts.

This corner for one cradle, this corner for another. All those little cloths, one after another until I think my back will break. Oh now shush, my apple, my goose. This to rub on the rash, this to smooth in the creases. This (oh, but you must stop crying) to calm the ache in your stomachs which will not stop.

Looking back, I'm quite sure something had gone wrong in my head by then, time slowing as if I were underwater, a woodenness to my thoughts, a longing but with nowhere to put it, nothing to do with it. Perhaps I went crazy, lost some sort of footing. Sometimes I think it was the events of my life that led me there. Other times I'm not so sure, look back and see myself from birth as a windup top, headed for a spin no matter what. Who can say? I fed myself, kept myself alive, though I was not sure why. Whole months passed without my noticing. Seasons changed, and I barely looked up.

For three years I went on like this; I might have been a

woman in a madhouse, except I had no keeper. My sister Harriet died during this time. My mother came out to tell me, and all I could think, watching her flat with grief, was how it should have been me, not Harriet. I wish I could say I mourned my sister, but I had no room left. Life itself seemed a foolish, grinding thing, easily left behind, yet my own heart beat and beat, keeping me in the world. All day long I spoke to my children, and to my mother: "Hush now, goslings," and "Here, Ma, look how she takes the apple, look how she has your eyes." Sometimes in my mind I shook my mother, screamed at her, but other times I said I was sorry, I wished it hadn't all come out this way, and couldn't we sit, still, in the fields as the wind came up?

The year I turned twenty I woke up a little, like an animal coming out of a long, slow sleep. I do not know what made this happen. My mother would say it was time healing wounds, but I do not think so. It was more that I got tired of not feeling the edges of the world, or knowing where I ended and it began. I remember herbs started to have a taste again— the sharp sweetness of mint, the piney taste of rosemary. *Enough*, I remember thinking one day as I sat listless by the bog. It did not replace *why*, but rather sat beside it, like two words on a chalkboard.

After that, I tried not to speak to myself out loud so much. I cleaned my house and trimmed my hair. I started to carve things for my mother—lace bobbins and pine cooking spoons with faces carved into their hollows. The gifts stacked up beneath my bed.

16

Just when I thought I might actually leave a present on my mother's doorstep, Amos fell in the woods. It was a hot afternoon in August the day I found him. One of my chickens had wandered off, and I was walking through the woods calling for her—*here chick-a-chick*—and click-cluck-ing with my mouth. My hair, I remember, was loose down my back. My arms were brown and bare. It was the sort of day I liked, the kind when I was simply living where I lived, wandering like a cat, the sun warming my scalp.

When I was little, Jeremiah and I had played a game we called Finding, where you walked or even crawled through the woods with your head bent low, looking for something to find. It might be a jack-in-the-pulpit or pitcher plant; it might be a piece of stirrup, a hair ribbon or newt, or even the gleaming droppings of a deer. It had to be a surprise, something you didn't know was there, and you couldn't ever find the same thing twice. When you found it—whatever it was you were not looking for—you clapped three times and yelled *Finders Keepers*. Then the other person came and looked. Between the two of you, you decided how many points the thing you'd found was worth, on a scale of one to ten.

It was a silly game, but as a girl I had loved how it made me feel like the woods were full of promises, and I loved the moment of finding something and opening my mouth to call. The day I found Amos, I was singing out and looking for my chicken. I was not watching the ground for hidden findings; I had only one thought—where was she, and could I find her before she was taken by a fox? I might have walked right by Amos—he did not call out, too proud—but something (an arm, the cloth of his shirt, the eyes I have grown to love?) caught my attention, and I stopped.

"Oh," I said. "Pardon me."

He remembers that, how I looked as if I had come down from a cave in the mountains but spoke as if I had walked into a parlor and surprised him there. He was lying on the ground, propped on one elbow, his wooden leg in his arm. I had seen him before, passed him in town a few times, but I did not know his name, or who his family was, or why he was lying in my woods. I might have turned, then, and gone. It crossed my mind—to say good day and leave him there. Or I might have startled as if I'd seen a ghost and called I'm sorry and run off. I was used to myself, by then, and company confused me. My arms were bare, and this was a man who had one leg and was cradling a second, wooden one like a doll.

I stopped in front of him. "I—my chicken has run off."

Amos nodded. "They'll do that."

"She's—" I wasn't sure why I was telling him, but the words kept tumbling from my mouth. "She's brown and white, mostly, speckled. She's much too stupid to find her own way back—" I stopped then, aware, all at once, that he was squinting up at me, looking at me hard as if I were some sort of creature he'd never seen. "I'm sorry," I said. "Are you all right?"

Amos nodded.

"But your—I mean, can you put it back on?"

He shrugged. "Blasted thing just won't sit right, and now the strap is broke and my—" He flicked a finger toward his stump. "It's not healing so fast, I guess. I figured I could be up and walking again in no time, but it's—" He shook his head hard. "I'm fine, I reckon. You better go along and find that chicken before she gets gobbled up."

I kneeled then. I sat close to him and did not say a word, just lifted the end of his pantleg to see where they had taken off his leg. The bandage must have fallen off for the wound was right there, caked with dirt, lined with blood and jagged stitches, the skin still blue with bruise. Amos sucked in his breath when I touched the cloth, but he did not stop me. Later he told me he was too surprised to do anything but watch—this girl in the woods singing like a chicken, her hair loose, her eyes wary, her hands reaching out to touch a stranger's leg.

"One minute," I told him, and I ran. To my house for a bucket, to the stream for water, back to my house again, for I had forgotten rags and a length of string. As I made my way back to where he was, something lifted inside me—a tiny waking of excitement, a steadiness of purpose. And then, as the water sloshed from the bucket, wetting the front of my dress, a warning voice: he'd be gone when I got back there. He was just a vision, some figment of my mind, from spending too much time inside myself. And then my mother's voice: *Don't touch.*

Amos was still there, sitting all the way up now, his leg once again covered by his pants. "Never mind," he said. "I'll be all right."

I put down my bucket, kneeled. "It's covered with dirt. It'll fester."

"It doesn't matter," said Amos.

"Here—" I handed him the wet rag. "You do it, I won't look."

I stood and turned my back to him, waited there feeling his presence, another breathing person in the woods. Then he spoke again.

"I—I can't," he said. "I can't touch it, it makes me—I get sick, I know I should be cleaning it but—"

"I could . . ." I didn't know what else to say. Clean it, touch you, wash it off, help.

"Only if you don't mind," Amos said. "It's not a pretty sight."

"I saw already."

He nodded. "And you don't mind?"

"No."

I sat by his side, lifted the cloth and cleaned. I hummed while I worked and did not look at him. Instead, I moved the rag in light, careful circles, over and over the wound. I would have thought that touching something so raw and open would have made me recoil, but I felt calm, almost happy: here was some dirt, here I might wipe it away. I cleaned until there was nothing more to do, and then I wound the stump with some fresh rag and rigged up the string to hold the leg on until he could get the strap fixed. At one point as I was winding, he reached down to help and our hands brushed. How warm, I remember thinking, the way only a person can be.

We finished tying on the leg, and I stood. He had dropped two crutches when he fell, so I handed them to him. Slowly he hoisted himself up and took a step.

He smiled then—a thin, quiet smile, but a smile nonetheless. "Let's find that chicken of yours," he said.

"It's all right, I'll find her. Your leg must hurt."

"When did she wander off?"

"I don't know. I only have three and they just poke around outside. I need to make them a house. I went to check that they were all there an hour ago and she was gone."

"You go this way," he said. "And I'll go that."

"But your leg—"

"I need to practice."

"But you still need to walk home."

"You go this way," he repeated, "and I'll go that."

And so Amos and I hunted for my chicken, the two of us calling out—*here chick chick*—so that our voices sometimes crossed in the air, and I'd look over to see him hobbling along through a stand of trees. We looked here and there, under branches and inside bushes, and it was like when I was little, playing Finding, so that I almost expected to glance through the trees and see my brother's shock of blond-white hair. We couldn't find the chicken, and after a while I called out to him that I thought we should give up.

"All right, then," said Amos, making his way to where I stood. He didn't thank me. He didn't ask if he could come out here again. I would have liked to tell him he was always welcome—Welcome Tired Stranger To Our Home. Instead I said nothing, and he saluted me like a sailor and turned to go. Watching him hobble away, I imagined how I might have invited him in, heated the water, made him tea in my chipped cup.

No, I told myself then. No, don't be silly. A total stranger and a man.

After he left, I went back into the woods to look a little longer for my chicken. *Here girl*, I called. *Come home come home*, but I knew she never would. The leaves were matted where Amos had been lying, and I sat in the hollow and hugged my knees close to my chest. Something came over me then—a deep, deep tiredness at being so alone. *Enough*, I thought again. *Please find me*. And I might have been talking to Amos, or I might have been talking to my mother, or I might have been talking to my chicken, who was probably in the mouth of a fox. I remembered the girl in the forest, the good and bad eggs, and lay down on the forest floor and slept.

It took him almost a month to come back, but one day I looked up from making a basket and there he was, a bag slung over his shoulder.

"Morning," he said. "Found her."

"You didn't."

"Yep. Found her over in my own coop, must've followed me. She made herself right at home." He opened the bag and pulled out a white chicken with a red comb. He set her down, and she started pecking at the ground.

"Oh," I said. "She's so changed, I hardly recognized her."

"Just like the trees," said Amos. "Happens every fall."

How strange, a voice inside me was saying. How strange to talk to nobody and nobody, and then along comes this man, and here we are joking, and how strange that it hardly feels strange at all.

"How's your leg?" I asked.

"Dirty," he said, "as a skunk's behind."

And so. And so one thing led to another, and I found myself a little less alone. I was twenty when I met him. Amos was twenty-four, proud and disappointed. If it hadn't been for him, perhaps I would have come back to my parents or gone into the town to marry someone like Karl Smith. Only for so long can a soul go on so stiff and solitary, talking to the air. But Amos was like me, on the edge of things and lonely. After I had known him a few months I told him about my children and he said he knew already, of course, but if I liked he could arrange with a friend to get a notice into the Boston papers asking for their whereabouts.

"It won't work," I said. "I don't even know if they're in Boston, and why would anyone answer a notice?"

"Do you want to do it?"

I nodded and began to love him.

Seeking two children, age four, age six, age eight. Seeking one child, for perhaps the two of them were separated, though my mother had said that they were not. Seeking a child with its mother's gray eyes and the chestnut hair of both its parents. Or its grandmother's green-brown eyes. I could only guess. Seeking a child, or two children, taken from their mother in Lowell, Massachusetts, on February 2, 1846. To see, not to reclaim. I knew it was too late for that. To see as an aunt or sister. To see as a friend. Seeking a boy and a girl, or two girls, or two boys. I grew dizzy with the possibilities, put in one notice, sold more baskets, put in another notice, giving it to Amos to send to Boston. Nothing ever came back.

Amos fell, and I cleaned him off. I wonder if he thought of me as fallen, and that was why he let me touch his wound, or later, touched me how he did.

First once a month, then once a week, then more often, he would come see me, and my days become moments stretched between those visits. He brought me more chickens, helped me build their shed. Each day I looked among the hay for eggs, smooth gifts. Later he brought me my rabbits, just a pair of them at first. You can spin thread, he said, make things out of their wool, to sell. Sometimes Amos lay with me. I was stiff at first, and scared. Amos too. Slowly I came to know the hollow in the middle of his chestbone, the small of his back. Slowly I peeled back my layers of cloth for Amos, one careful layer at a time.

At first I thought only of how I did not feel so alone when I was with him, of how his skin was salty and his lashes brushed my face like blades of grass. At first I thought of nothing but the moment, and he did not find his way inside me, but rather held me quietly, gently, encircling my waist, and we tasted each other, but in the quietest, slowest way.

I am lucky, I thought. Funny how I am so unlucky, but then somehow I am lucky too.

One day, a few years after he had started coming to see me, it came to me how we might make another child. It was such a simple thought, but for some reason it took a long time to arrive.

Once, twice, I thought, now it could happen a third time, like in a fairy tale. I was still young, but not so stupid now; this time I would know how to keep it. I did not say anything to Amos, but the next time he came to my bed, I did not turn away after a time the way I usually did.

"All right?" he whispered as I pulled him toward me.

I pressed my hands into the small of his back and felt him climb deep inside me.

Go on, I whispered to my insides. Turn to fingers and toes, ribs, a skull, a heart.

Afterwards, I lay in his arms and knocked on the wood frame of the bed. I could not even speak of it to Amos, for fear of scaring the third, last chance away.

My mother came out once after he had starting staying with me sometimes and said, "People are talking again, you heap trouble upon trouble."

I leaned over and stroked my rabbit's ears.

"Are you talking of marrying? You do know that man is godless and deformed, hasn't set foot in a church in years, never mind wash his face. Folks around here pay him to do nothing, out of charity, but we all know he's spending it on drink. Oh, he feels sorry for himself, but he could have married, he could have stayed with the church instead of watching through the window like he does."

I scooped up my rabbit, held her bulk against my chest.

"You are, aren't you?" she said. "You're talking of marriage to that man."

I shrugged.

She sniffed. "I know what you're doing, everybody knows."

I looked up at her. Near my feet were the presents I had made her, hidden under the bed. Over my head in the rafters were the letters she had sent me at the mill.

"You should hear what they say about you," she said. "I thought maybe you were coming to your senses, maybe things would be all right after a time, but then you take up with a cripple, let a man visit you out here for hours, days at a time. You *make* your life the misery it is, don't you see that? You do know if you have a child it could be deformed? Deformed and a bastard. You do know that, don't you? You'd really bring a child like that into this world?" Her cheeks were pink, her eyes shining. "If you heard what they said, you'd never hold your head up again."

"You know nothing about him," I said softly, locking gazes with her. "He's a good man, more charitable than . . . He's—" My voice broke. "He's good to me. Don't you see, I'm all alone out here."

Meet my eyes, I pleaded in my mind. For a moment she did.

I thought maybe she would say: I know, come home, child, it's been long enough, for both our stubbornnesses. Or if she could not say that, then at least she might say: I know, I do not approve of his visits, but I understand the chalky feeling in your fingertips, your throat, when days passed, days then weeks, and no one came.

It may have been long enough, for both our stubbornnesses, but they had hardened on us like a glaze. I did not look down, nor let my longing through my eyes.

My mother's eyes dropped, and she turned to go. "Enough," she said, her voice flat. "I don't want it anymore."

It was the last time she came to see me, and that time, she did not leave me any food.

When I hear my own story in my head, it sounds like someone else's life. At each moment, it might have happened otherwise. It is easy, now, to say what could have been: I could have bowed my head and moved back with my parents, married a man who was slow of mind but good of heart, learned to walk with a gentle air of shame. Before that, Eliza or Constance could have stayed at the mills, staving off my loneliness, or the penny-sized disc in my loom could have remained whole that day so that William would have had no reason to appear. Jeremiah, my brother, my Jeremiah could have stayed healthy and lived long, or earlier, he could have been working in the fields instead of climbing up into the loft.

My mother could have helped me to keep you, instead of taking you away. But then who am I to point a finger? She raised me from the cradle, taught me everything I know, and everything I have had to unknow. I have done nothing for you.

I could have been named Charity or Grace, been stronger, or more yielding. I could have been further from my mother, or closer; further from William, or closer. I could have been born a child who walked the middle road; instead, I needed both solitude and touch with a hunger that left me breathless, split in two.

It does not matter.

It does not matter because I left home, and Jeremiah died, and into my sorrow came my broken loom, and into me came William, and out of me came you. This is how lives are born, out of the climbing of a ladder, the breakdown of a machine. Believe me, it is nothing I regret.

My regret is that I did not struggle more to keep you. I might have taken you here to this house, fed you on my own milk and the vegetables from my garden. It would not have been easy, the winters cold, but my mother might have softened when she saw you, taken us in for the worst months. The people in town would have looked away from you at first, but children can move through almost anything with their clear gazes and sweet breath. Or I might have taken you to Boston, where people move unknown through crowds. I was a good worker, I might have found a way for us.

I might have named you . . . I do not know what. Now every name rings too solid for your ghostliness. Now, if you have made it past childhood, you are women with names I do not know. Now you are catching a glimpse of yourself in a mirror or staring out a window thinking of something you can hardly get a fix on, a stirring of something beyond. You think it is heaven, this thing that comes to you between chores. You think it is God's finger brushing back your hair.

It is the finger of your mother's thoughts.

I was sixteen, stupid and scared. I did not know the way to Boston, or how to plant and harvest my own garden from start to finish, or how, when you lose something, it may leave your side, but it never leaves your head. My mother wrote to me and told me she had found a home for you, and for all those months I could not think my way around that, not with my body so tired and heavy, sleep muffling me, my belly pushing out in ways I could not change.

This is not an excuse. I have no excuses. I am only trying to help you understand.

17

I am staring into nothing when the door creaks and Amos peers in, slung limp over his crutches, a sour expression on his face.

"Afternoon," I say.

He does not answer.

"What's wrong?"

He has not been out to see me for over a week. He shuts his eyes for a moment, then says how it's been a bad few weeks; part of his roof caved in and he can't climb up to fix it. Winter is panting round the corner—a mean one it'll be. He can feel it in his missing leg.

"God-awful lot of effort it takes," he says, lowering

himself onto the bench and throwing his crutches with a clatter to the floor. "Too much effort if you ask me."

"You having trouble getting around?"

"I get around." He knocks on the wood of his leg. "I always get around."

"What is it, then?"

He gestures widely at the world. "What is it? You tell me."

"Some of those boys will climb up and fix the roof for you." I put the kettle on and go for my rag to clean him off, and a bottle of my bog wine. "Ask at the church."

But then I remember he won't go near the church—not because they won't have him, but because he won't have them. I hand him the bottle, and he tilts back his head and drinks.

"What about you?" he asks after a long swig.

"What about me?"

"Winter cold as a witch's teat coming on."

I laugh. "Better a witch's teat than the taxman."

"What? They've been out here pestering you again?"

They gave up long ago, those young men with ruddy cheeks and squinting eyes who used to trudge out to my house with their collection books.

"No. They know there's nothing out here but me, and this pile of sticks, and my rich, lazy rabbits. Not worth the trip. I only meant—"

"Ice, hail and sleet. I'm not getting any younger, hauling those supplies out to you in the middle of—" He takes another drink. "You ever think about moving into town?"

"Town?" I echo softly, as if it were a word I'd never heard before. Really it is a word that has come to mean too many things to me: the world out there, everything I am not, everyone who does not know me or wish to know me. I

understand that it is not truly all these things. It is different
people, town—different houses and gardens; cats and dogs;
women, men and children. It is my childhood schoolmates
still living here, or not. Friends of my mother, or not.

"Town," I say to Amos. "No."

He nods. "I didn't think so. You'd rather freeze to
death out here."

"Me, freeze to death? After all these years?" I have
been getting ready for winter, making preserves and saving
eggs to store in oats for the months when the hens don't lay.
"You have enough to worry about," I tell him. "Don't add
me to your list."

"Good. You're not on my list. Listen, I'm dirtier than
the devil."

"I've heated water. Did you bring soap?"

He hands me a cake, leans back and pulls up his trouser leg.

I clean him. Sometimes I clean him briskly, like a
nurse. Other times I clean him as if he were the piece of
china I found buried in the yard as a child, its pattern coming clear beneath my cloth: one bright bluebird and part of
another, half a bridge, the pearly whiteness of the air. Still
other times I clean him as if he were my son—lovingly, but
with the greatest familiarity, as if I had made him myself.

This time, I kneel down and clean him as if he were a
handsome youth, and I the girl I used to be, pretty as an
angel on the outside, aching like the ghost of Amos's leg
within. He puts down the bottle and makes a low noise in
the back of his throat—a moan caught between pain and
desire. I can tell that the hands he feels are the hands of a
girl who is just beginning to touch things—bright hands,
avid, itching to know the world.

He leans back, eyes shut. Outside, close at hand, something splashes. A fish jumping? A stone, dislodged by the foot of a spying boy? I brush at Amos's leg with my hair, and then his hands, once again, are on my head, and I am a hurt, stubborn woman still almost a girl, and he a young man with his leg in his arms, fallen in the woods right by my house. None of their business, we tell each other. They with their churches and children, jobs and festivals.

I touch his good leg through the cloth of his coveralls. I undo the boot, peel off the wool stocking and stroke his toes. They are tensed and white, downed with fine brown hairs—delicate toes with a look of youth still about them; they curl around my fingers like a hand. Behind his knee on the back of his good leg, I touch the skin that stays soft on everyone, no matter how hard the work they do. Then I see how he swells before me, so I undo his trousers and take him in my mouth, and I am a child nursing, or the earth coaxed open by a root.

Watch if you will, I think to the thing that made the noise in the pond—fish or boy, animal or human eye. Watch and tell, or sink back down into the black water and be still. Sometimes I grow giddy with how little I have left to lose. *The mouth of a strange woman is a deep pit. He that is abhorred of the Lord shall fall therein.* I picture my mother watching through the window from among the trees, her hand clamped in horror and disgust over her mouth. Yet what do I know about her hidden life? My mother was a woman for whom touch, despite herself, was food; I could tell from the way she braided my hair.

Everywhere, people clean each other off, rest upon each other's shoulders and backs, crawl as far inside each other as they can, which is not so far, and yet still they try—and again. Perhaps it is because I am often alone out here, but I find this a remarkable thing.

"Ah," Amos sighs, and his hands tighten on my hair until the roots begin to sting.

Gently, I untangle his fingers from my hair, then lace our hands together, nook to nook. What comes from him is somewhere between milk and water, salt and sweet.

After he has shuddered and spilled, Amos leans down and reaches for my skirts. "Come," he says, "come here."

"Wait," I answer, though another, silent part of me is calling out for him to hurry. I know I am not easy around love. Half of me wants him in me, filling me up. The rest of me worries, round and round: Remember the girl who wanted too much and was left with snakes and thorns.

Amos kisses my cheeks and forehead as I kneel before him, his face on mine, the familiar scratch of beard. I do not pull away, but nor do I lean into him, and after a moment he turns and straps on his leg. Then he goes over to the bed, where he lies back and watches me.

"Somebody will fix the roof," I tell him. "You know what you tell me—you can't be too proud to ask."

He does not answer, my words no comfort at all, so I go to him, and he slides over on the narrow bed. For a moment we lie there straight and narrow, not touching. I breathe in my ceiling, beams and floor; my salt lick, bench and spinning wheel. Amos.

"Come here," I whisper.

"I am," he says.

One by one, Amos parts my layers, blowing on his hands to warm them. Cotton and wool, yarn spun from my rabbits' fur; he parts until he reaches skin. I slide my hands under his shirt, unbutton him, pull him to me. His collarbone, his stretch of neck, the longings of his tongue—I know these as if they were my own. "You *make* your own misery," my mother said to me once, and in some ways she was right, but this, too, I have made, with Amos. A funny little life. A life. Something like happiness, here and there, stumbling and slow. Is this what I was looking for when I was a girl? It is quieter than what I had hoped to find, and more fragile. This—he rises and falls against me—is love between two bodies missing pieces of themselves, two imperfect souls.

It used to be I was waiting for his seed to make a child. Each time I wondered afterwards, hoping for another chance. I thought Amos and I might even marry, build a room onto my house, carve a cradle together. Once there was a child here, a path might be worn between my mother's house and mine. Amos and I never spoke of children or where our touching might lead. He never asked me to marry him.

"Come here," I said, again and again, out of my twin hungers for him and what the two of us might make. Month after month, year after year. Nothing. Something inside me must have gone sour, or perhaps it was a problem with his seed.

Now, when Amos spills inside me, I know it is unlikely we will make anything. I feel how he presses up against my insides and wonder if he can tell how full I am in there already—one and two, you and you. In this darkness, this slipperiness, I can almost lose track of what is in and out. I am a mouth, a breath, a wall of cheek, and he is visiting. And then he is not visiting but simply *there*, and for a few seconds going and leaving are words I do not remember.

Then he is leaving, going. Once again I am myself inside myself.

Two days later, Amos says, "We could get married."
Something tumbles in my stomach. It is early evening. We

have been sitting in my house drinking bog wine and using knives to even off the bottoms of my brooms. Outside it has grown chilly. I have let my chickens come indoors, their wattles blue with cold. When they edge close to Amos, he makes hissing noises and kicks them away.

"Cope cope," I tell them. "Cope cope."

It is the noise my father used to make to calm the horses in a lightning storm; now I use it to calm my chickens and myself. I do not know how to answer Amos because I am not sure how he means his words, which he delivered in the flattest of all tones. He might be joking; he often is, but something tells me he is serious—perhaps the way he will not meet my eyes, or how he keeps trimming the broom long past where he should.

"Married," I say softly, trying to keep my voice as flat as his. "Why? I mean, why now?"

He shrugs. "I never did. You never did." He squints at me. "Did you?"

I shake my head. "But after all these years?"

Again he shrugs. "Never mind. It was just a stupid idea. Too much wine, never mind about it."

No, I want to tell him: I'm waiting for you to tell me why and ask again. But he is silent for a long while, so finally I continue on.

"Where would we live?"

"Never mind." He stands and pushes at the air in front of him, as if to swat me away.

"No, tell me, where do you see us living?"

"I—I reckon I'm fairly settled where I am, in my cottage. It's big enough, you could—"

"I reckon I'm fairly settled, too." As the words leave my mouth, I realize they are true; this shack has become an old friend to me. I am not sure when, exactly, it stopped being the place I went to nurse my wounds and became the place I lived.

"So—well, why not?" says Amos. "We could each stay where we are. I could—visit . . ."

"The way you do."

He nods.

"So the reason for it would be—"

He takes a swig from the bottle. "Don't know, really. Having done it, I suppose. Getting buried—you know—" He laughs, a short bark. "Oh you know, next to someone—all that old talk about Their Bodies Are Buried in Peace, and the Mingling of Bones."

"You're counting on me to go first and save a place for you," I say. "Otherwise you won't be next to anyone at all, not till I join you. When do you have set for me to go? If I know ahead of time, I can make provisions for my animals."

"Oh, Aimee—"

He swallows another gulp, and I see how he has entered his sloppy, sweet stage of drunkenness. As he looks at me, his eyes water and overflow. I take another long swig to hasten meeting him there, for my head is still much too clear inside. He lowers himself down next to where I sit on the crooked bench we built together years ago and presses my hand between his hands.

"Don't go talking like that, Aimee."

"Supposing we go at the exact same minute? That would be a miracle, unless we *made* it happen. Still, where do you expect to be buried, side by side with me? You know they won't have us in the churchyard."

He winces. "I won't have them. In the woods somewhere, I guess. Up in a birch grove or next to some rock. There's a nice big rock over by the Green River. Doesn't matter, really, just the thought of lying there all alone with the worms—"

"I'm not planning on going tomorrow," I say and reach out to knock on wood. "With any luck, we both have a lot of years left."

"Yes," he says, "I know. With any luck."

"But when we *are* buried, what about here?"

He looks around at the walls. "Here?"

"With the chickens grubbing on your head. No, I meant out there—in the bog."

"With all those witch people? I know it's just a bunch of stories, but you want to be buried with all that?"

I nod.

"I don't know," he says. "Why? Have you settled on it?"

"I live here, is all. Not by some rock or in a birch grove. That's all. But I know it's not the same for you."

"No ashes to ashes, dust to dust in this place," he says. "Not with all those minerals in the water. They'll find you a hundred years later with the string of your bonnet still tied under your chin and your final expression stuck on your face—sour or pretty, it won't matter."

"I don't mind."

"Somebody'd have to agree to it. They'd never agree in town. They have rules about this kind of thing, more every year."

"I'll put you there," I say, "if you go first."

"Who has plans for who? Anyway, I'd like to see you dragging me from where I drop, all the way up to this godforsaken place. I'd like to be around to see that."

"And if I go first . . . you'd let them—"

He shakes his head. "I'd see it happened how you wanted."

"And the one who goes second?"

"Shush now! All this death talk. See what I started with this stupid marrying idea. Forget about that—"

Amos reaches out to encircle me. Outside, night is falling, darkness pressing up against the window. I lean over to light two candles, then look at his craggy, kind, familiar face in the yellow light. All at once I wish he had asked me before the mills, before any of it, when his proposal would have meant sewing white linens with my mother, standing at the altar with the blessings of the town wrapped around us, walking home leaning on Amos's arm, both of us so young. But he was in love with someone else when I left for the mills, and anyway he would have seemed to me like all the others: all knobs, and edges, and dull, shortsighted eyes. I, with my own eyes short-sighted in ways I could not see, would not have looked twice.

The one he loved and was going to marry was from this town and lives here still. Five children, he told me once. A house with gas lights. A husband she does not love; he is sure of that. It was frostbite Amos lost his leg to, turned to gan-grene. The woman he loved brought him soup and mustard poultices, and when he was better enough to get fitted for a wooden leg, she told him no.

"What if we had married a long time ago?" I ask. "Before I left, or right after I came back?"

"If, if. You know you wouldn't have."

I wonder how he is so sure.

"Before," he says, "we were just children. But I would have asked after you came back. I'd never seen such a pretty girl, or such a sad one."

I shudder, remembering how like an iron box I felt, how like a red sore. "When I lived out here?"

"I would have asked," says Amos, "except I was a cripple and you had this . . . way about you, a fierceness. People thought you'd gone mad. I used to watch you when you came to town, even before we met out here."

I trace his shadow, lit by flickering candlelight, on the

wall. "I wanted, you know—I hoped we might make another child."

"I know." His voice is not soothing, but hard.

"Would you have wanted that?"

He nods.

"It never happened," I said. "I kept wanting it to, but it just never did."

"I know."

Now the questions fly from my mouth. "So if it had, would you have stayed?"

He nods.

"But it never happened. And it probably never will."

"No," he says. "Probably not, although you never know. Look what happened to Sarah, long after she gave up hope. Funny how some things happen and others don't. That leg hadn't given me trouble for days, I thought I could walk clear to Canada on that new leg, and then it falls off right outside your door."

"You let me clean you."

"So kind of me."

"No," I say, "it was. I was dying out here."

"No, not you. Too stubborn. *I* was dying, flat on my back in the poison ivy."

"You saved my life," I say.

I can feel him shrug.

We marry the next day at dawn, just at the time when the sun would come up if the day were clear. This day is thick with rainless, snowless clouds. We do it ourselves, with a glass of wine and a little of the Bible and a broomstick to step over and back. I wish Plumey could be our guest, but worry that she would think the whole thing too strange, especially now that she is more in the world.

Afterwards I take out my quill, and we write a letter on a page torn from the *Farmer's Almanac:* our names, the date, *Married to Each Other on This Day.* Then we sign it, our names wedged in between the phases of the moon.

"What should we do with it?" Amos asks.

"Bury it? Throw it in the bog?"

"Which?"

"The bog. Throw it in the bog."

We put the page in an empty bottle with some pebbles, seal the top with wax, stand together and send it into the bog pond. Then I give Amos a basket of eggs, the twig brooms and two jugs of wine in a burlap sack, and he slings the sack over his shoulder and starts down the path.

"Good-bye, wife."

" 'Bye, Amos."

What surprises me, watching him make his way around the edge of the bog and out of sight, is that I am not really surprised.

Week by week Plumey grows older, surer—grows away from me, and also toward me, in a movement difficult to trace. Even if she is a sort of daughter to me, she, like all children, will leave her mother for the world. Already it has begun. She came to me a few weeks ago and said she thought she might have made a friend, a girl who had just moved to town. She said the word *friend* with a slight stutter. I could tell it was a miracle to her.

"Will you bring her to see me?" I asked.

She nodded.

"When? I'll be sure to have some tea."

"I don't know."

She was talking now in sentences, just like any other girl. I knew she would probably rather invite her friend for tea in the Doctor's parlor, not beside my bog. They would eat cookies there, and look at dress patterns in magazines. On a thick rug by the fire, they would whisper and braid each other's hair.

"You have a new ribbon," I said. "Pretty."

She reached up to touch the ribbon on her braid. I did not point out to her how sweetly she was growing into her body, her girl fat dissolving to show strong bones. It would only have made her hunch. Someday soon she will be a graceful woman, not beautiful, but with a kind of firmness about her, an air of knowing. She is only eleven, but already lines show on her brow. She is a girl who grew old and lost everything, and then began again. I think, hope, that this will give her strength.

It grows cold these weeks; the rain could almost have been snow. Last night a rainstorm littered the countryside with branches. Now, when Plumey steps into my house, she looks surprised to see me.

"You're here," she says.

I have built a fine fire in the stove. I pat the bench where I am sitting, and she joins me.

"You thought I'd be washed away?"

She takes off her gloves, laces her fingers together, and stares down at her knuckles.

"You know it would take more than a little rain," I say and hand her a clump of the rabbit wool I am picking through.

"Yes," says Plumey, but I can tell what she is thinking—how once before, the world disappeared in a matter of a few sleeping hours, how I might have been struck by lightning or hit by a falling tree, or simply turned to water by the rain. Those things would not seem like freak accidents to Plumey. The accident is that at night the sun sets and the rain falls, and the next day anything remains.

"Did you come to check on me after the storm?"

She shrugs and reaches into her pocket, then hands me a small tub of storebought salve and a heel of bread. She is learning the sullenness, the withholding pose, of a girl-woman. I remember when I learned it myself.

I put the bread on the stovetop to warm it and open the salve. "Thank you."

She must have noticed how I have been moving stiffly; I hurt my back last week when I was hauling water. Or perhaps Amos gave her the salve to bring to me. In its tub it is milky gray and smells like peppermint.

I remember smoothing salve on my mother. She had hurt her back in giving birth to Luke, and a few days later she could still barely move, lying stiff on her side with the baby suckling her. She handed me the salve and told me to pull up her nightclothes. My father turned away then, and disappeared into the other room, leaving me to fumble up under the bunched white cloth to my mother's back. At first I barely touched her skin, as if she might burn me or I burn her, but then she told me to rub harder, push into the muscles.

I rubbed and pressed, felt the backbone of my mother, the wings of her shoulder blades, the long stretches of her skin. I saw how she had freckles in places I had never seen, a pale brown spattering. I rubbed until she told me I could stop, but no longer; I did not like to see my mother lying there like that. With her nightclothes bunched up around her neck, she looked bare and helpless, very young or very old, and her backbone felt as fragile as knobs of hollow glass attached by string. I wanted her to be standing on her feet again. Or, if she had to lie there, I wanted to be not myself but my baby brother, eyes shut, fingers blindly feeling for her.

Plumey is not my daughter; I will wait for Amos to rub the salve. She picks up the rabbit wool from where she put it down on the bench and starts to comb through it.

"It was raining and raining," she says. "I thought the bog would flood."

"It never does. You shouldn't worry."

"The house should be back away from it. You could drown."

"I'm not going to drown. I'm staying right here. You're the one who'll go away, when you get married or want to see the world."

"No no." Her voice is that of a small girl once again. "I'm staying here too."

We could build a little room for her off the side of my house, or even two; maybe with more space, Amos would come to stay. With three of us here all the time, we could let more rabbits kindle, make a whole farm of it, get the long-haired ones from England with their fine white fur. Out of the money we made, I could buy a china set and make cakes, so that she would invite her friends from town.

She might say yes, if I asked. She is still a frightened girl, and this, in its way, is a gentle place. I know she loves me. I must not ask her. She is just beginning to unfurl.

Instead, I begin to tell her bits and pieces of myself. That way, when she leaves me, I will stay with her and have a home in a back corner of her mind. Each time she visits, I tell her a little piece, not in any order, but tumbled, as they come. She seems to like it and stares hard at me as I speak, as if she is trying to see through my face to imagine the girl I once was. It is not difficult for me to tell her my stories, not most of them, anyway. I have rehearsed them, telling them to my blood children. Telling them, in the rough edges of half-pictures, to myself.

I talk; she talks. I tell her about being ten, she tells me about being five. Her brothers who slung her over their shoulders like a sack of grain. The corner of the house where she put a doll's bed a neighbor had made from twigs and carved with her initials.

"I put Mary and Felicity in the bed," she says. "And my—my Mama gave me a piece of calico for a blanket—"

She tries to tell me more about her mother, but instead she sits gasping, trying to fill herself with air. I cannot tell if her brothers loved her gently or tossed her about, if her mother loved her well and now was gone, or had not loved her enough.

"It's all right," I tell her, and put my finger over my mouth to show her I understand. Part of me wants to know everything—what her mother looked and sounded like, what she smelled like. Did she hold Plumey in her arms the way I long to but do not? I have no right to these memories. Plumey does not call me mother, it would be wrong and strange. She does not call me Ma'am. For a long time I think she thought of me as Rabbit Lady. Now, because I have told her it is all right, she calls me Aimee. She does not say it often, and still with awkwardness. In her high voice I hear the deep voice of my mother calling my name, and the voice of her mother calling hers.

I tell her about my father and getting chocolate for Christmas, about the house I grew up in, the crannies in the beams where I used to hide things. I would like to tell her something, anything, about my mother, but find I do not know how to begin.

"That house is still there," I say. "Just a thirty-minute walk across the fields."

Plumey nods. "Who lives there?"

"People."

"Which people?"

"A new baby, for one, called Abigail Susan. That's what Amos tells me, anyway."

She is silent, thinking. Perhaps she knows. Then she looks up at me with her frank gaze. "Abigail Susan," she says, "is a pretty name."

"You like it?"

"I might name one of my daughters that."

"How many will you have?"

She counts off on her fingers. "Six."

"And how many sons?"

"One."

"Just one?"

She nods. "The last one will be a boy."

"Oh? How do you know?"

I know, I would have said at her age. *I just do.*

Plumey shrugs. "I'm only playing."

"You'll be a good mother when you grow up," I tell her. "Your children will be lucky."

"I'm *playing*," she says again, something grim and full of sorrow in her voice.

I tell her the story of the woman whose husband put salt in her skin. I add on the ending my mother sometimes used and bring the woman up to heaven.

"Like that other wife," she says after I finish.

"Which wife?"

"The one who turned into a pillar of salt."

"You mean Lot's wife? Did you hear that at church?"

She shakes her head. "With Amos."

"Amos told you? When?"

"I told *him*. On the path—he makes me read things out loud."

"He's helping you with your reading?"

"Lot's wife," she says, "looked behind her and was turned into salt. She didn't die, like the other one, but she couldn't move ever again."

"It sounds scary," I tell her, "but it won't happen to you."

"I play the preacher," Plumey says. "And Amos plays the town."

One morning, when a brief, first snow has dusted everything, the flakes melting on her hair, I tell her about Jeremiah dying. My favorite brother, I say. When we were very young, I had pretended we were twins.

"Was he your same size?" Plumey asks.

"No. First he was smaller, then he was bigger."

"Oh." She tilts her head in thought. She could be any girl then, asking questions, listening to a story.

"But was he your size in between, for a minute?"

I picture my brother and myself—the small, pale boy, the tall, sun-browned girl; the lanky, red boy, the smaller, itching older sister. And the passing. Was there a time when we had been the same size? Could it have been the moment in the barn?

"No," I say to Plumey. No matter how much I tell her, still I do not come to my children or touching my brother. Part of me thinks I should tell her—as a warning, what happens to a girl whose hungers open her too wide. But Plumey is not like me; already life has made her careful.

Not telling her about my children is something else. This

I might tell her more easily; perhaps an orphan like Plumey would understand. But she is a young girl unversed in the ways of love. I might tell her I had children, but I cannot tell her how or why. At first I thought I could slant the truth, play with it, just as long as I told her the most important things. To simplify, I could invent a husband for myself. Then I remembered my mother wanting to invent a dead husband for me. No, I had said. Liar, I had thought. I cannot let Plumey think I was a harlot, but nor can I invent a dead husband from years ago—not when I have stayed true all these years.

Besides, I can hear her voice: "But why didn't you look for them? Why didn't you get them back?"

Somehow I think she might have found a way.

19

I go to see my mother in my mind.

The path to the house is familiar and not, the smell in the air outside old and new at the same time—a mix of bleach and rising dough, smoke and the lemon scent of her hair. I walk up to the door, the same old slab of oak. Someone has put a knocker on it, a lady's hand clutching a brass ball. No one but my mother is home; I can tell as I stand by the door. Luke is not there, nor his wife, nor their babies. It is a still, quiet house, emptied of family.

Please, I say softly, and I do not knock.

Inside she is waiting. Stubborn girl, she says. How many years?

I show her my hands, palms up.

Stubborn, stubborn girl, she says. You always were.

I reach for her. My hand is no longer a child's; hers seems younger than it used to. When I touch her, her knuckles bend, her fingers soften.

It's cold out, she says. Oh, your hands are cold!

I nod.

Did you knit that shawl yourself?

From my rabbits' wool.

You need to reknot there, she says, pointing to a frayed edge of fringe.

I take up the loose end, twist it into a knot, but the yarn breaks off.

Sit, she tells me.

I sit by her feet, rest my head on her knee.

Aimee, she says, her voice the saddest sound I've ever heard.

I know, I tell her.

It means too many things, and she understands them all.

I will go to see my mother. Not in my mind; I have dwelled there for too long. It is a Sunday afternoon; Plumey is with the Doctor and his wife. Amos drank long and hard last night, stayed with me and went off in the morning to sleep the day away at home. I brush my hair, pin it to my head with my shell comb, take it down. I peer into the mirror, see myself startled and glassy-eyed, sit on the edge of my bed.

Never mind, maybe tomorrow.

Why didn't you find them? I hear Plumey asking, though she never actually said it. She would mean my children, not my mother, but the difference hardly matters anymore. Some things are lost without the possibility of return: Plumey's family, Jeremiah, my father, Anna, Harriet. My twins, lost but not, breathing—this I am sure of—but not where I can sit and watch.

Some things are breathing over the next hill.

Go, I feel Plumey saying, impatient.

I put on my shawl and cloak, leave my house, stand for a moment on the edge of the bog, and draw a deep breath. Then I remember. Under my bed—presents for her, from years ago.

Back inside, I kneel slowly, but I cannot bend far enough to reach under the bed. I use a stick of kindling to grope; one by one, I coax the objects out. A small, carved bird, crude and dusty. She will laugh at it: why this, after all these years? I could make a better one by now. I wipe it off, set it on the floor. Then, like a fisherwoman, I use the stick to fish for other presents. When I am finished, there are four: spoon, bird, basket, lace bobbin. I gather them inside my shawl, put on my cloak and leave.

In my thoughts the path was clear, the trip short. In truth I had forgotten how great is the distance between my house and hers. I remember how to go, but only barely. The world is sharp, cold and sunny, and I walk through the woods, then the fields, then the woods again as if I were coming home from an afternoon of wandering as a girl. I would arrive breathless, brambles in my hair, my ears burning from the cold. Table to be set, she'd say, potatoes to be peeled. Look, I might tell her, opening my fist to show the fragments of an empty robin's egg or a cardinal's feather. For an instant my mother would pause to see what I had found.

With each step I take, I grow less sure. How do you mend something that has been broken for so long? If you leave the fragments of china unmended after the cup breaks, in time each piece gets new chips, tiny ones, until the edges will no longer marry.

I married Amos, I might say to her. I have a daughter named Plumey. My blackberry jam would please you. My knitting is straight and true. When Plumey is ill I give her barky, bitter mixtures, like the ones you made for me.

And then the old anger again, stopping me in my tracks. Because I married Amos but not as she would have wanted me to. Because even in my mind, I must lie to please her, Plumey not my child, not really. Because my mother took them from me, forcing me to lose not only them, but also her.

Step by step I go forward, stop, turn back a little, pivot and go on. Hours pass; finally I get close to the house. Outside, a thin, honey-colored dog raises his head when he sees me, but does not bark. A breath of smoke comes out the chimney; someone has propped a pitchfork by the door. I might knock, a child might answer, or Luke or my mother. They are probably sitting down to Sunday supper around now.

Hello, I could say, for this is what people—strangers, family—say to each other at doors.

I walk up the path and whisper hello to the dog, who sniffs the air, then settles his head on his paws. I curl my hand into a fist, but I cannot seem to knock.

I leave the carved spoon propped against the door.

The next Sunday I return with the basket. I expect, almost, to see the spoon lying, still, where I put it, but it is gone. As I turn to go, I am sure I feel eyes on my back, someone watching. My mother, from a window? My brother Luke? Amos, who always seems to know where I have been?

That night, lying with him, I tell him. "I left my mother a present."

"Oh? When?"

"Today."

He nods, and I feel his fingers twining through my hair. "Why?"

"It was something I made for her. Years ago, before I knew you."

"But you didn't leave it years ago."

"No."

We lie there for a while, drifting. Just when Amos draws close to the edge of sleep, I find I need to tell him more. "Amos?"

"Mmm?"

"I keep—I just keep thinking about Plumey, how she came to see me, you remember, when she couldn't even talk, and she'd lost everything but she brought me things anyway, and maybe she stole them or found them, but she didn't even know who I was and she brought me presents. I kept thinking I'd help her, get her to talk. I—I showed her the alphabet, you know, and how to weave, and she sat there like an idiot child, but the whole time she understood things—"

I know I'm not making much sense. I'm not sure, even, what I need to say, but I can feel words stacked up inside me, vast piles. Amos strokes my arm from the border between sleep and waking.

"She can never find her mother, no matter how hard she tries," I go on. I sit up, so awake, suddenly, that I can feel blood moving through my veins, the places where bone meets bone. "But mine—"

I lie down and reach for him, needing his breath. Though he kisses me back, I can tell he is surprised by my sudden swervings.

"I'm sorry," I say after a moment, pulling away. "I don't

know what's come over me. And you lost your mother, too, I didn't mean to—"

Amos sits, dragged fully into the waking world. "It's all right. Did she like the present?"

"I don't know. I left one this week and another last week. I didn't knock or go inside."

"Did they see you?"

"I don't know."

"Do you want her to?"

"No. I don't know."

"Bring her another one," says Amos, lying back down. "But knock this time."

I leave another one. I do not knock. I am running out of patience with myself, but I cannot seem to find another way. Like a schoolgirl with a crush, I approach with my offerings, then dart off.

Here, here. For you. Nothing, really, something small I made.

They may think the objects are from a child, for one of their own children, or for Luke or his wife. Surely I am the last thing on their minds. *My sister? My daughter? Oh, something went wrong in her head, we never see her. She manages fine on her own, may as well be a stranger, never goes much of anywhere. She was always the wild one in the family, brought us all kinds of shame. Every bushel of apples has its sour one.*

After a month of gifts, just when I need to start making more, Luke comes to call. I know it is him because I have watched him from afar over the years. He is a strapping man, tall, blond and wide, with big, red hands like my father's and cheeks so bright he looks feverish. I see him through the window and sink back onto my bed. When he knocks, I find I cannot answer.

"Hello?" he calls. "Anyone home?"

I hold my breath, as if exhaling might give me away.

"It's Luke," he says, knocking again. "Your brother." Something falls away in his voice when he says the word; a coldness creeps in. "Let me in."

I rise, put one foot forward, then another. I open the door, and he ducks inside my house. His eyes take it in—how small, he must be thinking, but also perhaps, how *right*, filled with what she needs and nothing more.

"You've been leaving things at my house," he says. "Why?"

I perch on the bed, wishing my rabbit were inside so I might hold her.

"Why?" he repeats, but I stare at my knees.

"Please," he says. "Just answer me."

And I remember how small he was, how blond and rosy in my arms, and how much I hated him and loved him. He is all she has left now, this child of her late years, who nursed from her until he was too old.

"For her," I say softly.

He nods. "I gave them to her. But you should have left a note."

Like a child, I want to ask *Did she like them*? Did she praise the workmanship, admire the effort, prop them on top of the pie-safe?

"She's doing poorly," he says. "She's more and more feeble-minded and in poor health. She's—" he shrugs, "not at all well."

"I'm sorry," I say, for I see, all at once, how he is the one who has lived his life with her; how he, not I, will feel the vaster hole when she is gone.

"She says your name now and then. In her sleep, or other times. I thought—I reckon Mary and I thought it might do her a little good to see you." He laughs, a harsh, croaking sound. "Either that or send her to her grave."

I stand up and smooth my hair. "Tomorrow?" I ask, meaning can I come then, but it sounds as if I'm asking if tomorrow she will go to her grave.

"She's not well," he repeats, and I hear how tired he is. "Come in the morning if you're coming, when the rest of us are at church."

He bends his head to duck out the door. My brother, the one I never really knew.

"Luke?"

He turns toward me, his face half-hidden from the glare.

"Thank you," I say.

"I'm doing it," my brother answers, "for her."

I rise the next morning at dawn and heat water for a bath. Outside, the air is cold. Inside, the house grows foggy from the steam. I sit in my tin tub and scrub my outsides clean. Not the body of a girl, nor that of an old woman; I am, for the moment, in between. I pour water over my head and wash my hair, comb it out, twist it into a knot. I cannot peer into the mirror, for it is all fogged up. I put on my cleanest dress, my newest shawl. Slowly the room grows lighter, day finding its way in. I make a cup of tea but cannot drink it, lift a piece of bread to my mouth—too dry. I walk outside to feed the rabbits and chickens.

"I'm going to see my mother," I tell them, and they take no notice, which somehow comforts me. It is too early, still, for me to leave, so I bring the blind rabbit inside and brush her, saving the fur to use later on. I smooth my dress, repin my hair, chew on a cinnamon stick to freshen my breath. I knit a little, card some wool, return the rabbit to her lean-to. Finally the sun is high enough.

Leaving my house, I walk. This time I do not stop or stumble, turn or pause. The air smells like snow, but the ground is bare, the ash trees gray, the birches peeling to show their pale pink underskins. This time my hands are empty; I bring my mother nothing but my self.

The house, when I get there, seems hushed and quiet, a scrap of paper pinned to the door: *come in.*

I turn the handle, open the door.

No, I think, the old hungers and angers, fears and aches rising like food into my throat. But there I am—*come in*—and I know I cannot turn away.

"Hello?" I say softly, and receive no answer. "Hello?"

I find her sitting by the stove in the kitchen, her back to me, her head bent toward her chest. She might be sleeping, rocking a little in her dreams, the nape of her neck pale and bent, her hair in a neat, coiled braid. For a long moment I stand there and simply watch her from behind—my mother, with eyes in the back of her head. I'm sure she knows I am there and so I wait for her to turn, but a minute passes, then another, and she does not move.

"Hello?" I say again, and her head lifts up.

I walk in front of the chair to where she can see me. "Hello," I repeat, the only word I remember how to say. My mother looks up with her mossy eyes and for a moment everything inside me drops to my feet, and I am empty and calling—*hello, hello*—a girl again, and then a baby—*mama mama*—and then an infant sounding out in wordlessness, a long, fierce howl.

Then my pieces come back to me. I am visiting my mother, years and years have passed. I am myself.

"It's me," I tell her. "Aimee."

She squints at me.

"Hello," I say again.

"Hello," my mother says, and her voice is not the one I remember, but a higher, reedier voice, and somehow also flatter too.

"I—I left you those things, the spoon and baskets—" I falter. "I made them for you—a long time ago."

She looks in my direction and I kneel, wanting to get closer, but unsure, suddenly, if she can see at all.

"Did you get them?" I ask. "I wanted—"

"Sometimes," announces my mother, "the boys get back late."

"Luke?"

"John, Jeremiah, all the rest of them. I can't keep it warm, it gets dried up."

"Supper?"

She nods. "You can't *keep* meat cooking forever, don't you see? And then he says it's dry. You can't—" Her voice is unhappy, thin. She shakes her head, makes a rapid *tsk-tsk-tsk* sound that I remember well.

"They'll be back in time."

"Yes?" asks my mother.

"Yes."

She is here and not here, spinning in some other time. I think of Plumey, the way her words, when they first came, were almost always in the past. With Plumey I could speak that language, but I need for my mother to know me now.

"Mother?" I say, the word both foreign and familiar on my tongue.

She nods, seems to tilt a little toward me.

"It's me," I repeat. "Aimee."

"Aimee," she says. For a moment I look into her eyes to see myself reflected back, and something settles in me. Then I realize she may only be parroting my name.

"Aimee," I try again. "You know, your daughter. The one who lives on the other side of the land, the one—"

The one you told stories to, whose name you picked from *The Ladies' Pearl*, the one who heaped shame upon shame, lay with men, the one with the babies you made her give away, the stubborn one . . .

I start to cry, wordlessly, sitting at my mother's feet. I cry because she does not know me and years have passed; because I can explain nothing now, mend nothing; because she has lost her quickness, her vivid, lovely mind with its stories and sayings, commands and buried yearnings.

"Not enough," she says, her voice a whine now, a broken thing. "It'll never thicken."

You heap trouble upon trouble, I remember her telling me.

"More cornstarch, please, right in the pan," she says, and I hope she is saying it to some shadow that is me in another time.

We talk. Past each other, around each other. My mother talks of burned food and sick babies, of ants in the floorboards and on skin. Mostly her voice is troubled, but now and then she smiles and sounds happy: the calico has had kittens; the snap peas are coming in well. She names my brothers and sisters as I listen, but not me. I tell her about Amos and Plumey. My daughter, I say, lying a little but telling the truth as well. I tell her I'm sorry to have blamed her for so long for things I started on my own. I should have known better in the first place, I say, but still I wish I'd kept them. I say I cannot be sorry that I did not bend my head in shame. I could not live a life like yours, I tell her, and I remember how right from the start I went off to play on the edges of our land, not a girl who lived well in the middle, too much to taste, too many ways to go wrong.

My mother hears nothing, or not in ways I can see. After a while I have said enough, and so I talk with her about ironing and folding, and then in a way we *are* talking to one another, for she speaks, and I answer, and she answers back. We are not in this time, not in this world, but still we are somewhere making sense.

An hour passes, maybe two. I put more wood in the stove, make my mother and myself a cup of tea. I pull up another chair and sit by her side. Her hand shakes when she tries to lift the cup, and the hot tea slops into her lap.

"Oh," I say, rising to take the cup from her and get a rag.

"Hot," she says, but calmly, as if it does not hurt.

I find a rag and come near to swab at her dress. When I draw close, I smell the lemon scent of her hair.

And then she has lifted her hand and placed it on my head. My mother, after all these years. I cannot tell if she knows that I am me, but her hand is the hand I remember, and I stoop there trying not to move, feeling her weight on my thoughts. She strokes my head, up and down, back and forth, brushes a loose strand of hair from my face and tucks it into my bun. She touches my brow, my eyelids, pauses her fingers for a moment on my damp cheeks. I am no longer crying or spinning backwards; I am *there*, all bright, crystallized attention. Then she stops, and I peer into her eyes.

For a moment (I am almost sure), she sees me.

Say my name, I think. Luke says you say it sometimes. Please say it now.

"Not enough teeth in that boy's mouth," she says instead. "I worry they won't come in."

She is talking, I know, about Luke, whose teeth were late. I think we have had this conversation before, after I came back from the mills. Then, I must have clenched my own teeth, felt my tongue thick and angry in my mouth. Now I answer her.

"He'll be all right. He'll grow up big and strong."

"Yes?"

"And take care of you."

She nods. As I sit there, something in me mends a little, and I watch my mother drift quietly to sleep.

I leave before they get back from church. Before I go, I take the note off the front door, write a message on the other side and prop it on the table: *I will come next Sunday unless you tell me no.* To make her tea, talk to her. To be there when my mother says my name.

A cold spell settles, brittle, on the land. My window is crosshatched with frost, but I rub a peephole in its center. In the late afternoon, three days after my visit to my mother, Amos comes out to help me bank my house. He brings two boys from town; I don't know where he found them. He brings Plumey, all bundled up in a new gray cloak, her yellow hair covered with a scarf. When I see them coming in a crooked line, I, too, begin to put layers on top of my layers. This is a cold that reaches right through me. For several days I have been coughing, shivery and weak, something coming on.

By the time Amos gets to my door I must be scarcely

visible beneath my bundlings. He laughs when he sees me. I start to move past him, but he bars the door with his arm.

"Let me by," I say.

"I brought help. You stay in."

"What do you mean, stay in?"

For years we have banked the house together. This year, like every year, I have the leaves waiting, held in piles by branches crisscrossed up the sides.

"You were feverish last night." He touches my forehead. "You still are."

Outside I can hear voices, the boys laughing. I worry they are taunting Plumey. Amos blocks the door, so I go to my peephole and see that she, too, is laughing, her head thrown back. I realize I have never heard her laugh out loud like that. One of the boys says something, and she ducks her head, then darts a look back up, delighted and shy.

Be careful, I want to tell her. Where did she learn to look like that, so coy?

"Come in or stay out," I tell Amos, who is still hunched in the doorway, letting the cold air in.

He steps inside and shuts the door.

"Where did you find those boys?" I ask. I wish I could tell if they are the same ones who have made trouble here in the past. Perhaps Plumey has made friends with the boys who made her cry; nothing she does would surprise me much by now.

"In town. I bribed them," says Amos.

"With what?"

"A fine jug of your bog wine."

"You didn't."

He nods.

"But they're only children. When they come home

smelling to the sky, their parents will think I gave it to them.''

''What does it matter? They're here to help. They'll deserve something after their work to warm them up. Me, too, I'll deserve something. Why should they get left out?''

Amos wants me to stay in, but I follow him out into the cold. Outside, the children are already clearing the ditches left over from last year's bankings. The hollows have filled, over the summer, with brush and twigs, chicken feathers, part of an old sack. Plumey glances over but does not say hello. For a moment I am hurt, thinking she will pretend she does not know me. Then I hear her humming: ''I had a little nut tree . . .''—a secret song since the others don't know where she learned it. Her cloak is covered with scraps of leaves. I picture her silent, throwing maple leaves into the bog.

Around us the world is a sharp and fragile thing. Twigs snap, brittle, when we step on them; the shallow parts of the pond are sheeted with thin, cracked ice. We have not had our first blizzard yet, but it will not be long. Then the land will be blanketed, easier. As the children clear the ditches, Amos and I lift the cross-branches from the piles of leaves. Everything is matted underneath, turned from crimson and yellow to a red-brown color like dried blood. One by one, we free the piles from their stays. After we have put the branches in a heap behind the garden for next year, the children come to our leaf piles and take armful after armful, staggering, as if drunk already, back to the house, where they have pounded in stakes on the edges of the ditches to hold the leaves.

There they pad and muffle, leaf by leaf, building vegetable walls against my wooden walls until the piles almost reach my window. Plumey tries to outdo the others, moving faster, breathless, covered everywhere with leaves.

This is how I stay warm in winter, second-skinned. I would like, now, to burrow down inside a pile of leaves, for the cold air has crept deep inside my layers, making me tremble despite myself. I would like to dig down to where the soil still holds traces of summer—below the frost heaves, to where nothing is chapped or cracked. When I was a girl I could stay out for hours in this weather, hardly feeling it. Now I tighten my cloak and cough into my hands.

"Go inside," Amos says. "Go on," he says. "Go inside and get warm. Your throat."

"Your leg."

"What leg? You should try a wooden throat, it'll give you less trouble."

If the children were listening, they might think we sounded like a married couple. They do not seem to hear us, too busy in their tasks. I wrinkle my nose at Amos. I hope snow will fall tonight or tomorrow, making the land less bare. In the morning, then, I might wake to trails—a rabbit's prints, the scribble of a raccoon, the belly of a drowsy skunk as it drags itself, fat with winter, across the land between my mother's house and mine.

When they have finished half of the front wall, I go to it and begin to press it down, tamping the sides so it will not blow away. I move in order to stop the shivering, but I am shivering so much that it is hard to move. I would like to crawl inside the leaves and sleep.

"Look," I tell Plumey, and all three children stop for an instant and watch as I press the leaves with my palms. "You need to push it all together like this when it's done."

Plumey nods, but the two boys turn away from me and

continue on. Dusk falls fast around us, blurring the edges of the trees.

"They should go," I say to Amos. "Before it gets dark."

He looks at the house. Halfway up the front and side walls, everything is leafy and padded, as if the boards have sprouted leaves. Every year I love this transformation. Two walls still need to be done. Amos disappears into the house and comes out with one of my jugs, but I will not let him give it to the children. If they take it, they might drink to stay warm on the walk home and get lost, freezing to death in the woods. Or the Doctor might smell wine on Plumey's breath and forbid her from coming back. I go inside and find three pine-needle baskets, but Amos follows me in, shaking his head.

"That's enough for now," he tells the children when we go out. "You better get on home while you can still see. You know there's quicksand in these parts. When you come back and finish, you get the reward."

One of the boys kicks at a clump of leaves. "Some of that wine would warm us right up for the walk home. Maybe just half for now."

"When the job is finished, the reward will come," says Amos in his preacher voice, and though they scowl, they do not dare argue. Plumey's face shows nothing at all. I would like to keep her with me for the night in my half-banked house, but the Doctor and his wife would worry, and she probably wants to walk back to town with these two boys. I do not say good-bye to her at first, not in any real way. I thank all three of them. None of them look at me, even when I ask if they'd like a lantern to help them back.

"You don't have an extra one," Amos says.

I give them a rope so they can tie themselves to each

other in the dark, and in case the snow starts up while they are walking home. When I was a girl we walked to school that way in blizzards, a snowbound centipede.

"Walk her to her door," I tell the boys. One of them mutters something to the other. I picture them tossing my good rope into the high reeds the minute they are out of sight. Or worse, circling Plumey with taunts, or tying her and leaving her: *You pretend you're like the other girls now, but we see through.*

"Plumey, maybe you'd better come inside," I tell her. "It's getting darker by the second."

"It's still light enough," she says. "I know how to go."

"What are your names?" I ask the boys.

One of them mutters something—Jake and Roy Parsons—and I nod as if I know who they are.

"Let her go," says Amos. "They'll be fine. I know these boys."

"I told my aunt I'd be back by dark," Plumey says. "Tomorrow I'll come again."

I remember my mother standing in the doorway as I went off to the mills, and how later, looking back, I imagined her with a white thread in her hand—the longest piece I'd ever seen, and tied to me. Now she must be rocking, her chin tucked toward another time: *Come in, Jeremiah, Aimee— quickly now, you'll catch your death of cold!*

"Then go, if you're going," I tell them. "Before it's pitch dark."

"Good night," says Plumey.

"Yes. All right."

"This way," she says to the boys, and I watch her lead them through the dusk.

It is not until I sit down that I realize how out of sorts I am, my feet and fingers aching hot or tingling cold—I cannot tell. Amos takes off my shoes, then rubs my feet through the brown-gray wool of my stockings. Every winter I go through a spell like this, a week, sometimes two, of burning throat and aching bones. In the beginning when I was alone out here, these were the hardest times of all. Amos stokes the fire, touches my toes, presses on my arches, pushes and kneads until my bones begin to feel like hot water flowing from my feet through the rest of me. How tired I am, there in his hands. Though my feet burn, I find I am shaking, cannot stop.

I need

I need to lie down and my head is the heaviest thing I have ever tried to carry and Amos is tending the fire, lighting the lantern and the candle by the mirror, handing me a weak cup of tea. But I cannot drink, too hot inside, yet shivering, my head too heavy to lift up. I wave the tea away like a princess, like a lady. I do not mean to wave that way, but I seem to have lost track of my own voice.

"Aimee," he says, "I told you to stay in."

I slide over, and he sits perched on the edge of my bed, such a long, thin man, made taller by the low rafters of my house. Amos, my husband. It is a strange thought, and yet not strange at all, as if he were at once a total stranger, dropped down into my life, and a man I had married in my youth. He gives me a cup, filled with wine this time, and I raise my head and sip. Lying there, I think I can feel the weight of leaves against the walls, a palm pressed to my house.

"The rabbits," I remember. "I should bring them in by the stove."

"They're fine," he says, but I know it is too cold out there. I need to bring them—at least the blind one and the young ones—in, close to the fire, which makes its kissing sounds as it burns through sap.

I move to get up, but I am still shivering and cannot find the strength to rise.

"I have—" I begin, but he shakes his head.

"They're rabbits," he says. "With fur coats, remember? And anyway, they're fine. I checked them. You won't believe me, because you know I think rabbits belong in stew, not hopping live around the cookstove, but I did."

"You're sure?"

He nods.

I am burning in my bed, much too hot to rise and go out. I would melt the cold air, glow my way through it, a coal in the center of a snowball.

"I'd still rather bring them in here."

Amos sighs. "All right. Stubborn as a mule. If I die of frostbite out there, at least it will be for the sake of your blessed animals."

I try to tell him to take his hat from where it hangs on the rafter, but already a gust of cold air has come and gone, and he is out the door.

A girl comes to me and she says I am your girl. Another girl comes to me and she says I am your other girl. Their eyes are watchful, their chocolate-brown hair stiff with frost. I try to say take off your cloaks, sit by the fire, but I cannot find the words. They take off their cloaks. They sit by the fire. The icicles on their hair begin to melt, releasing them. With their hair plastered wet against their heads, they look younger, their foreheads wide and bare. I realize that I cannot tell girl from girl; each one is the perfect shadow of the other, and they speak in a half-language I do not understand.

Talk to me, I say, but one girl takes the broom and begins to sweep my house, and the other stands on my log stool, reaches up into the rafters and pulls down the wooden box where I have my mother's letters, my hair brooch, the threads and rag-bits of my past. Then she begins to read, in the halting voice of a child who has just learned: *My dear Daughter, The first of October Father hurt his foot . . .*

A boy comes to me and he says I am your boy. No, I tell him, I had girls. It was me you had, he says, you just don't know. A woman comes, tall and graceful, with a biscuit in her hand. I am, she tells me, your girl all grown up big. No, I say, you're my mother, remember me? Oh, she says. Aimee?

I find them reaching for me, new to this world and hungry, but I have no milk. Somebody has bathed them; they smell of soap and lemons. Somebody has dried their skin and wrapped them in white cloths. Carefully, I unwind them, draw them to me, cup the twin shapes of their heads. She and she, they are: twenty toes, twenty fingers, four open ears. I lay them down beside me, coo and caress, but their hands are fisted, their mouths stretched into wails.

Hush hush, I whisper. Cope cope.

To calm them, I tell them things: How, for a time, we all lived together in a high room where they swam like fish. How after that, I carried them to Boston, where I opened a shop that sold yarn and jam and they rode on ships and trains. Or I carried them home to their grandmother, and there they played Finding in the woods. Or I carried them nowhere, gave them up, but still they visited at unexpected moments—in the cast of Plumey's voice, the brush of Amos's arm, my mother's fingers on my brow.

My throat is raw and my tongue heavy, but the words come easily and my stories seem to soothe. The twins curl like nesting spoons, watching me. After a time, they sleep.

——⤖◆⤙——

They sleep, and my fever breaks. My floating limbs return to me, my skin settles, my tongue becomes the right size in my mouth. My house returns to me, its walls half-blanketed with leaves. I reach for the tea Amos made, the cup still warm against my hand. How thirsty I am, parched. I drink, and then some more.

Amos will come in from the cold with my rabbits and stay with me through the night. In the morning, Plumey will visit and tell me about Roy and Jake, and I will try to say yes and careful in the same breath. On Sunday, if I am welcome, I will make tea for my mother. *They came to me,* I'll say. *I came to you and then they came to me.*

There was a woman and what do you think?

From between the narrow hips of a narrow girl, the two of you were born.

ACKNOWLEDGMENTS

As a work of fiction written from a late-twentieth-century perspective, this novel is not meant to be read as "history," but in many of the details of its imagined world, it is nonetheless indebted to historical and scholarly texts. I have woven in a number of fragments from nineteenth-century poems, folklore, and letters. The chant on pages 3–4 and rhyme on pages 10–11 are adaptations of two nineteenth-century children's pamphlets: *The Two Sisters* and *The Funny Book* (authors unknown). Aimee's recounting of her first lie on page 27 is loosely drawn from Harriet H. Robinson's 1898 mill memoir, *Loom and Spindle: or Life Among the Early Mill Girls*, as are some of the phrenology and mill details in Chapters 9 and 10. The poem on page 66 and letters on pages 148–149 are collages/adaptations of ones in *Farm and Factory, Women's Letters, 1830–1860*, edited by Thomas Dublin. The fairy tales in Chapter 5 are versions of tales in *A Treasury of American Folklore*, edited by B. A. Botkin. For other mill and period details, I am indebted to John F. Kasson's *Civilizing the Machine: Technology and Republican Values in America, 1776–1900*; and David Freeman Hawke's *Nuts and Bolts of the Past: A History of American Technology, 1776–1860*; as well as to articles in *The Lowell Offering*, the monthly magazine written by nineteenth-century female millworkers.

For giving me gifts of time and space, I am grateful to the National Endowment for the Arts, the Barbara B. Deming Money for Women Memorial Fund, the Mac-Dowell Colony, and the Blue Mountain Center. Many people read drafts of the novel and offered insights and encouragement. Particular thanks to Susan Bernofsky, Scott Campbell, Alexandra Chasin, Robert Chibka, Darcy Frey, Matthew Goodman, Ellen Grimm, Michael Grunebaum, Ed Hardy, Danielle Herold, Pagan Kennedy, Suzanne Matson, Maritza Perez, Anne Whitney Pierce, Jim Pingeon, Lauren Slater, and Melanie Thernstrom, as well as to my parents, Suzanne and Lawrence Graver, and my sister, Ruth Graver. Thanks, too, to my agent, Richard Parks, and my editor, Jennifer Barth, for the enormous care they put into preparing this book for its journey through the world.